Rage of Winter
Terran Strike Marines Book 2

Richard Fox & Scott Moon

Copyright © 2018 Richard Fox
All rights reserved.
ISBN: 171883876X
ISBN-13: 978-1718838765

Chapter 1

Lieutenant Hoffman hurried through the maze of tree-lined boulevards, his boots crunching through ankle-deep snow as he ran, his breath fogging in the frigid air as he worked his stiff fingers against his gauss rifle. The looping lanes of ancient Koensuu City connected parks, fallow orchards, and ice-encrusted mausoleums. Narrow trees with white bark towered above his team, their branches heavy with snow.

He felt like the dead alien culture surrounding him was watching from beyond the veil of extinction, judging his efforts.

"You called it, LT. They cut straight through the alien quarter," Garrison said on the infrared radio tight beam. *"Don't fall behind. You'll get lost. I promise."*

"Wouldn't be much of a challenge if the spies only operated in Terran-built areas with checkpoints and alert security." Hoffman checked the map on his forearm screen. "Do you have eyes on the target?"

"Little help from above would be nice," Garrison said, breathing hard but not gasping. *"Your girlfriend is really making good time."*

"Surprising," Booker said on the IR, not winded at all. *"With that monster she calls a bodyguard, I figured they'd be walking half-speed."*

"Uh...LT, I'm gonna need some help with this intersection. Which of the eighteen possible turns should I take?"

Hoffman tapped his forearm and checked his tactical map. "The *Falstaff* says continue straight. Other paths are one uniform temperature." He spent three extra seconds double-checking the map, zooming out for the big picture. "The area they're heading for looks like it was designed for defense. Mountains on three sides and this tricky isthmus through the frozen lakes."

A cheerful, well-rested voice sounded in his earpiece. "Falstaff *One to Hammer Six, I'm seeing frozen marshlands mostly. Looks like Celtic knotwork from orbit."*

"Roger that," Hoffman replied to the captain watching down on him from orbit.

"Your target is within reach. C&C recommends a

snatch and grab, soonest. Target is breaching burial site KC-zero-zero-niner-alpha. Be advised, the structure looks solid."

Hoffman keyed his squad link. "Prepare to execute."

"Received and understood. Breacher up," Gunnery Sergeant King responded.

Hoffman hustled to a snow-dusted dome where King, Garrison, Max, and Booker crouched against the cover, gauss weapons shouldered and ready.

"Breacher, copy. Ready to violate ancient burial grounds," Garrison whispered. "Max, take the eye so I can open my kit."

"Ha, ha. You know ghost stories freak me out," Max said, tapping him on the shoulder to take over the point position.

Hoffman reviewed basic facts about the alien city from the mission brief. An advanced race had evolved on Koen, then allowed their technology and manufacturing levels to slide back several hundred years. Koen birth rates declined to post-apocalypse numbers. Faculty members of the Phoenix Anthropological Department argued this had been an intentional tactic to evade the Xaros advance. Now the planet was a human colony and a newly founded forward base in the war against the Kesaht—a foe few members of the Terran military had faced yet.

As Terran frontier worlds went, Koen earned mixed reviews. Military intelligence pointed to hard evidence of an Ibarran cell operating several safe houses in the city. Half the colonists wanted to level the ancient buildings and monuments, while the other half treated them like holy shrines. Deadly weather systems swept the planet with brutal regularity.

Hoffman was here to tie up a loose end before she could make it to one of the Ibarran safe houses. Memories of New Bastion and the blonde traitor kept him warm on this winter world. If the woman was here, she was after something important. And so was Hoffman—redemption.

Memories of New Bastion fought for his attention. He shoved them down, but he still tasted the arid climate and felt the sweat running inside his gear as the woman called him a coward and a traitor. All in contrast to the snow-damped silence of Koen. He'd nearly gotten his team killed trying to save her on New Bastion, and the fallout from that event had been a political nightmare for the Terran Union.

"You all right?" Booker asked

"Yeah."

"We got her this time," Booker said with confidence.

"Remind me when we're frog-marching her into the brig with zip ties on her hands and feet."

"We've never been this close to nabbing her since Nouveau Marsellie. She's running scared," Booker said. "Right, King?"

"I'm working here," King said. "Not chitchatting."

"Sir," Max said, "got another footbridge over a delightful frozen marsh-river. Targets came this way and tried to hide their tracks. I've got thermal signatures of footprints and brush marks from one of these Aspen-like tree branches."

"Can you confirm movement reported by C&C?" Hoffman asked, decreasing his distance from the point team.

"Straight as an arrow, sir. Right to one of these squished-down ziggurat buildings," Max said.

"Probably a tomb. Can you see the doors? Which way do they open?" Garrison asked.

"C&C can confirm. You are on target," Coltrane, the ship's captain, said. *"We're passing out of direct IR good hunting. Wide frequency comms will monitor in case of emergency."*

The IR comm links were working well today, Hoffman thought, *until the curve of the planet got in the way.*

"Can you imagine how cold it is without Strike Marine armor?" Garrison asked. "We're across. Setting up security. Max, I definitely saw a ghost."

Max cursed.

"Garrison, that's enough. Report to the PT deck on the *Falstaff* for a 10k timed run when this mission is over," King said.

Hoffman smiled. The powerlifting door breacher wasn't huge, but neither was he a runner. "Focus," he said, then confirmed the location of his team members on his forearm display, keeping it turned into his body for the sake of light discipline despite the early morning sun. "Bounding overwatch, two by two. Rally on the last point of cover before target structure."

His team crossed a series of footbridges leading toward the squat building. Each bridge reminded him of a little fortress full of secrets—buried treasure, dangerous trolls, squads of Ibarran legionnaires waiting to launch and ambush.

Beyond the sparse forest was the stark skyline of the Terran colony and spaceport. Few of the new human buildings rose higher than the top of the boreal forest and never too close to the ancient parks. The spaceport landing zones were farther away, in the center of the city on the highest level of a terraced plateau the size of Tucson.

Hoffman viewed the surreal dream world with tactical overlays displayed on the interior of his helmet visor.

He pointed his gauss rifle skyward, waggled the barrel twice to signal an advance, and moved after his point team—Corporals Eric Garrison and Austin "Max" Maxfield. Private Opal 6-1-9, the last doughboy in active military service, stayed close and on his left, the six-and-a-half-foot-tall brute moving with the stealth of a smaller man. He performed every military task with textbook efficiency programed into him by Ibarra's engineers during the Ember War.

Gunney King brought the rest of the team up the snowy lanes behind him. "The city's waking up. Lot of air and ground traffic from the colonists this morning."

Lights blinked on the signal arrays of taller buildings, warning airships heading to landing pads downtown. Local traffic moved lethargically as small ships and ground cars headed out for a day's work.

"Hoffman for Max, report."

"False trail leading past the structure," Max said.

"Duke, report," Hoffman said.

The team's sniper overwatching the alien quarter did not respond.

"I'm confident the hottie and the brute ducked in this morbid tomb," Max said.

"Garrison?" Hoffman asked.

"Best I can tell, door slides up into the frame. Which sucks. Hard to blow off hinges when there aren't any," the breacher said.

"Options?"

"If they run, we'll have to chase them," Garrison said, sounding disgusted. "I really wanted to breach this thing, but if I blow that door, we'll take our prisoners home in buckets. All I have now is this stupid aerial burst flash-bang."

"They're squirting out the back!" Duke's transmission crackled in Koen's unreliable atmosphere.

In one motion, Garrison stowed his breaching charge and pulled his special-use shotgun. "Permission to deploy aerial burst flash-bang?"

"Do it. Team, execute!"

Garrison shrugged his gauss rifle and breaching kit higher onto his back as he aimed the short shotgun toward the fleeing figures. He toggled from "frangible breaching round" to "aerial burst" and pulled the trigger three times.

A trio of rounds raced ahead of the spies, exploding around them in a triangle of blinding light and thunder.

"King, right flank and converge. I'm advancing with Opal for the takedown."

"Acknowledged," King said, sprinting into the maze with Booker hot on his heels.

"Duke, report. I want them before they get into the city," Hoffman said.

"They didn't like my little friends." Garrison laughed. "Second volley away." One, two, three more flash-bangs arced through the trees and exploded like an artillery barrage without teeth. Garrison raced after his shots.

"Opal, catch them!" Hoffman said.

Opal sprinted forward like a freight train, carrying his oversized gauss rifle at port arms as he ran. His boots flung up snow behind him like a charging horse and his pneumatic hammer bounced where it was strapped to his back. Mist exploded from his mouth with every breath and he made a sound that scared Hoffman each time he heard the doughboy charge.

Hoffman and the others followed. Within seconds,

Opal sprinted past Garrison and gained on Max, one of the fastest Strike Marines in the company.

The chase rushed around a turn as snow shivered down from branches. Gauss fire erupted just ahead of Hoffman's lead element, but no rounds came his direction.

"I'm hit," Duke reported, pain filling his voice. "Winged the big guy about the time he opened up with suppressive fire."

Hoffman and the rest of his team arrived seconds after Max and Opal engaged the spy and her hulking bodyguard. Gunney King and Booker emerged from a snow-packed lane and aimed their weapons, ready to fire on the spies from their flank.

King shouted, "Drop that weapon, Medvedev! Do it now!"

Hoffman instinctively took a headcount of his people and moved to support. Duke getting injured worried him. As the team's most senior operator, he normally predicted problems and solved them before the others had time to worry. Now the sniper was separate from the rest of the team and far from Booker, the medic, and first aid.

These tactical considerations and others flickered through his mind. Time crawled, then rushed ahead, then staggered as adrenaline affected his senses. "Masha! Tell the legionnaire to stand down. He's your bodyguard, not a martyr."

Medvedev pulled the blonde woman behind him as he fired his gauss rifle one-handed and they took cover behind a stone fence. The bruiser then whipped a compact gauss carbine over the edge of the wall and let off a single high-powered shot that blew through the snow packed on top of the wall like an explosion.

Max hunched forward, blood spraying out of his back, staining the snow. Strike Marine armor was tough, rated for anything but a direct hit. Whatever the Ibarran was armed with was designed to kill Strike Marines. Another round caught Max in the shin and took his feet out from under him.

The comm specialist's life signs flashed amber on Hoffman's visor: armor breached, massive blood loss, tissue damage, and a cardiac rhythm in danger of shock. The lieutenant realized what Medvedev had done; he'd fired to wound, to slow down the pursuers and buy the two a chance to escape.

Opal, still charging at Medvedev, raced right past Max as he lay bleeding and moaning in the snow. Medvedev stood up and aimed center mass on the doughboy. A burst of rounds hammered Opal's thick breastplate, deflecting off the heavier armor but managing to slow Opal's charge.

The Ibarran's barrel glowed red-hot as Medvedev popped the capacitor out of the weapon and pulled a new battery from his belt. High-powered shots were energy hogs, and the Ibarran had just left himself vulnerable.

"Enemy!" Opal roared. "Kill enemy!"

"Alive, Opal! Alive!" Hoffman ordered as he ran toward Max. "Medic to the front!"

Opal swatted the carbine out of Medvedev's hands, but the bodyguard ducked the doughboy's meaty fist and drew a pistol from inside his open jacket with expert smoothness. Medvedev jammed the muzzle into the seam of Opal's armor and fired the pistol on full auto, stitching along Opal's chest. As the doughboy twisted aside, recoil swept the pistol away. The last rounds in the gun sparked off the wall, and Masha, huddled against the stone, shrieked.

Opal, blood dripping from his armor, swung a lazy hook that Medvedev blocked with an elbow. For an instant, the two giants were face-to-face with Opal having the slight advantage in height and weight. Snorting like an angry bull, Opal smashed his forehead into Medvedev's nose, and the bodyguard flailed back and bumped into the wall. He sidestepped Opal's snap kick and the doughboy's foot only managed to knock off a layer of ice. Opal grunted and swiped a backhand that glanced off the bodyguard's head and sent him facedown into a puff of snow.

The doughboy raised a foot and Hoffman thought he was about to crush the Ibarran's head, then Opal set his boot heel between Medvedev's shoulder blades. The bodyguard snapped over and rammed a knife into the thin armor behind Opal's knee, the blade sinking home with a meaty thunk. Opal opened his arms wide, let himself fall forward, and flattened against the Ibarran.

Hoffman heard an ugly groan as all the air was knocked from Medvedev before Opal raised a hammer fist and struck his opponent on the temple. Medvedev's head lolled from side to side and he went limp.

Opal kept one hand loosely around the Ibarran's neck and pulled the knife free with his other hand. He dropped the bloody weapon to one side and pointed at Masha.

"No run."

Masha, her blond hair peeking out from beneath the folds of a knit cap, raised her hands with a sneer. One hand kept moving toward the back of her head.

"Don't!" Hoffman came around the wall, weapon

trained on Masha. "You're wanted alive. My orders didn't say anything about bringing you in with both hands."

"You're that good of a shot?" Masha asked. "In this cold? All that adrenaline throbbing in your veins. Pull that trigger and you'll probably blow my face off."

"Try me." Hoffman took a step closer, the crosshairs of his holographic sights on her right wrist. "Please."

Masha glanced over at Medvedev, unconscious and pinned beneath Opal.

"You almost had us on Tarkara," she said sadly. "I thought giving you the slip then would have gotten you fired."

"Got you now." Hoffman motioned up with his rifle. "Extend your arms up and lock them out. King?"

"Sir." The gunney came around the other side of the wall.

"Search and secure," Hoffman said as he caught sight of Booker working on Max. He ached to go check on his Marine.

"I demand a female to search—hey!" Masha's protest was cut short as King grabbed her by the scruff of the neck and slammed her face-first into the snow. He cuffed her hands behind her back and tossed the cap at

Hoffman's feet. A thin spool of metal glinted in the moonlight.

Masha sputtered, snow clinging to her features as King quickly patted her down.

"Booker busy?" she asked Hoffman. "Oh, then where's Adams, your other lady Terran?"

King pressed a knee into the small of her back and slapped black rings onto each of her ankles. He touched a button on his forearm screen and the rings locked, binding the spy's legs together. He covered the bottom half of her face with a plastic muzzle, muffling her protests. A silk hood went over her head and tightened loosely against her neck.

Masha thrashed in the snow, trying to scream words Hoffman was sure weren't pleasant.

"'Bout goddamn time," King said.

"Secure the brute," Hoffman said and then turned and ran back to where Max lay in the snow.

Booker and Garrison knelt next to the wounded Marine, his armor open and the bare flesh of his torso exposed. Garrison held a light and heat lamp over his friend as the medic worked.

Hoffman leaned over Garrison's shoulder. Max's left flank was a mess of dark blood and exposed muscle.

His breath fogged in the light as shallow wheezing came out of his mouth. Booker's medi-gauntlet was alive with holo projections and data as she ran a probe around the wound.

"How's it look?" Max asked through gritted teeth.

"Like you caught a golden ticket back home for some extended leave," Garrison said. "I'm sure it hurts a hell of a lot worse than it looks, you big wuss."

Max coughed and blood spattered Garrison's visor. The breacher reared back slightly but didn't wipe the blood away.

"Sir, press here." Booker grabbed the lieutenant by the wrist and guided his hand to just over Max's sternum, setting his palm against the man's bloody, slick skin.

"Give me an update, Doc," Hoffman said.

"He's got a through-and-through wound to his left abdominal cavity. Secondary damage to his right lower leg. His suit's integrated tourniquet has the wound under control," Booker said as she ran a line tipped with a small box from the side of her armor to a port on Max's collarbone. "Time for some good stuff, Max."

She looked at the other two Marines. "Hold him down," she said.

"Ah…not the spike." Max writhed from side to

side. "I'm not hit that bad. I'm not! My wife hears I got the spike and—"

Hoffman pressed against Max's chest and put his other hand on the man's shoulder.

"On three," Booker said.

"It's…not…" Max slurred, and Hoffman realized he was going into shock.

"One!"

There was a pneumatic snap and Max yelped as a needle broke through his armor and jabbed into his carotid artery. Fluid raced through the line connected to a reservoir of drugs within Booker's armor and Max's eyes lost focus.

"I still need some help here, and a medevac," Booker said, her normally cool voice laced with concern. She raised her gauntlet arm and surgical probes popped out of their housings.

Garrison picked up Max's smashed visor. "Um, Doc?"

Booker let out a slow breath and holo fields popped up on the inside of her visor. She splayed out her gauntlet hand over Max's wound and the probes reached into the bloody, torn flesh.

"Medevac…now," she said. Her fingers moved slightly and the probes sank deeper into Max.

"OK," Hoffman said, "we can have a Mule down from the *Falstaff* in…nineteen minutes."

"Shit!" Booker said as blood squirted out from the side of one of the probes. "He doesn't have nineteen minutes. Call in the city's ambulance now, sir, or I'll lose him."

"What are you doing?" Garrison said, a tinge of fear in his voice.

"I've got to do artery clamps. In the dark and the snow. Damn it, Max!" She took a small wand off her belt and the tip lit up, red-hot: a cauterizer.

"I have to do this ugly," she said as she sank the tool into Max's exposed guts and red smoke wafted up.

Garrison glared over her head at Medvedev. "Your ass is mine when we're done saving my friend's life."

Medvedev was still unconscious and bound with more restraints than the now-calm Masha.

King stood next to Opal. The doughboy's breastplate was open and deep-green blood dripped into the snow.

"Max hurt?" Opal asked, heedless of his own injuries.

"Got it! I think I got it. Blood flow has nearly stopped." Booker rocked back on her knees and wiped the back of her hand across her forehead. Glancing at her forearm screen, she frowned. "Shit on a stick, his armor spalled. The bullet fractured his inner lining and he's got fragments in his chest cavity. LT, we need that medevac ASAP."

Hoffman opened a channel on the local emergency defense network.

"Doc," came a voice from the tree line.

Hoffman swung around and raised his rifle but relaxed when he saw Duke come out of forest. The sniper had his rifle across his back, and under one arm was his helmet, which he tossed at Hoffman. The visor had an ugly bullet strike at the upper edge of the visor glass.

"They had help," Duke said. A thin sheen of blood covered one side of his face from a cut on his forehead. "Countersniper about a kilometer out. Set up on a school roof."

"You OK?" King asked.

"I'm embarrassed is what I am." Duke took a can of chewing tobacco from his belt and tapped it into a palm. "Should've done my sector search a lot more carefully. Good thing the other guy had some local defense rifle and not a top-of-the-line model like Buffy." He jerked his head toward his rifle and put a wad of dip between his cheek and gums. "Lowest bidder came through for once." He kicked snow at his helmet.

"What about the other sniper?" Hoffman looked back to the city lights.

"Took him out," Duke said. "Local police are already scraping him off the walls."

"There's an Ibarran cell here," King said. "Intel told us these two were the only Ibarrans here."

"Then we need to get the prisoners off world before their friends can mount a rescue," Hoffman said.

"OK," Booker said. "Max is stable enough to move, but I need to get him to a trauma center." She took a bundle from the small of her back and unrolled a tactical stretcher. "Help me load him and strap him down. We can use the pressure to hold some of these wounds closed." The medic and Garrison went to work, and Max moaned in pain each time they tightened a strap on what looked like a complicated body bag.

"Air ambulance is three minutes away," Hoffman said, reading off a text alert on the inside of his visor. A second shuttle was also en route, one with a military call sign. He keyed a transmission to the support ship in orbit.

"Falstaff, need an immediate dust off," the lieutenant sent.

"Negative, Hammer 6," the captain said. "Orbit command just redirected us to investigate a graviton reading near the outer moon."

"*Falstaff*, this is a priority-one mission from Phoenix High Command. We have jackpot on two Ibarran operatives and the city is not cleared." Hoffman looked over at Max, thinking ahead about how his team was about to be split up.

"Well aware, Hammer," the *Falstaff* officer said. "Mule 99 will transport you and the prisoners to Hadronus Spaceport. Sit tight there until we can make the trip back to local orbit. Then we'll punch out back to Earth."

Hoffman watched as Booker gave Duke a quick once-over.

"Time frame on that, *Falstaff?*"

"*Squat and hold, Marine.* Falstaff *out.*" The line went dead.

"Sir," Booker said, hurrying over to the lieutenant. "I need to take Duke to get checked out. It's his head wound. I noticed a gait disturbance when he walked out of the woods—unsteady on his feet and speech is a bit off—likely a concussion."

"Agreed. The only one who can take a bullet to the face and walk it off is Opal," Hoffman said.

"Gunney." The lieutenant waved a hand over his head and pointed to a nearby clearing as he jogged toward the open area. "We've got birds inbound," he said, switching to IR as he left the team behind. Hoffman removed a small cylinder the size of a pinkie off his belt, banged one end against his thigh, and tossed the strobe toward the tree line.

"Adams should be doing that task, sir," King said, his weapon still trained on Masha and Medvedev.

"We're shorthanded," Hoffman said. "Casualties aren't helping."

"When's command going to give her back? Or replace her?"

"We should be off clandestine ops once we hand over the Ibarrans." Hoffman tossed out two more strobes, marking the landing zone for the approaching shuttles. "Then life can get back to normal."

An alert popped up on Hoffman's visor: Max's blood pressure was falling dangerously low. Booker raced back to his side and went back to work on him.

"Come on, come on," Hoffman muttered, looking toward the horizon. It was his duty to remain calm and in control, even as the cold pit in his stomach continued to grow. He'd lost doughboys during the Ember War. He didn't want Max to be the first Marine he ever lost.

Finally, running lights peeked through bare branches.

"Duke, Booker, you're on litter duty," King said. *"Stay on the medevac bird with Max. Rest of the team will provide security for the prisoners. We'll link back up once the mission allows."*

The rumble of approaching engines filled the air and a white-hulled ambulance shuttle hovered over the clearing.

"Max, you hang in there," Garrison said. "You need blood or someone to keep the nurses off you, I'll be there soon as you call."

Hoffman raised both arms over his head and guided the shuttle down. Snow whipped up as Duke and Booker carried the wounded Marine to the open back ramp, where a team of medics was already waiting.

Hoffman knew the statistics. Since he'd got Max into next-level care while he was still breathing, the chances he'd survive were near certain. But he was still worried about his Marines, still sure that his leadership had failed Max, the Marine's wife, and all the children he had waiting for him at home.

Chapter 2

Hoffman removed his helmet and melting snow sloughed off the side, spattering against the Mule's deck. The shuttle's interior was cooler than his suit's internal settings, but the brisk air was a nice reprieve after hours inside his helmet.

Masha sat next to Hoffman, cuffed to the bench, her head still hooded and her chin resting against her chest. Her bodyguard was at the other end of the cargo hold, where King stood nearby with his rifle slung across his chest. Garrison looked after Opal, spraying the doughboy's wounds with a saline solution.

Still unconscious, Medvedev sported a hasty bandage over a cut on his face, and bruises mottled one side of his head.

The oddly sweet smell of Opal's blood was in the air.

The bio-construct was largely immune to pain and infection, and the fluid that served as his blood was laced with large amounts of carbohydrates. Opal didn't flinch as Garrison began suturing the doughboy's skin together with a small device that resembled a pistol.

Masha swayed from side to side and her shoulder brushed against Hoffman's. She tapped the side of her foot against his armored boot, then pulled away. The lieutenant removed her hood and she blinked at him with ice-blue eyes. She looked over at her bodyguard, then stared daggers at Hoffman, her mouth working behind her muzzle.

"He's fine," Hoffman said. "Got off lucky, if you ask me. Opal would've ripped his limbs off if he wasn't human."

Masha's nose crinkled and her eyes tightened with pain. The lieutenant unsnapped the muzzle and she opened her mouth to stretch sore muscles.

"Your sniper's dead," Hoffman said. "Want to tell me who else you've got in Koensuu City and save the trouble of a long and unpleasant interrogation?"

"We had one other asset on this planet." Masha looked back at Medvedev.

Hoffman chuckled. "Sure you do."

"Fine. The entire planetary defense force and all the

police are Ibarran agents," she said. "Release me now, hand over your weapons, and I'll see that you're well treated."

"Your lack of cooperation will go in my report," Hoffman said.

"You mention our first meeting in any of your reports?" she asked. She sat back and her demeanor changed. She relaxed, almost as if she were the person in charge. "Hot summer day on New Bastion. You, a Terran lap dog on a kill team order. Me, an agent just about to make her escape from a minor setback. Not many people have such an auspicious first encounter. Fate is the only explanation."

"You fouled up my team's mission," Hoffman said. "I thought you were a Terran POW. Had I known who you really were—or all the trouble you'd cause Earth and my team—I would've blown that air car the first chance I had."

"Don't think I, or the Ibarra Nation, didn't appreciate your help on New Bastion." She gave him a quick smile. "Granted, having you and your devil mutts bothering me on subsequent operations has really lost its charm."

"You and the Ibarras are traitors to Earth," Hoffman said. "Illegal colonies. Attacks on aliens. All that is coming to an end and you're going to help."

"You think I'm going to give up the location of

Navarre, our home world? Please. Lady Ibarra makes us better than that," Masha said.

"What were you doing in the cemetery?" Hoffman asked. "Why are you on Koen?"

"Such a beautiful night." She let her head tilt gently to one side. "You ever go walking in the moonlight? Brisk air gets the blood going." One of her eyebrows danced.

Hoffman shook his head.

"Granted, I would have appreciated better company." The spy looked over at Medvedev and she whistled a bird call.

Medvedev jerked awake. He pulled at his restraints, his face flushing as his muscles fought against the short chains keeping his wrists bound on either side of his knees. Opal growled at Medvedev. King tapped a finger against his rifle's trigger guard and Medvedev relaxed.

"Wakey wakey." Garrison put the cap back on his spray bottle and refastened Opal's armor around his massive frame. He leaned close to Medvedev, almost eye to eye. "You didn't kill Max. You tried, though. Managed to hurt him pretty good. You know he's got kids? Wife back on Earth? You almost took their father away."

"I don't care what happens to traitors," Medvedev said.

"Traitors?" Garrison grabbed Medvedev by his bloodstained coat. "You Ibarrans broke away from Earth. How are we the traitors, you ugly son of a—"

"Ease up," King said and Garrison let the bodyguard go.

"You want to know a secret about your animal?" Medvedev raised his chin toward Opal.

"Opal is a hell of a lot better man than you'll ever be," Garrison said.

Medvedev mumbled something.

"What was that?" Garrison leaned closer and Medvedev reared back and head-butted Garrison just below the left eye. Then Medvedev lashed out with a kick, launching Garrison against the wall.

Opal roared, lurching across the deck with fists clenched and veins pulsing through the mottled skin of his neck and head. King got between the two and braced his rifle across Opal's chest, then Hoffman sprang out of his seat and ran down the cargo bay.

"Opal, stand down!" Hoffman said.

"Opal crush!" Opal said as he reached over King's shoulder toward Medvedev. The Ibarran stared into Opal's eyes, a look of smug satisfaction on his face.

"No hurt team! Opal crush!" Opal's thick arms

bumped Garrison—one hundred ninety-five pounds of muscle in addition to armor weight—off his feet while reaching for Medvedev. Garrison jumped up, wrapped his arms around Opal's neck, and tried to pull the doughboy off-balance. The Mule lurched sideways from the shifting weight of the Strike Marines.

"Settle down, kids," growled the pilot, Lieutenant Sakkatos, over the intercom.

Hoffman shouted orders as King shoved Opal back and Garrison slapped his hands over Opal's eyes. Opal braced his arms next to his body and howled, a primal roar that stopped Hoffman in his tracks. He hadn't heard Opal yell like that in…years.

"Play the damn video, Gunney!" Garrison shouted.

King flipped up a screen on his forearm and typed in a code.

"Happy! Happy trees, right, Opie?" Garrison asked.

"Trees…" Opal said as tension raced away from his shoulders.

"I got one," King said and held his gauntlet arm up in front of Opal's face. Garrison took his hand away from the doughboy's eyes.

The angled screen displayed a dark room with a Caucasian man in out-of-fashion clothes holding a painting palette and standing before a blank canvas. His hair was like an alien, twice or maybe three times the size of his head, and tightly permed in the shape of an afro.

The man in the video spoke. "Let's do a little winter scene…" He began swiping a wide brush with phthalo blue across the canvas. "A little touch of alizarin crimson. Just a touch." His words were gentle as he continued to narrate while he painted.

Medvedev cocked his head to one side, his lips pulled into a frown.

Opal's gaze lost focus as he watched the video. Garrison sighed with relief and slid off Opal's back.

"There's nothing wrong with having a tree as a friend," said the man in the video as he added detail to the outline of a tree that was thicker and greener than what grew on most of the Koensuu peninsula.

Garrison touched his cheek and winced, then took the rifle from King and stood outside Medvedev's kicking range.

"An explanation is in order," Masha said, her voice hard and dark. "Your toy was about to murder a prisoner!"

"I wanna get you to be creative on canvas," the painter in the video said. "Just take your time with nothing in mind. Just have good feelings and be happy…in love with life…"

"We had to condition Opal to fight your bodyguard," Hoffman said. "Doughboys won't normally harm humans, but he's stuck in an aggression loop—because Medvedev keeps provoking him. It takes a few missions to straighten out the calming protocol the engineers put in to break the loop," Hoffman said. "The video triggers his underlying conditioning. He's made to kill enemies and break shit, and your legionnaire is an enemy."

"That's what you tried to do," King said to Medvedev. "You wanted Opal to snap your neck."

"You can't ask questions of the dead," Medvedev said.

"And the dead can't fight for the Lady," Masha said, rolling her eyes and giving her bodyguard a dirty look.

"If you feel good about yourself and the world, good things will just happen. Happy trees. Just go crazy. But not too crazy. Don't try too hard. Just have fun." The video continued as the ship stabilized.

"Opal watch," the doughboy said as he returned to his bench.

"Don't forget to turn him back on," Hoffman said, relaxing as Opal calmed down.

"Chuck Norris doesn't do push-ups. He just…" Garrison started.

"Save it until we know the crisis is over," Hoffman said. "And only one joke about the legend at a time. We don't know what two Chuck Norris jokes would do to Opie." He went back to Masha. "Let's finish our conversation."

"What do you want to talk about, Lieutenant?" Masha asked.

"Why don't we talk about the Ibarran terror cells in Koensuu City?"

"*Terror* is such an ugly word. You wound me, Thomas Hoffman. I am an explorer. More like one of your Pathfinders than—"

"Than what? A spy?"

"I thought we would be friends." She smiled at him with beautifully intense eyes and complete confidence in her abilities. "We know what you did for the Dotari. The Ibarran Nation salutes you. They have ever been faithful allies."

"Not relevant to this mission," Hoffman said.

"Such tension in your voice. Do you have something against the Dotari?"

"They fought well during the Ember War."

"Oh, come now, Lieutenant. We are not talking about ancient history. You saved them from the phage. You personally destroyed the last Xaros probe in the galaxy—we can all hope and assume. My hero."

Hoffman controlled his expression. Details regarding the Dotari salvation were classified at the highest level.

She smiled at him despite the uncomfortable wrist ties.

"Tell them nothing!" her bodyguard growled.

"How can I say no to this face?" Masha said, winking at Hoffman.

"That is not his face," Medvedev said.

Hoffman felt a chill pass through his chest. Years ago, when he led a doughboy platoon, he'd bore the face of Jared Hale, brother to the Ember War hero, a bio hack that made his doughboys latch on to him as their leader. After the war, and after all his bio-construct soldiers—except for Opal—had died off, he'd returned to the face he was born with.

Masha and her bodyguard were toying with him, playing mental tricks by dropping hints that they knew far more of Hoffman's background and mission than he did of them.

"Permission to deploy the nonessential prisoner to the surface via anti-grav pallet," Garrison said.

"We don't have an anti-grav pallet," King said.

Garrison shrugged. "Details."

Hoffman yanked his thumb across his neck, silencing Garrison, then faced Medvedev. "You're not among your people, Medvedev. You're my prisoner. If you tell me where the rest of the real traitors are, I will mention your cooperation in my report."

Medvedev curled back his upper lip and muttered something in his native language.

"Lieutenant," Masha said. "We should start over—focus on what we have in common."

"In common? What do we have in common?" Hoffman said.

"Humanity…a number of mutual enemies."

"We can trade notes later." Hoffman put the muzzle back on Masha's mouth and she looked at him with big puppy-dog eyes.

Hoffman stepped away from the prisoner and went to the cockpit, where snow whipped past the glass.

The pilot, a well-built man with an infectious smile, tapped his headset. "My comms are working."

Hoffman motioned for Lieutenant Sakkatos to

remove the noise-cancelling ear protection. "I don't want any chance of this going across the networks. You get any requests about your cargo?"

"Nope," he said. "We're flagged to you and the *Falstaff*. Secret-squirrel time. Ping as normal system traffic to all the IFF."

"There are still Ibarran spy cells in Koensuu City. If they realize we've got their agents onboard…" Hoffman said.

"Scope is clean." The copilot rapped a finger against a radar screen. "Ain't nothing but ice, rocks, and those big moose things from the city to Pohja Base."

"Pohja's nothing but navy," Sakkatos said. "Think those two have friends there?"

"Keep things quiet just in case," Hoffman said. "HQ says the installation was scrubbed and cleared. I don't exactly know how they did that, but the sooner we get them off world, the better off we'll all be."

He looked at the communications screen on Sakkatos's control station. The temptation to send a message back to the hospital and get an update on Max and Duke was almost overwhelming. But the mission demanded radio silence. No matter what he felt.

****

Hoffman lingered in the door to the cockpit, considering what Masha seemed to know about top-secret Terran missions—which was too much. Was she dropping hints to scare him off from asking questions? Asking specific questions belied a Terran Union knowledge gap that the Ibarra Nation could exploit, but if Masha and Medvedev never saw their renegade faction again, then it didn't matter what kind of questions he asked them.

Hoffman scowled. Cloak-and-dagger double-think was a far cry from his days leading a platoon of doughboys.

The pilots and copilots tensed up. Sakkatos scanned his view screens with new intensity and his copilot, Weber, bent over the comms panel.

"What's happening?" Hoffman asked.

Sakkatos pointed at a headset. Hoffman put one of the plastic nobs against an ear and listened to planetary defense forces chatter across several radio frequencies about ships entering the atmosphere. Hoffman's stomach suddenly felt hollow. In the distance, flashes of light looked a lot like gauss cannons firing.

"The Ibarrans attacking?" Hoffman asked.

"Not them," Sakkatos said as he cycled power to the

engines. "Definitely not their ships. Last transmission from the *Falstaff* showed a pretty significant hostile force en route to the planet."

"Last transmission?" Hoffman asked.

"She got off a data packet before the enemy destroyed the ship," Weber said, hands flying across the comms keyboard. "Picket ships haven't been able to slow them down."

"Yeah, that's about right," Sakkatos said in a low voice. "It's going to get hot, Hoffman. I assume your men are trained on the turrets?"

"We are," Hoffman said, trying to remember if Garrison or King had outscored him on the last simulation. "Can we still make Pohja Base?"

"Yeah, sure. No problem," Sakkatos said. "Well, maybe. This is a Mule, not a fighter. If you jarheads could avoid provoking a fight or doing anything to get us noticed, your flight crew would appreciate it."

Point defense systems fired on the horizon as waves of assault craft filled the atmosphere like a meteor storm. Blips appeared by twos and threes on Weber's radar screen.

"Talk to me, Weber," Sakkatos said.

"We have a problem. A wing of bogies is closing on us. Fast. Too bad we had to leave our crew chief back on the *Falstaff.* Can't have uncleared personnel around the prisoners." He gave Hoffman a dirty look. It was the Marine lieutenant's order that left the Mule shorthanded. "You think Jim made it to an escape pod?"

Lieutenant Sakkatos banked the Mule hard, leaning his weight into the control stick as he piloted the armored transport ship around the side of a mountain. "It's no good. Those are combat fighters bearing down on us. You better tell your Strike Marines to lock and load."

"Garrison, King. Turrets," Hoffman shouted.

"Way ahead of you, sir!" Garrison shouted from the other side of the Mule.

"How long until we can get inside the base's air defenses?" Hoffman asked Sakkatos.

"Strap in!" Sakkatos lowered the craft into a valley. "Friend-or-foe radar's got the bogies as…Kesaht. They're mean as hell but not ace pilots, if you ask me. They rely on numbers and swarm tactics."

Sakkatos whipped the mule up and to the right, then dove like a brick when the first fighter attacked. Two energy bolts flashed past the cockpit, shaking the ship.

"Pohja's gone off-line," Weber said. "I'm not getting anything on the comms anymore."

Hoffman gripped the doorframe as the Mule banked

hard. He made it back to the cargo bay and saw Opal helping Garrison up into the hatch for the ventral turret pod.

As soon as Gunney King saw Hoffman was there to guard the prisoners, he slammed down the hatch for the dorsal turret and locked himself inside.

"Let me help," said Medvedev, who'd just woken and was tugging against the restraints holding him to the wall bench. "I can't do anything from here."

Hoffman hesitated for a second before disregarding his prisoner's offer to help. His eyes fixed on Masha next to her legionnaire bodyguard.

"I can fly anything in your fleet," Masha said, lounging against the wall as though her restraints meant nothing.

"Opal, either of them try to get loose, you snap their necks." Hoffman ducked back into the cockpit. "Lieutenant Sakkatos, I'll do fire control and leave you and your copilot to your work," he said.

"Roger that," Sakkatos said, banking the Mule around the side of a cliff. "We'll be flying low."

"I heard the Kesaht eat their prisoners," the copilot said, "which doesn't work for me at all."

Sakkatos shrugged, then dropped into a canyon and

accelerated. The red and gray canyon walls were a kilometer apart but felt closer at the speed the Mule was moving. Winter storms covered the sky and filled side canyons with ice and snow.

Hoffman got into the crew chief's seat, strapped himself in, then grabbed the side of the tactical display with both hands. In his Strike Marine armor, the cockpit felt painfully small.

The screen showed camera views from the forward, aft, dorsal, and ventral sections of the ship. Radar and infrared images were overlaid across directional hash marks that moved with the rapidly changing scene. Hoffman adjusted the contrast with a few quick motions of his bare hands. Gauntlets reduced the finger acuity needed to use the workstation optimally. Strike Marine gear was not a tool for subtlety.

"King, you have two crescent fighters popping in and out of cloud cover," Hoffman said.

"I see them. Can you confirm range?"

Hoffman tapped a series of commands on the computer without looking at his fingers. Distance and atmospheric information zipped over to King's turret.

"Garrison, you've got nothing. I repeat, no targets for the ventral turret," Hoffman said.

"Why doesn't that make me feel better?" Garrison asked. *"Anyone know why these Kesaht are so pissed off?"*

"Target's about to enter range," King said. *"Permission to engage?"*

"Sakkatos?" Hoffman asked.

"They definitely see us," the pilot said. "No point trying to hide."

"Cleared to fire," Hoffman said.

King's gauss turret thumped over and over and Hoffman felt vibrations through the hull.

"No hit. I repeat, no hit. Bogies are unaffected," Hoffman said without emotion.

"Roger," King said.

Along one side of Hoffman's tactical screen, he saw the camera view from Gunney King sweeping the clouds for his adversaries. From King's magnified point of view, rock spires and canyon walls alternated with swirling cloud cover as the Mule lumbered onward at best speed.

"Garrison, I think it's your turn," Hoffman said. "You've got five incoming crescent fighters. Brace yourself for the main event."

Garrison opened fire with his turret gun, cycling gauss rounds at the enemy as fast as his weapon could spit them out. Rounds ripped past the fighters. Heartbeats later,

Garrison scored a direct hit. One crescent fighter disappeared in a ball of flames as its comrades continued onward. The Kesaht ships closed the distance, rushing into the canyon with their afterburners glowing behind them.

Sakkatos climbed out of the canyon, crossed over another mesa, and dropped into another maze of cliffs and rock spires. "How are we on fuel?"

"More than enough," his copilot answered.

A bolt of energy punched through the cockpit, leaving a hot scar across Hoffman's vision. The Mule wobbled up and down as wind howled through the cockpit and sparks erupted from the copilot's station. Weber reached for fire-suppression controls, but his left arm ended in a blackened stump and bounced off the controls, leaving an ugly smear of blackened blood.

"Hoffman! What's going on? I've got a swarm of crescent fighters," King shouted over the IR comms.

"Same here." Garrison's natural boisterousness vanished as Sakkatos juked the Mule left, right, and down to avoid the new swarm of enemy fighters.

"Weber needs a tourniquet!" Sakkatos shouted, glancing at his copilot again and again.

"Hold fire, King." Hoffman struggled out of his seat. "I say again, hold fire. You have three dropping down on you, but it's a screen. Sakkatos, if you see them, move to give King a shot."

"Evasive climb," the pilot said, and Hoffman braced against the seat, "...in 3, 2, 1."

Hoffman flexed his legs and abdominal muscles to resist the sudden g-forces, but Weber made no effort to brace for the maneuver. His helmet flopped back and sideways against his seat as his arms dangled in the air, under no control from the man.

Hoffman lurched out of the seat as the climb ebbed and got to the copilot. An ugly black hole smoked on the man's thigh and Hoffman's boots slipped in the blood pooling against the deck.

Sakkatos flipped the Mule on its side as a Kesaht crescent-shaped fighter zipped past the Mule's cockpit. Hoffman held on for dear life and mag-locked his boots to the deck.

Gauss cannon shots zipped over the nose and there was a flash as an enemy fighter exploded in the clouds.

"Get some!" Garrison yelled.

"Weber?" Sakkatos shouted as he maneuvered into a new vector.

Hoffman lifted the copilot's head and looked into his half-open eyes. Blinking red alerts flashed on the copilot's visor.

"He's KIA. Sorry." He lowered Weber's chin to his chest and looked over the copilot's station. "King, your friends from round one are making another pass. Weapons free. Garrison, you don't have a shot but get ready to engage if they make a turn after their attack run."

Energy bolts ripped past the cockpit and Sakkatos cursed. He banked the Mule hard and Hoffman's shoulder bounced off the bulkhead, cracking display screens. There was an ugly shriek of tearing metal and the Mule began rolling over and over, the centrifugal force pinning Hoffman to the back of the cockpit.

"That was our port wing!" Sakkatos shouted as he struggled against the controls and Hoffman's ears filled with shouts and warnings from the two gunners.

The Mule leveled out and Hoffman fought back to the crew chief's station.

"Hoffman," the pilot said, breathing hard, "can you give me a damage report, besides the obvious holes. This old girl is getting real sluggish, real fast."

Hoffman scanned tactical menus. The Mule was losing altitude quickly. A wire diagram of the aircraft pulsed on a blood-flecked screen.

"Port wing is half-gone," Hoffman said. "Capacitor

banks one through five are off-line. And…trim control is failing. What's trim control?"

"We're going to land a bit short of Pohja Base," Sakkatos said. "Well short."

"The anti-grav clusters are functioning at less than seventy-five percent and the ailerons are blinking red. I have a feeling that's bad too."

Sakkatos laughed grimly. "Yep, we are definitely going down. I have to get us across these mountains or we'll be in a real world of hurt." He gunned his remaining engines, climbed, and clipped a jagged protrusion of rock.

Sakkatos scraped the bottom of the Mule against another ledge, nearly removing the ventral turret. "Valley we're in now is a straight shot to Pohja Base. Easy hike for a bunch of Strike Marine studs like you guys."

"With injured and a prisoner," Hoffman said. "Through mountains in a storm."

"Weber's not injured; he's dead," Sakkatos said, fighting the controls as the entire Mule vibrated. "I bet he'd love the chance to freeze his ass off down there."

Hoffman reached for the pilot. "Shit…your arm."

Sakkatos looked at his right bicep where a piece of metal had lodged. "Well, that explains why this control stick feels so heavy. Huh. What crap luck."

"Can you land?" Hoffman asked. "One of my prisoners is a pilot."

"We're not going to land. We're going to crash. I'm gonna fly this bucket all the way to the crash site."

"Masha!" Hoffman shouted and ran back to the cargo compartment.

She smiled back at him from the cargo bay, eyes wide and innocent.

"No time!" Sakkatos shouted. "Everyone strap in and hold on. Close up the turrets or you'll eat them when we hit." He fought for altitude as pine-tree analogs reached up to swat the clumsy Mule from the sky. Garrison cursed as the bubble around his turret struck treetops.

"I need to get out of this!" he shouted.

Hoffman grabbed a yellow and black handle on Garrison's turret hatch and yanked it up. The hatch snapped open and Garrison scrambled out.

"Seats in their upright and locked position." Garrison jumped onto a bench and drew a strap across his chest.

Hoffman looked up and stepped aside as King dropped out of the upper turret.

"Protect the prisoners!" Hoffman strapped himself in next to Masha, locked an arm across her chest, and gripped a metal rod on the bulkhead, bracing her against the ship.

The Mule hit a tree and lurched to one side. The ship rumbled as more trees broke against the hull and Sakkatos yelled from the cockpit.

The Mule slammed into the ground and the dorsal turret broke through the deck. There was a crash and the Mule tipped up. Hoffman's world went upside down and the straps across his chest failed. He had a brief sensation of falling before he hit the roof face-first.

Chapter 3

Hoffman awoke to the distant sounds of Xaros drones flying overhead, the thrum of their anti-grav systems ringing through his ears. Muffled explosions flashed at the corners of his vision. Doughboys died by the hundreds in the Utah Mountains as he struggled back to consciousness. The flashback always ended the same way: armor soldiers firing rail cannons and annihilating a Xaros construct before it could tear through the St. George fortress.

Silence buried the chaos. His ears rang. He opened his eyes to stare at the silhouette of a giant blotting out a sky. Snow swirled around his massive friend.

"Sir! Sir! Wake up." Opal knelt over Hoffman, ignoring the sliver of metal protruding from his side. Blood had frozen around the untreated wound.

"I'm here, Opie," Hoffman said, sitting up. "Hoffman for King, report."

No answer. The Mule was a disaster, upside down and the hull ripped away like a kill ravaged by wolves. Small fires traced through the electrical systems, the cockpit crushed against a rock outcrop. Black soil was mixed into the snow, tracing a path along their crash route.

"Help me stand, Opie."

The doughboy's big hands grabbed Hoffman and lifted him in one motion. "Sir called Opal 'Opie.'"

He looked at the doughboy. "Is that OK?"

Opal stared at him with wide eyes and furrowed his brow. "Opal is Opal 6-1-9."

"You're hurt. We need to get you fixed up and check on the team."

"Others here," Opal said. He marched to the form of Gunney King lying akimbo ten feet from the Mule wreckage, pointing at the downed Strike Marine with a plate-sized knife hand. "Gunney King."

Opal marched closer to the wreckage. "Corporal Garrison. Arm hurt." The other Marine sat next to a hunk of the outer hull, one hand gripping his gauss rifle, the other arm clutched against his side.

Hoffman stretched his neck right, then left as he

followed the bleeding doughboy to a thick pine tree where Masha and Medvedev were tied up facing away from each other. "Prisoners."

"Good work, Opal." Hoffman shivered against the cold. He reset his armor and waited for the warming elements to ramp up from sleep mode to combat readiness.

"Opal thirsty."

"Sit down and rest. You've lost a lot of blood. I'll have a look at your wound in a moment." Hoffman walked to Garrison and squatted down. "How bad is it?"

"I'd be smeared all over this planet if it wasn't for my armor," Garrison groaned. "Left shoulder throbbing like a son of a bitch. Mule tried to tear me apart when we landed."

"Get your ass up and find the ship's emergency kits." Hoffman looked at his forearm screen and frowned at an ugly crack across the display. He touched Garrison's icon and the computer responded. He sent an order for Garrison's armor to administer a quick dose of stimulants and painkillers.

"Ha, the good stuff. I knew there's a reason I liked you. Is Opie OK?" Garrison asked, rolling into an upright position and adjusting his gauss rifle sling to his right hand.

Hoffman nodded. "He has the worst wound of the

team, as usual. Get to it, Marine. I need to rouse Gunney."

Hoffman stood over King's form.

A few paces away stood Garrison, facing the prisoners with his rifle ready. Glancing over his shoulder, he said, "He looks so peaceful. Hard to imagine him yelling at me. Can I just draw a couple simple things on his armor before he wakes up?"

Hoffman gave him *the* look.

"Right. I'll just move a little closer to the hot spy chick and her freakishly large bodyguard. I wonder what he can bench press."

Hoffman linked his IR band to King's armor CPU and checked his vitals. The man was unconscious, but his armor didn't read any major injuries. Hoffman sent a command for King's armor to send a whiff of ammonia into his helmet.

"Gunnery Sergeant King, report."

The man groaned for half a heartbeat, then scrambled to his feet. Standing too abruptly, he staggered around, pointing his side arm with his right hand and pawing for his rifle with his left. "Team, rally. Rally around the crash site. Set up security. Pancakes with strawberries. Pancakes with strawberries. Can I get some service around here!"

Hoffman spread his hands as he calmed his top NCO. "Easy, Gunney. Take a second to get your bearings."

"What? Ahh...I'm OK. I'm good." King grunted and cursed under his breath as he circled the wrecked Mule. "Team, sound off, by the numbers."

Garrison's IR mic chirped on their squad net. "Garrison, checking the wreck."

"Opal, guarding prisoners."

Silence.

"That's the entire team," Hoffman said. "We split for the extraction, remember?"

"Yes, sir. Are you OK?" King asked, hesitating before adding, "Did I say anything unusual?"

Hoffman patted him on the shoulder as he walked past him. "I need to work on Opal. Check on Garrison and the prisoners, then salvage what you can from the Mule."

Smoke swirled toward the sky from at least three locations. The Mule had broken apart after shearing a path through Koen Aspen-like trees and plowing into the side of a mountain. Fat snowflakes fell straight down without wind to divert them. Visibility shrank to less than a hundred meters as the sun set.

Hoffman found Opal digging through the wreckage like an angry demon. The doughboy flung a door panel over Hoffman's head, then grabbed one of the benches and tore it loose. "Where rifle?"

Hoffman looked up at the sky as snow fell into his face. Silence ruled the forest.

"Opal. Your rifle can wait. I need to look at your injuries."

Opal tugged something from a tangle of metal. "Arrrrrgh! Broken! No! Opal kill enemy. Rifle kill enemy. Arrrrgh!" He pulled back his right fist and punched a section of metal, ringing it like a gong. Seconds later, he slammed the broken rifle against the metal, then dropped it, then started tearing the remains of the Mule apart. "Broken!"

Hoffman reached out to calm the mottle-faced doughboy, then jumped back to avoid an arm thicker than his leg.

"No! No! No!" Opal slammed both fists on the canopy of the Mule cockpit.

King slid to a stop next to Hoffman. "What the hell?"

"Calm down, Opie! You can use my rifle!" Garrison yelled from where he was standing guard on Masha and Medvedev, wincing in pain as he tried to placate the doughboy and guard the prisoners at the same time.

"He's cracked. Is this what they do when they shut down?" King asked.

Hoffman stepped in front of King and pushed down his gauss rifle. "He's just angry. Doughboys get attached to their rifles. Part of their programing."

Opal's all-out fury continued until he staggered and fell from exhaustion and blood loss. "Rifle broken…"

Hoffman ran to his side, surprised by the distance the doughboy had covered during his tantrum. He assumed a defensive stance. "Easy, big guy. I need you to follow my orders."

"Play that stupid video," Masha suggested.

Hoffman gestured at the smoking wreckage of the Mule.

She nodded at his tactical sleeve with her chin. "Use that. Think outside the box."

Hoffman ignored her. His armor was covered with blood, debris, and snow. "Go slow, big guy. Listen to sir. Follow my orders."

Opal stood at attention, slowly because of the frozen metal protruding from his side. "Yes, sir."

Hoffman opened a combat first-aid pack. "Lie down on your right side and hold on to that rock. King, I'm going to need help with this. Second thought, switch with Garrison. He's stronger."

"Garrison, you heard the boss."

Garrison slung his gauss rifle and hurried to Hoffman's side. "That doesn't look good."

"I hope you've been eating your performance bars. You must pull that out in one try. No slipping. No hesitating. I'm going to cauterize it and glue down the skin flaps as fast as I can."

"Are you giving him pain meds?" Garrison asked.

Hoffman shook his head. "They don't do anything for doughboys. On three. One, two, three."

Garrison gripped the twisted piece of metal with his right hand and pulled. "Come out, you son of a bitch."

"Opal, let go," Hoffman said.

Opal relaxed his latissimus dorsi, the muscle running from his upper back almost to his hip like the flank of a horse, and Garrison yanked the metal scrap free. Hoffman plunged the cauterizing tool into the muscle and swept it along the length of the wound.

"By the Saint," Garrison muttered.

"Didn't know you were religious," Hoffman said as he wiped the sizzling mess with disinfectant squares. "Why didn't you use both hands? I told you to use all the powerlifting muscle you're always bragging about."

"Left arm is still a bit wobbly."

Hoffman looked at the arm in question. "You mean broken?"

"Probably. Call it a stress fracture. With a dislocated shoulder thrown in for good measure."

Hoffman shook his head. "We don't have time for 'who's the toughest Strike Marine?' If you're injured, I have to know."

"Yes, sir," Garrison said. "The meds my armor sent into my system have my teeth buzzing right now. My left arm doesn't hurt as much, but it's not moving right either."

"Opal? Status?" Hoffman asked.

"Unit fluid levels are suboptimal," answered the programming deep in Opal's consciousness.

"Drink some…we don't have any water, do we?" Hoffman looked around. "Snow. Eat some snow, Opal."

The doughboy picked up a hunk of dirt-encrusted ice and bit into it. Squeaks and cracks came from his mouth as he broke down the ice between his massive molars.

"He going to make it?" Garrison asked as Hoffman unrolled a sling from the medical pack and tied down Garrison's left arm.

"Doughboys are made tough," Hoffman said. "His

system will replace his blood loss quick enough. None of his organs were damaged. No need to worry about shock with him."

"Lucky guy," Garrison said. "Course, he doesn't get the benefit of synthetic opioids and amphetamines at the same time."

"You weird out on us, I'll trigger the antidotes," Hoffman said.

"Kind of wish Booker was here," Garrison said, his teeth chattering.

Hoffman helped the corporal move his rifle sling into place. "I'm going to watch Opal for a few minutes. You're on prisoner duty. We're moving ASAP."

"Not a lot of inventory in this Mule," King said. "Best not to stay here for too long. We left a trail of burning fuel for half a kilometer—like an arrow pointing straight to us."

Hoffman helped Opal up to a sitting position as the doughboy continued stuffing his mouth full of snow. The green and brown of Opal's skin pulsed as new fluid flooded into his system. He looked up at the overcast sky as snowfall flitted through the wreckage and evaporated in the flames. The distant roar of fighter engines and crump of explosions carried on the wind.

"We need to get moving," Hoffman said.

"Yes, sir," King said. "You think the Kesaht will come for us?"

"They know where we crashed. I'm going to assume they will."

"Lieutenant, can we…get…some of…that…fire…action?" Masha said through chattering teeth.

Medvedev stared at Hoffman, ignoring his minor injuries and his guard.

"I'm…freezing…over here," Masha said.

"You and me too, sister," Garrison said.

"Such a gentleman, Corporal Eric Garrison. Would your armor fit a poor little thing like me?"

"No," Garrison said. He looked around. "What? Everyone knows it won't. I'm not a heartless jerk. It's just that my armor only fits me. And it really creeps me out when the spy uses my full name."

"She doesn't need armor," Hoffman said.

Masha glared at him.

Hoffman turned his back on the prisoners. "Opal, sit them by the fire. Not too close."

Darkness and a special kind of cold came quickly in the mountains and Hoffman adjusted the internal settings of his armor. "Team, minimize comfort settings. We need to conserve battery power. I'm going to attend to the pilots."

"Roger," King said.

Hoffman found Sakkatos first and stared at the tangle of metal and composite plastic. Extracting his body was like taking apart a three-dimensional puzzle in a snowstorm at night. He took the man's dog tags and scanned his identification as KIA. "Sorry, Sakkatos."

He searched the man's gear for a token of Saint Kallen or other religious artifact but found none. Exhaustion spread through his body without warning. He craved silence. No matter how hard he tried, he could only remember the beginnings of prayers.

Weber was just as stuck, but the crash had done less damage to the man. Hoffman had expected to find a bloody rag doll in the copilot's seat, but other than the missing hand and bloodstains, the copilot could have been sleeping.

"This is taking too long," King said and he smashed open an ammunition crate. "We should be kilometers away by now."

Hoffman tried to mark the crash's grid coordinate, but there was no connection to the GPS satellites. "Agreed, but let's not rush to failure. Koen is looking like a bad planet to be lost on."

"I have the survival kits, including a pair of light enviro suits. Do you want me to give them to the prisoners?" King asked.

"Give me a minute." Hoffman stared at Sakkatos and Weber and did some quick mental math on how long it would take to extract them from the wreckage.

"You should give them a proper burial," Medvedev said. "They were brave men."

Hoffman planted his gauntleted fists on his hips and stared down at the man. "They'll get it…just not right now. You're an Ibarra legionnaire, aren't you? What does this tactical situation call for?"

"That we move out before the enemy catches up to us," Medvedev said. "We are exposed to an air attack."

Hoffman didn't answer.

Missiles streaked across the sky, falling from high orbit toward the nearest navy base. As King finished gathering supplies, Hoffman watched the distant light show, explosions reflecting through the gloom that shrouded the mountain peaks.

King lifted two shrink-wrapped bundles. Hoffman nodded.

"You had enviro suits and allowed us to suffer? That is a clear violation of section nine of the Hale Treaty and the Articles of War," Masha said.

"Do you not want them?" King asked.

Masha shivered uncontrollably.

"Put them on. Take in some nutrient paste and water. We'll be on the move in five minutes," Hoffman said.

"I will untie you to put the suit on, then bind your hands in front because I'm such a hell of a nice guy and I don't want you falling down the mountain. One wrong move…and we will make other arrangements to transport you." King tossed the first pack onto Masha's lap and untied her from the tree.

Hoffman went to the case of emergency supplies and looked through the contents: a half-dozen packs of nutrient paste, a first-aid kit, water-purification tabs, two emergency beacons, and four all-purpose battery packs.

In normal combat conditions, Strike Marine armor carried enough power to operate for three days without resupply. The cold weather would be a constant drain on the systems, and moving over rough terrain would sap the reserves even faster. The spare battery packs were designed for the lighter, more efficient void suits Mule pilots and crew would wear and might buy the Strike Marines a few more hours of performance apiece.

Opal tossed Hoffman a beat-up cardboard container from the wreckage, a "box of nasties"—meals carried onboard. Hoffman opened it up and slipped a bag of nuts and a frozen ham sandwich into a pouch on his belt. He picked up a cup of coffee with a sealed lid.

Shivering still, Masha zipped up her enviro suit. Her lips were blue. The lieutenant warmed the cup of coffee with a pull tab and handed it to her, saying, "Tell me about the Kesaht."

She worked her fingers against the container as it warmed up and held the thermos near her body. "You don't know about the new threat to the Terran Alliance?"

Hoffman motioned to Medvedev, and King tossed the Ibarran the other enviro suit.

"One mission at a time," Hoffman said. "I know of them. Just never faced them in battle."

Masha laughed.

"That's the first genuine sound you've made since we met," Hoffman said.

"Oh, Hoff. You're so sweet. I just find it amazing that nothing has changed in the Strike Marines. Admirals and politicians love their comms lockdowns," she said. "The Ibarra Nation's been skirmishing with them for a few years, mostly on artifact worlds, though they have launched a few raids. You don't know anything about the fighting on Oricon or Balmaseda?"

"The Ibarrans provoked them?" Hoffman asked.

"They hated us—Terrans and Ibarrans both—before we even made first contact," Masha said. "And the Kesaht were raiding systems before the Ibarra Nation and Earth had our latest…impasse. Who do you think attacked New Caledonia?" Masha asked.

Color drained from King's face. "What are you talking about?" he asked.

Masha ran her hands down her arms and tugged gloves built into the suit over her fingers.

"We can catch up later, yes?" she asked. "We're better off someplace that's not so exposed."

Medvedev had almost changed into his enviro suit.

"We're waiting on you two," Hoffman said. "Why are the Kesaht attacking us here? You said you'd run into them on artifact worlds. Isn't that why you're here? The Koen ruins?"

Masha shook her head. "I'm just here for the skiing. The Kesaht are here in numbers. This isn't a raid. It's an assault."

An animal screamed in the distance as a predator tore it apart. The keening death cry could have been a child or a lost soul disintegrating. A mob of killers yipped and screeched at the moon, snarling and snapping at each other as they rendered flesh from bone.

"Wolves?" Garrison asked, shaking his head. "Aliens and traitors aren't enough. Now we have to get eaten?"

"Maybe we're not to their taste and they'll only kill us," Medvedev said.

"Not. Helpful."

Hoffman pulled King aside. "I'm clear on what's working against us—depleted team strength, injuries, hostile environment, and responsibility for two high-value prisoners. Give me good news."

"We're not going to run out of ammunition. Well, not if things go well," King said.

"Plenty of ammo. Good." Hoffman watched Garrison and tried to estimate the extent of the breacher's injury.

"Nutrient paste. Water. The issue is power packs. We need to move under minimal power. I recommend restricting battery usage to basic warmth and sensors," King said.

"Standard survival stuff."

"We have no contact with satellites," King

continued. "Not sure where we are, but close to the navy base."

Hoffman's gaze flickered involuntarily toward the Mule crash where Sakkatos and his copilot were entombed. "We need to blow the ship. Make it look like a total loss. No survivors."

"We can do that. Are you sure you want to use the denethrite? We're not exactly a walking armory. Garrison won't be happy to waste his precious stockpile."

"He likes blowing things up. That's why he's the breacher," Hoffman said.

"With a broken arm."

"He says it isn't that bad," Hoffman said. "His armor's designed to keep him going."

King wiped frost from his visor. "We'll see."

"I don't like all the missile fire from orbit. This is looking like a full-scale assault on the planet."

Explosions lit up the underside of distant clouds as the snowfall relented.

"We're OK. I think the base is in worse shape than we are."

Opal trotted over to Hoffman and handed the lieutenant a gauss rifle with a banged-up stock.

Another series of orbital bombardment strikes

thundered with increasing fury. Hoffman looked down the long valley that led to Pohja Base as explosions marched across the distant landscape. Hoffman zoomed in with the rifle's optics and saw buildings on fire and crumbling. Fighters streamed across the sky, trailing fire and exploding in the air. Gauss cannon emplacements fell silent. Larger, direct bombardment explosions bloomed silently among the defenders. Mushroom clouds reached silently upward.

"Nukes?" Hoffman asked, not wanting to hear the answer.

"No." King scanned the devastation through his binoculars, adjusted the filter, then studied the gray mushroom clouds again. "Not nukes. High explosives with what I think were thermobaric warheads. No radiation fallout."

"We're not going to Pohja, are we?" Garrison asked.

"Mountain range runs southwest toward a river that leads back to the Koensuu City," King said.

Hoffman checked his own HUD map and listened to a wing of crescent fighters cutting across the sky. "Time to go. Garrison, blow up the Mule. King, hide our tracks. We'll move on foot until we locate a better option. Opal, bring the prisoners and follow me. I'm sending our first way point on team comms."

Garrison slung his rifle over his back and unpacked his demolition kit. He used two hands, but Hoffman could tell he was favoring his right. His left remained tight to his body, locked in place by his armor and used only to hold the detonation cord. He spooled it out with his right hand, working fast and efficiently.

"That one knows what he is doing," Medvedev said. "I've worked with legionnaires like him."

Hoffman didn't wait for Garrison to finish. He took Opal and the prisoners along an animal trail and stopped near the stream bed he had designated as their first rally point. An explosion thundered from the crash site.

King and Garrison rushed down the trail.

"We're moving out on foot to Koen City," Hoffman said to the prisoners as he checked the restraints around Medvedev's wrists. "You cooperate, you'll be taken care of."

"Give me a weapon." The bodyguard motioned to the pistol strapped to Hoffman's chest. "I'm no good to Masha with my hands tied."

"Yeah, listen to him," Masha said.

"No," Hoffman said firmly. "You two keep up. Try and run off and you'll die tired." He tapped the back of his hand against his pistol.

"The Kesaht fighter patrols are heading away from us on the other side of the valley," King said. "We should step off now."

"Maybe they aren't even looking for us," Hoffman said. "First thing to go right today. Let's move out. King, take point."

"That's my job," Garrison said.

"You're injured. Let's move."

Chapter 4

Duke ignored Booker's third offer of pain medicine and grit his teeth as he stared at the door to the critical care room. Duke wore a hospital gown over his bare upper body. His pseudo-muscle layer was unzipped and the upper half dangled from his waist. His upper body armor and sniper rifle lay on a chair while the medic worked on his face.

Max is solid, Duke thought. *Good guy.* Memories of team get-togethers with Max's family kept fighting to get to the fore of his mind. He didn't envy Hoffman's duty to inform Max's wife of the injury…or what might happen next if things took a turn for the worse.

"If you can't relax, I'm going to have security hold you down and give you pain meds. Do you really want me to stitch up your face with that expression on it?" Booker asked. "Make it stay like that forever?"

Duke exhaled and tension drained out of him. "I'm worried about him."

"He's a Strike Marine," Booker said. "We don't take in the week. Plus, he's in with the trauma surgeons right now. The local docs were more than competent when I turned him over. All the worry you can give won't help him right now."

"How is he, really?"

Booker covered his final stitch in antibacterial ointment and waited for it to dry into a second skin. She looked him in the eye when she answered. "He's in real bad shape, but stable. Needs blood transfusions. A good percentage of his upper intestines need to get reknit. Liver took more damage than you've done to yours with years of cheap booze. He's got enough painkillers and antibiotics in his system to keep him out of sepsis or feeling like he's anywhere but a warm, fuzzy cloud. Other than that, he's down for the count for the next few days."

"That's a shame. He's always been one of the better comms operators."

"Make sure you tell him that. He respects the hell out of you, can't imagine why. We'll peek in on him soon as he's out of surgery and the drugs wear off," Booker said.

"I'll make a note."

Duke tensed as air-raid sirens spun up in the courtyard of the hospital. He hated the sound. He was somehow able to sense—maybe feel—them before they reached audible levels, and once they were at full volume, they tortured everyone within a kilometer.

"All personnel, report to battle stations. Noncombat personnel, report to your assigned work areas. All supervisors are to complete a headcount within fifteen minutes and log it," a voice said over the public-address system. "Civilians are to shelter in place. Repeat, civilians are to shelter in place unless they have been designated critical augmentation staff. This is not a drill. This is not a drill."

Duke looked at Bunker. "That's a citywide alert. What the hell?"

Booker, eyes wide, nodded and hurried to check on Max through a window to the surgery ward. Duke pulled off the hospital smock, zipped up his pseudo-muscle layer, and reattached his armor plates in less time then it took most men to button a shirt. He hefted his bundled sniper rifle onto his back.

Booker hesitated in the doorway. "Where are you going? I'm not done with you."

Duke pointed upward. "I'll be on the roof."

"You can't just...wait for me."

"Move your ass." He was still pulling on one sleeve of his pseudo-muscle layer as he ran the stairs, a complicated and graceless procedure while holding a heavy gauss carbine in one hand and his sniper kit over one shoulder.

Kesaht crescent fighters blasted over the city. A second wave came in slower, strafing the city seemingly at random, while only a few antiaircraft guns returned fire. Duke could see Planetary Defense Forces soldiers running to air defense batteries on roofs of surrounding buildings. He glanced at the doorway to the roof. "Get up here, Booker. It's game time."

He dropped his pack and unfolded it. In seconds, he had his kit set up—a shooting mat with magazine patches sewn into it between sections of burlap camouflage strips. From a prone position, he could hit targets out to two kilometers, even in a rush like this. Unfortunately, his target selection presented unusual problems.

He took a knee and swept the sky with his sniper scope. The rifle was heavy in this position, but precision fire was still possible.

Booker burst through the doorway, dragging her

own kit and rifle.

"Set up and start spotting targets," Duke said.

"How about I shoot my own targets?" she asked, grunting the words between clenched teeth as she rapidly deployed her gear and hefted her weapon. Then she hesitated.

"As soon as you earn an actual sniper rifle," Duke said.

Crescent fighters fought in three levels: void space, high altitude, and right above the rooftops. Enemy ships not engaged in the battle for void and air superiority now moved slowly or even hovered over targets in Koensuu City. The city defenses spooled up too slowly and the Kesaht pilots took full advantage of the surprise attack.

"You'll take your own shots with the rifle you have. First, we need to be a team. And when it's time for you to drop some targets…"

"I know, I know! Breath control! Relax! Don't I look relaxed?" she asked.

PDF point defenses engaged several fighters that almost immediately broke off their attack. Others swept around the defenses and blasted critical targets with their ship guns. Duke swore as one of the point defense batteries disintegrated under a hail of kinetic rounds.

"OK, I'm set," Booker said. "We have clearance to fire?"

"I didn't ask permission."

"Wait, wait, wait," she said. "If we do this, we make the hospital a target."

"Everything in the city is a target. They just haven't gotten to this one yet." Duke tracked a fighter begging to be shot.

"Max's in this hospital. There are civilians here. Children."

"Now you've gone and made it ugly," Duke said and then squeezed off a round, punching a hole through the canopy of the crescent fighter. It flopped over and crashed into the river meandering through the city.

"Duke! We have to move to another building before we start a shitstorm!"

"What makes you think the Kesaht care if there's wounded in here?" He swept his rifle ten degrees to his left and shot another slow-moving crescent fighter as it dumped rounds into one of the walking parks that wove through the city.

"If they notice you, they *will* care about blowing up this building!"

Duke hesitated, drawing back from his rifle for a

second and lowering the barrel a fraction of an inch. "Fine."

Duke was on his feet with his kit rolled up and his rifle slung across his back before Booker realized she had won the argument. He considered yelling at her to *move, move, move* but took the time to pack a dip of tobacco into his lip instead. The slight stimulant buzz of nicotine calmed him. Always had.

He held the can out to her.

She rolled her eyes, hefting her gear in a surprisingly neat bundle.

He shrugged once, then hustled toward the roof access door. A lot of banging downward and handrail grabbing later, he emerged onto the street level and followed the wall to the shadows of an alley. He dropped his hastily repacked sniper kit and shrugged farther into his pseudo-muscle layer. His lightweight sniper armor was already attached to it but not strapped down properly. He was about as un-squared away as he had been in years.

Booker moved past him and took up a position on the corner of a building. Civilians ran from structure to structure. A ground car sped up the street at unsafe speeds. Somewhere in one of the buildings, a baby cried as the mother screamed for someone to hurry up. Air-raid sirens groaned in the background, contributing to the low-level headache that was the foundation of Duke's awareness.

Fires spread through the city. Emergency-response crews drove past a burning building on the way to another, more serious explosion.

A truck full of PDF soldiers came around the corner and slowed to make the turn. Duke ran forward, jumping onto the side rail. "Where you going?"

"Got reports of landings outside the city. We've been ordered to the outer defensive lines," the soldier said.

Duke glanced at Booker, who shook her head in the negative. He thumped his hand on the side of the truck. "Sounds good to us."

"I need to stay at the hospital. They already have wounded streaming in, civilian and military casualties," Booker said, hefting her sniper kit higher onto her shoulder.

"Is she a medic or a sniper?" asked the driver of the truck, eyeing her from head to toe and taking his time about it.

"In the Strike Marines, we do it all," Duke said. He leaned closer to Booker. "You're a field medic. We're going to need you at the front."

She looked at the hospital, then climbed in with the other soldiers. Every one of them stared at her, almost completely ignoring Duke. "I'm worried about Max. But you're right."

"So what's new?"

Chapter 5

King set an aggressive pace, moving under the cover of tree branches and intermittent snow. Hoffman kept the prisoners between himself and Opal while Garrison brought up the rear.

"Maintain visual contact," Hoffman said over the IR comms, shivering from one of the random stabs of cold air penetrating his suit. The armor could button up for void and high pressure environments, but adjusting his armor to be warm and toasty would drain his batteries, and he had to err on the judgment that no resupply was coming. Moving would keep his Strike Marine armor warm and conserve battery power as the armor recaptured some of the kinetic energy of locomotion. Each time they stopped, the battery would drain faster. He needed to keep his team moving.

King paused, looked back, and acknowledged with a hand signal.

"Lieutenant Hoffman, I'm freezing," Masha said. "No amount of exertion will warm me up. Not on this planet."

"These enviro suits are just as warm as their Strike Marine armor in low-power mode," Medvedev said. "Do not show them your weakness."

Masha muttered something in Basque.

"I'm your bodyguard, not your mother," Medvedev said.

Hoffman took Masha by one arm to keep her moving. "The Kesaht will kill all of us if they catch us."

"Of course," she said. "But I am *cold*."

"We're all cold. It could be worse," Hoffman said.

"LT, you know Fate can hear you," Garrison squealed. "Don't tempt her."

Near the top of a trail, King held up one fist.

"Freeze. Don't move," Hoffman relayed to the team. "King, report."

"Might be the remains of a moose or whatever passes for a large forest-dwelling herbivore on Koen. Looks like moose. More fur. And it was spotted gray and white, I think," King said.

"You think?" Hoffman asked.

"Something ate most of it."

"We're coming up the trail," Hoffman said. Watching the prisoners and the terrain, he calculated they were moving too slowly to clear the area before Kesaht crescent fighters completed their grid search. He'd already been granted one stroke of luck when the enemy was drawn away by fighting elsewhere. "Garrison, tighten up our line. We need to move faster and find shelter."

"Acknowledged," Garrison said. He puffed up the trail and joined Hoffman and the others at a scene of primal carnage. "Wow, what'd you do, Opie?"

Opal gave him a blank look.

"Why can't I get a rise out of you, big guy?"

Hoffman recorded a short video entry for his log, then answered his broken-armed breacher. "He knows he didn't kill this moose-thing. Probably thinks your question is stupid. How's your arm?"

Garrison lifted his right arm and flexed the pseudo muscle under the composite armor plate. "Nothing but a gun show."

"Your other arm."

"Kind of aches."

"Aches?" Hoffman stepped closer and engaged him on a private IR link.

Garrison swallowed hard and held Hoffman's stare for the first time in hours. He looked worried, almost guilty. "I've done all I can without Doc Booker. The armor's like an exoskeleton, good at supporting my actual skeleton. The compression protocols are cycling—and hurt like hell half the time. I've taken the maximum dose of anti-inflammatory pain meds. Sorry, LT."

"Not your fault. We'll get you to sick call and fix you up soon as we can."

"The base doctor will probably want to give me a couple extra weeks leave. On Hawaii or something. Just guessing. Someplace warm."

Hoffman shook his head and went to check on his prisoners. A moment later, he heard King yelling at Garrison.

"Watch where you step! There's blood all over this scene."

"Understood. Wouldn't want to make a mess."

"Just…" King sighed. "Garrison, you meathead. Just get your act together. I can't do everything."

Hoffman squatted next to Masha and her bodyguard, grateful they couldn't hear the IR net. "How are the environment suits holding up?"

Masha hugged herself as she had been for the last kilometer. "Good enough."

"You're trembling."

"I told you I was cold," she said. "We should get

moving. You promised me the exercise will warm me. And I don't like the look of that dead animal. Did you measure the size of the bite marks?"

"No."

"Whatever brought that thing down is probably ninety kilos and has a mouth like a wolf."

Hoffman didn't disagree. "Water and nutrient paste. Two minutes. Then we're moving."

The animal cry he'd heard on the wind hadn't sounded like a predator but something dying badly. He possessed a memory of coyotes killing a brace of rabbits in the night. The sound was hard to identify at first because he hadn't known rabbits could make a sound. The pain and anguish in the sound had been horrible—a wailing squeal like a thin soul leaving the world.

Looking out the window into the Phoenix trailer park, he'd seen shadows racing away from the kill—never a complete coyote, just a gray flank, a leg, an emotionless snout smeared with blood. The dying Koen moose bellowed like a tortured cow in the night. Feeding howls from the wolves increased in volume and number.

"Time's up. Let's move," Hoffman said, realizing Medvedev had shifted between Masha and the sound of the night hunt.

"Thank you, Medvedev," she said. "I hate the sound of the pack."

King took point. Garrison brought up the rear, his left arm held close to his body and his gauss rifle slung to his right hand.

"Why do you keep the doughboy?" Masha asked as they moved down a trail.

"Why do you keep breathing?" Hoffman asked.

"That's right," she said. "You can't help it. You're a Hale model. Changed your face, though."

"Watch your step. It's dark and this trail is narrow," Hoffman said.

"Two things, LT. It's creepy how much she knows about us, and two, the wolves are coming," Garrison said.

Hoffman ran back up the trail, standing by Garrison as he addressed King over the IR. "Get back up to high ground. The prisoners are the mission. Garrison and I will catch up."

"Acknowledged," King said.

"I can't see them yet. They're half a klick back at least but hauling ass by the sound of all that hyena howling," Garrison said.

"Let's give King a two-hundred-meter lead and follow," Hoffman said. "I don't think these things can outflank us on this terrain. Thoughts?"

"If these wolves are smart enough to flank us, I'm going to freak the hell out," Garrison said. "I don't really do animals and wilderness. Or freezing cold darkness."

Hoffman shook his head. "Words I never thought I'd hear from a Strike Marine. Garrison, you're still tracking blood from the moose-thing kill."

"I wiped my feet back there!"

"Let's move," Hoffman said. "King, we're following at two hundred meters."

"Acknowledged. Reached the bottom of the switchback. Climbing to high ground now."

Hoffman and Garrison rushed down the trail, across a stream, and started to ascend the steep path. When he looked back, Hoffman saw shadow creatures on four legs bounding down the mountainside like nightmares. Moonlight broke through the low, flat clouds and slashed the monsters like harbingers of slaughter.

"Your man has blood on his feet," Medvedev muttered.

"Sue me, traitor. I'm sure it'll be wiped off by the time we reach Koensuu City," Garrison said.

"That's almost forty kilometers," Masha said. "At least a day of hiking in the best conditions. Will our battery power last that long, Lieutenant Hoffman?"

He didn't answer, but he did check his armor's diminishing power levels.

The lieutenant got a good look at the first three wolves as they blasted through the half-frozen stream—shaggy fur that looked heavy enough to turn a blade, spikes behind the ears and down the back, and beaky mouths full of small teeth. The last detail should have been a relief, but thousands of small needles looked like the edge of layered saw blades.

"Ugly bastards!" Garrison said.

"King, report."

"We're at the top of the trail. Not great for a pitched battle against combat troops. Might work for natural predators. Can you reach my position?"

"A little help from a sniper overwatch would be helpful," Hoffman said as he pushed his legs and his armor hard up a trail that seemed to grow steeper with each step.

"Medvedev is demanding a weapon to help fight the wolves," King said.

"Negative. Tie them up if you have to. The prisoners are the mission. They can't be allowed to escape." The howling-screeching sounds of their pursuers sent ice down his spine.

He reached the top of the trail and motioned Garrison onto the defensive perimeter King had set up—two felled trees dragged across the flanks of the small trail-top clearing. Beyond the flat space was another steep trail barely wide enough for one person to climb at a time.

"You have a sidearm you cannot use simultaneously with your gauss rifle. Give it to me and I will defend Masha. One less problem for you," Medvedev yelled at King.

"Negative, Medvedev," Hoffman grunted.

One of the rampaging wolves whimpered as a bullet hit it in the shoulder while stronger members of the pack snarled and bark-screeched.

"I really hate that sound," Garrison said, firing one-handed. "Contact."

Hoffman searched for a target and saw something blur along the edge of his night vision. "Use infrared."

"Not good when targets are moving this fast," King warned.

"You can't leave us tied to a tree!" Masha yelled.

"Can!" Opal roared as he cranked down the safety cord to hold the prisoners against a tree. "Prisoners stay!"

"Hoffman, let me fight!" Medvedev shouted.

Opal rushed to the defensive line of Strike Marines

and fired a pistol, the weapon looking like a toy in his huge hand.

"Got one," Garrison said.

"Got two," King grunted. "They're getting cautious. Stay alert."

Hoffman swept his rifle across his zone as the hunters changed from flashing shadows to circling sharks. Eyes reflected flashes of lightning as they peered around trees, disappeared, and reappeared in new locations. Clouds boiled over the mountain-scape. Starlight and moonlight came and went with the wind-driven clouds.

"Opal!" King shouted. "Your buddy is loose."

The wolves rushed up the mountainside, busting from underbrush and bounding over fallen trees. Hoffman shot one in the mouth as it appeared right in front of him, teeth flashing from its snout-beak.

"These things can't be this hungry," he said as he reloaded and scanned for another threat.

"They're territorial," King said. "And pissed off."

Hoffman, King, and Garrison fell back from the perimeter as a wave of snarling killers swarmed their position. Gauss rifles cut them down methodically.

Medvedev slipped his hands beneath the rope and shimmied the chain between his cuffs against the rope, which disintegrated in seconds. He snapped to his feet, wrists still bound together. He tried to free Masha when a pair of wolves rushed him from behind. He kicked one in the mouth and caught the other by the throat. He swung around and crushed the wolf's skull against the tree trunk.

Hoffman did a double take when he realized Medvedev was free. The glint of eyes in the darkness behind the legionnaire promised another attack by the pack.

King fired, turned, fired, turned, fired, and reloaded. "Defensive perimeter, fall back!"

Hoffman fired over Medvedev's shoulder as the Ibarran sidestepped the second Koen wolf's attack, catching it in his thick arms and using his cuff chains as a garrote. Opal crushed the wolf's skull with a whack from his pistol and reloaded the weapon. King fell back until he was shoulder to shoulder with Hoffman.

Garrison struggled to reload with one hand. Slick with blood, injured, exhausted from the pace of the fight—he let the weapon hang for a second and popped his Ka-Bar out from his forearm. He retreated as he worked for a better position. "I really miss Adams right now."

Medvedev grabbed Garrison's rifle by the barrel and swung it like a club into a wolf as it lunged for Garrison's leg. The blow snapped the wolf's neck with a wet crack. Medvedev flipped the rifle in the air and caught it by the grip.

"Hey, give that back!" Garrison reached for his weapon.

Medvedev shouldered Garrison and knocked him flat. The legionnaire shot a wolf creeping up behind the Marine. The bullet blew out the back in a glut of blood and fur, striking a second wolf in the leg, severing the limb. The wolf turned and limped away, yipping in pain.

The howls faded into the forest.

Garrison rolled to his feet and popped his Ka-Bar out of his forearm sheath.

"My rifle," Garrison said, his voice firm and level.

Medvedev snorted and looked back at Masha and found himself staring into the barrel of Opal's pistol.

"Not yours," the doughboy grunted.

Medvedev flicked the safety on the gauss rifle and gripped it by the barrel. He held the butt end out to Garrison. The legionnaire's gaze remained fixed on Opal.

Garrison snatched his weapon back and Opal lowered his pistol.

"How'd he get loose, Opal?" Garrison asked.

Opal's face flushed, his green and brown complexion fluctuating as the doughboy tried to discern an answer.

"Temperatures below freezing make the polymers in the rope brittle," Medvedev said. "Weak against torsion."

"I knew that," Garrison said. "So did Opal. Right, Opal?"

"Hello?" Masha called out. "Damsel here. Distress is over but being tied to a tree and covered in wolf blood is not helping my composure."

"King, give me an ammo count," Hoffman said as he reloaded his rifle. "Opal, get the other prisoner loose."

The lieutenant squared off against Medvedev.

"Opal's programmed to kill you if you threaten the team," he said. "You touch another one of our weapons again and it won't end well for you."

"You keep her safe," the legionnaire tilted his head toward Masha, "and I won't have to do your job for you."

"Sir," King said, "weather's starting to get worse. I think I saw a cave while we were killing the local wildlife. Shall we investigate?"

"Lead the way," Hoffman said as Medvedev helped Masha off the ground and brushed snow off her suit.

Chapter 6

The wall didn't enclose the outlying city and wasn't well-positioned for the rigors of modern battle. The Planetary Defense Forces had augmented it as best they could and continued to improve it in the face of the new threat. Duke climbed down the steep bunker stairs with Booker right behind him, his gear feeling heavier than normal. Adrenaline could only last so long and he'd lost a good bit of blood from his wounds.

"Tight quarters in here," Booker said in a low voice just for Duke. "Another great reason to be a Strike Marine instead of pulling garrison duty."

"Agreed. The sooner we're out doing our job, the better. We need to avoid getting pulled into grunt work before Hoffman gets back," Duke said.

"We should have heard from him by now."

"The lieutenant's solid. He's got the rest of the team to watch out for him, including Opal, who's about as fanatically loyal as it's possible to be," Duke said.

"Masha's dangerous. We should be there."

Duke studied young PDF soldiers as he made his way down the narrow, low hallway. Stairs went up and stairs went down, depending on the contour of the wall foundation around them. Leaning toward Booker's ear as they turned a sharp corner, he whispered, "None of these kids have been in a fight."

Booker nodded. "Sergeants look frosty."

"This way, sir," a non-com said. Nearly middle-aged, the man had battle scars on the side of his neck.

Duke followed the sergeant to a briefing room with maps and computer screens.

"Captain Pine," the sergeant said, pointing Duke toward an officer consulting with junior officers. "He'll tell you where and when to die."

"I thought that was what sergeants were for?" Duke asked.

The sergeant shook his head. "Nope. I just tell you to stop whining and do it."

Duke saluted and presented himself to Pine. "Sergeant Duke, Strike Marine sniper. This is Sergeant Madilyn Booker, medic. I'm cross-training her now."

The young captain stared. "General Allan didn't tell me we had Strike Marines on the planet."

"We're on a priority mission, supposed to be hush-hush, but there was some shooting and I forgot to duck. My team leader's outside the city, finishing our mission, but we're looking for something constructive to do."

"Details of your mission?" Pine asked.

"Need to know, sir," Duke said. "Sorry. But nothing related to the Kesaht."

Pine studied him, then took a good look at Booker. His attention lingered on her more than Duke liked.

"Info would be helpful," Duke said, spitting into a corner. "But if you don't have it, we'll just go outside and start killing shit."

Captain Pine waved them closer to the map table. "All right, Strike Marines, this is the situation. Kesaht have landed here, here, and here. Our fleet is engaging them in void combat but are just as outnumbered up there as we are on the surface. Expect more landings to occur over the next few days." He paused. "Our fleet's holding their own...for now. It's tight, probably going to get tighter. But at least we can keep the Kesaht from slagging Koensuu City like they did Pohja Base."

"What about ground forces? Do they have a beachhead?" Duke asked.

"Yes and no. The Kesaht use different tactics and

strange timelines, compared to what we're accustomed to seeing. They landed outside the city almost at random. On the sides of mountains, in thick forests. They're moving on the city piecemeal, not organized like Vishrakath or Naroosha assaults," Pine said. "None of the precision of a Xaros attack."

"You fought in the Ember War?" Booker asked.

Captain Pine cleared his throat and moved icons around on the map table. "We studied it in the academy. Shall we continue?"

Duke and Booker nodded, expressions blank.

"Our garrison is well trained and equipped. We pushed them back after the initial assault but lost contact with outlying cities Yeansuu, Brona, and Haegs—all sites built on or near ancient cities. Our outlying towns have seen some fighting, but the Kesaht are pushing hard on the city. General Allan wants us to hold the Kesaht as far back as we can. If they get their artillery in range, it won't go well for the civilians. The Kesaht aren't brilliant. We've enveloped and subdivided their lead elements. It's still a bit touchy beyond this perimeter. Lots of meeting engagements. Sudden ambushes."

Duke continued to listen without commenting. He understood where the briefing was heading and what would be asked of him.

"You need reconnaissance," Duke said. "Which is half of what being a Strike Marine sniper is all about."

"The other half?" Pine asked.

"Gauss bullets through foreheads." Duke jerked a thumb at Buffy, his sniper rifle.

"Less good news," Captain Pine continued for Duke and the junior officers also standing by. "The Crucible is damaged. The other gate within jump range is on Malmo, which is also under attack. We're not expecting reinforcements any time soon."

Booker swallowed hard.

"On the upside, the Kesaht won't be getting reinforcements any sooner than we will, which is good news, since they already outnumber us ten to one." Pine said. He faced Duke. "I could use your help with reconnaissance. Identify routes the enemy are taking into the city. The isthmus is two miles wide, easy to monitor even with most of our strength dedicated to defensive lines. There are a lot of places we can harass the Kesaht before they get that far. I want them bled white before the main battle."

"What about comms?" Duke asked.

"That far out, radio comms are inconsistent at best.

Too unreliable to trust. The IR relays are as bulletproof as always. Fiber-optic lines still function. I'll require you to report back using the relays. Are you up for a little side mission?"

Duke checked with Booker, then smirked. "You have any carrier pigeons?"

"Ha ha," Captain Pine said. "We'll have a Mule drop you in the Teunsaa Valley. Got reports of enemy troop buildup in that area before we lost our satellites."

****

Red lights flashed along the walls of the bunker as alert tones sounded on the public-address system. PDF soldiers hustled to battle stations, up ladders and stairs or to gun ports. The powerful thumping of flak turrets firing from the surface resonated through the underground tunnels.

"We may have found the main event," Booker said.

Duke nodded, grabbed his gear, and headed for the stairs as the pace of defensive gunfire increased. "Move. Out of my way. Strike Marine coming through."

"Sorry about my friend. He hasn't killed anyone in hours. Excuse us. Pardon me," Booker said, hurrying through the narrow space behind Duke.

He emerged aboveground and ran onto the wall.

"Duke!" Booker yelled.

He turned in time to see a Kesaht lander burst into flames, pieces of its short wings flying apart as it dove at them—intentionally or unintentionally, it was hard to say. Duke squatted almost to the ground and threw his right arm up to protect his head while his left held the bulk of his gear over his shoulder on a heavy strap. Heat singed the surface of his lightweight sniper armor.

The Kesaht pilot fought for altitude, pulling up right before impact. The burning, broken craft hit the ground hard, remaining mostly intact. The side doors exploded outward as though fired from an explosive charge. Rakka shock troops swarmed forward with crude firearms, wicked bayonets, and bone-handled pole arms.

Duke drew his carbine at the same time Booker drew hers.

"Isn't that sweet," she said, shooting the first Rakka in the face as he outran his feet in his enthusiasm to attack her. "He wants to eat me."

Duke fired on three targets, one after another in the space of two seconds.

The lead Rakka charged, wild hair flying, alien face

contorting with battle rage and hatred.

Duke's patrol rifle came up smooth and fast. He fired two gauss rounds in the front runner's chest and one in his head, then moved to another target. He stepped backward and sideways, then advanced. Knees slightly bent and flexible, his vertical motion was nonexistent no matter his speed. Enemies and friends danced unpredictably in the close-quarter battle.

A squad of PDF soldiers flanked the swarming Rakka, cutting them down in droves with enfilading fire until the mass of aliens turned on them and charged. Two of the young soldiers went down immediately. Others planted their feet in wide shooting stances and opened fire. Their gauss rounds knocked back a row of Rakka but the simultaneous machine-gunfire of the Rakka wiped out most of the PDF squad.

The sergeant from earlier cursed his men as he walked through them with a pistol in one hand. "You have to move and shoot, shoot and move. This isn't range day! I taught you better than this!"

"On me, Booker! We're going at them!" Duke yelled. Side by side, they cut through the chaos to the corner of the wall. Using it as a strongpoint, they pivoted back on their pursuers and slaughtered them with accurate fire.

Duke grabbed Booker and yanked her behind cover as bullets ricocheted. He dropped to a knee, so low he was almost sitting, leaned out, and fired the moment he had a target. Booker stretched over his shoulder, murdering one Kesaht after another with head and throat shots.

"This close-range stuff is easy," she said, excitement and adrenaline causing her words to tumble out too quickly to be understood.

"Take a breath. We roll these assholes back, then recover our gear."

"Understood," Booker said.

Above them, a turret swiveled around and fired down into the Kesaht shock troops, blowing them into pieces.

PDF troops staggered around the battlefield, crouching beside wounded comrades or just staring at the carnage. Smoke rose to meet falling snow.

"Grab your kit, Booker," Duke said. He covered her as she moved, despite the apparent security the flak turret had provided. She returned the favor when he moved.

In the distance, dozens of Kesaht landers streaked toward the surface.

Chapter 7

King led the team higher into the mountains, almost to a pass that would lead down to the main river, as storm clouds dropped low and dumped fat snowflakes straight at the ground. Hoffman could barely see Opal and the prisoners five feet in front of him.

"Find shelter," Hoffman said, his stomach rumbling, his body aching. Garrison and Masha shivered and complained every ten steps since the Koen wolves attacked. Universal tape imperfectly covered the gaps in the legionnaire's enviro suit. Opal's wound was leaking inside his suit, which generated alerts sent to Hoffman's command unit. King barely spoke.

"King," Hoffman said.

"Go."

"You good?"

"Just missing the rest of the team," King sent over IR. *"Come on up. It's a cave, defensible entrance and might be deep enough to conceal a fire if we run out of heat packs."*

"Copy that." Hoffman saw the cave a moment later. The opening was small, the angle of entry uneven. "Opal, help the prisoners down, then climb in."

"Opal hungry," Opal said as he lowered Masha into the darkness.

"Be careful with her," Medvedev said.

Opal ignored the legionnaire.

Hoffman waited for Garrison, then ducked inside, sinking past his knees in powdery snow.

****

The passage cut horizontally into the mountain, dropping away and expanding like a cathedral to old gods. Layers of rock reflected from a single glow stick on a frozen pool on one side. Hoffman looked back as lightning flashed in the small opening. A vertical column of snow added to the drift they had clambered through on the way in.

"It's dry if you come far enough inside, out of the

wind and prying eyes of the crescent fighters," King said. "I didn't see anything for a fire."

"Opal, search the room. No enemies," Hoffman said.

The doughboy took Garrison's rifle, paused to stare at Medvedev, then methodically cleared the cavern.

"Didn't your guy clear this delightful place before he invited us in?" Masha said, thrusting her chin at the snowdrift forming near the entrance. "Will we be able to get out?"

Hoffman addressed Medvedev. "What do you think? Do legionnaires value a second set of eyes?"

"Any leader that retreats into a cave with one way in or out deserves to die," the legionnaire said. "But it is getting damn cold out here."

"I suppose your doughboy could dig us a different exit if needed," Masha said, "and I'm shivering. Cocoa with marshmallows, anyone?"

He ignored her questions and asked his own. "What do you know about Kesaht aircraft? Will they operate in this weather?"

Masha shrugged. "The pilots do not fear for their safety. Their commanders are ruthless. Should they fly in a snowstorm? I doubt it. Will they? Of course," Masha said.

"Don't think we can get ahead of the aerial search during the storm. We'll just end up walking in circles and freezing to death while I complain the *entire* time."

"What'll kill me first? The storm or the nagging?" Hoffman motioned toward the entrance and they got out of the cold.

King collected spare battery packs from the team as they entered, then set the packs in a small mound and covered that with large rocks, pressing the battery leads down. The field expedient space heater clicked on. Hoffman popped his visor and felt a wave of heat from the rocks. The heater would keep a small radius warm without the problems that came along with a smoky fire in a confined space.

Opal returned, wearing fatigue on his face but showing no other evidence of pain or fear. "Big room clear. Small hallways too small for team. Only fur friends fit through."

He held up three—or maybe five—creatures in his palm that were either rats, cats, or shaggy white spiders the size of his hand.

"Are you going to eat them?" Garrison asked.

Opal furrowed his brow. "No eat fur friends."

"Put them back, Opal," Hoffman said.

The doughboy, holding the bundle of animals in one hand, moved away from the glow stick and heat-pack cluster.

"I think that was just one creature, wiggling enough to look like a basket of cats," Garrison said. "Wonder what they taste like."

"Chicken, I imagine," Masha said.

"Rest and recuperate," Hoffman said to the team and the prisoners. "King, follow me."

Hoffman climbed from the cave, moving quickly to one side of the opening as King emerged to cover his own zone on the other side. With only two of them, their fire lanes would be expansive in the event of a fight. He heard nothing but freezing night wind and the sound of wolves in the distance.

"Break in the storm. Won't last," King said as he scanned the valley below them with handheld binoculars. "We're in a bad spot, LT."

"Worse than an alien starship swarming with mindless cyborgs bent on tearing us limb from limb?" Hoffman asked.

King lowered the binoculars and smiled. Moonlight painted his face with stark shadows. "You split our team for that mission as well. I'm not criticizing. I was part of that decision."

Hoffman did his own scan of the area as King stood security for him. "Epic view when you can see it. We need to get over this range, down to the river, and cut back to the city. The waterways around the isthmus make more sense from this vantage point."

"I don't like it. This entire planet gives me the heebie-jeebies," King said.

"The line between natural and artificial landscape is less defined than I first thought," Hoffman said. "Once we have comms with base and they regain air superiority, we can request extraction and support."

Several minutes of silence elapsed as wind howled through a mountain pass and raised a cloud of snow from the treetops down in the valley.

"She's the woman from New Bastion," King said. "Can't believe we finally caught up with her. How much more do you think she knows about the Kesaht?"

Hoffman nodded. "Our mission is capture and transport, not interrogation."

"A certain amount of intelligence gathering is implied in all missions," King said.

"True." Hoffman put away the binoculars. "The temperature's fallen five degrees since we came out here.

Visibility will favor the enemy fighters. We should move under cloud cover if we can. All we need to see is one foot in front of the other."

"That storm on the horizon looks worse than what we just came through. Sheltering here is a risk. Might be avalanche season by the time we're on the move," King said.

A pair of the crescent-shaped fighters emerged from a pass across the valley and swooped low over the trees kilometers away.

"Good call, LT. Never doubted you for a second," King said.

The fighters selected a trail through the forest and strafed it with energy weapons as a battle flashed from the direction of the navy base.

"There's a strange rhythm to a bombardment. Easier to appreciate from this far away," Hoffman said.

"That was just a strafing run," King said.

Hoffman lifted one hand, acknowledging King was right. "Today a strafing run, tomorrow airstrikes guided by their version of our recon teams. Let's get inside. I'll learn what I can from Masha and her bodyguard. Follow my lead, and when in doubt, keep your mouth shut. She's better at word games than both of us put together."

"Sir." King saluted.

They climbed through the deepening snowdrift and made their way to the warming station where his people and the prisoners were eating, more or less.

"I never thought I'd be excited about nutrient paste," Masha said. "Must be the altitude."

No one else spoke. Easting paste from a tube wasn't much of a dinner event, although Opal displayed the most fastidious table manners. Hoffman and the others watched him methodically roll up the tube after each sip until it was compacted into a neat cylinder. He then stored the leftovers in an empty ammo pouch.

Medvedev ignored the food paste until he'd knelt on one knee and prayed for several moments, his quiet words following a familiar rhythm.

"Prayer to Saint Kallen?" King asked skeptically.

Hoffman nodded. "He's not pretending."

King made no response.

Battle noises moved farther from the cave with an occasional flyover at supersonic speeds. Hoffman noticed a change in Masha. He watched her watching Opal.

****

Garrison sat next to the big legionnaire, watching him eat with undisguised interest. "I bet you could destroy an all-you-can-eat buffet."

"Best place to store food and water is inside the body," Medvedev said. "Harder to lose it."

"What's your deal? Why are you babysitting the hot blonde on this forsaken planet?" Garrison shifted to relieve the pain of his injured arm and shoulder.

"Orders," Medvedev said.

Garrison tipped back his head and squirted a bright-yellow substance into his mouth, wiping the back of his hand across his mouth when he was done. "Is it cheese? Is it roast beef? Is it a hamburger casserole combo meal? We don't really know, do we? I was just saying you look like you train hard and eat a lot. I respect that."

"My good friend Medvedev has a healthy appetite. There still Chinese buffets outside the Marine barracks in Phoenix?" Masha asked.

"The General Tso's plate at Asia Ma Ma is the best of them all," Garrison said, then he stopped suddenly. "Wait…you've been to Earth?"

Masha waved away his concerns. "No."

Hoffman sat back to watch the show, wondering at the spy who seemed to talk too much.

"What's best to eat on a buffet? Sirloin steak? Lobster?" she asked.

Hoffman leaned forward from his seat near the edge of the group. "What have you two been up to since Bastion? Other than when we almost had you on Nouveau Marsellie and Ticonderoga."

Garrison pointed a finger gun at Masha. "I didn't really appreciate what you did to us on Bastion. We nearly died saving your ass."

"Hardly," Medvedev said.

"Be polite, Medvedev," Masha said. "I never had the chance to say how impressed I was that your team got me away from Fellerin and gave me the opportunity to kill that Haesh bastard myself." She nodded at Hoffman, then King, and finally Garrison—her eyes wide with innocent appreciation of their prowess. "I was more impressed that Earth managed to sweep the incident under the rug…for the most part."

"You had to make it ugly," Garrison said.

"What were you doing on New Bastion?" Hoffman asked.

Her smile expertly mixed naughty and nice. "A little bit of this, a little bit of that."

Hoffman knew what she was doing but still enjoyed

looking at her. Garrison was spellbound for several moments.

"What were you doing here? Skiing?" King said from his position guarding the entrance, bursting the scene like only a gunnery sergeant could.

"Good guess," Masha said.

Opal woke up in the middle of the conversation and stared at Medvedev across the heat packs warming the pile of carefully stacked stones.

"I'd advise against a staring contest," Garrison said, "unless you want to make a wager."

"I do not. It is a doughboy. An organic machine. Not so dangerous by himself. If there were a squad of them, I'd be worried," Medvedev said.

"No wager?" Garrison asked.

"No."

"Not even a little one?"

"No."

"Opal bored," Opal said.

"You see, Med, Opal isn't your ordinary doughboy. He's fought banshees—"

"That's enough, Corporal," Hoffman said.

Masha stood, drawing all eyes. "We know all about your fight to save the Dotari home world from the phage."

"The details of that mission are still classified. I like Garrison. He's a good Marine. Don't get him court-martialed, Masha," Hoffman said.

"Understood, Lieutenant Thomas Hoffman. And I agree. Your corporal is a good fighter. Even though he is injured far worse than he will admit."

Medvedev leaned forward, planting his elbows on his knees and talking to Garrison as though he were a green recruit. "Your shoulder is dislocated. I have seen this injury many times. The armor you wear is little different from what we are issued in the Ibarran Legion. It will keep you going longer than is healthy. You will require surgery if you don't set it properly."

"It will require surgery anyway," King said.

Garrison glared at King. "Why did you have to bring that up? We all know that, but why talk about it?"

"You've had surgery before," King said.

"And the pain meds *do* things to me. I say funny stuff. My squad mates—"

"No pain medication is necessary. I will help you. I will set the bone and allow the armor to do the rest. With luck, there will be no more fighting and you will heal very well," Medvedev said. "I saw you fighting the wolves. You weren't at your best."

Hoffman looked to King for advice.

King shrugged. "It won't heal on its own. And if it hurts a lot, Garrison might shut his mouth for ten minutes."

Garrison held his left arm with his right and stared angrily at Medvedev. "Let you put those mitts of yours on me?" He shook his head. "No way. You might slip and snap my neck. I saw what you did to Max. Miss that guy. Hope he's OK."

"Why do you suddenly want to help us?" Hoffman asked as thoughts of Max rekindled his anger at the Ibarrans, emotions he concealed for the sake of the mission.

"You won't give me a rifle. Won't let me fight. The best way to keep Masha safe is for all your team to be healthy. I swear by the grace and honor of Saint Kallen."

"Opal," Hoffman said, "if Medvedev moves funny, you crush his skull. Med, let's see what you can do."

Opal stood quickly, feet already in a fighting stance. "Opal crush."

Medvedev turned toward the doughboy, watching him for several seconds before acknowledging Hoffman's permission. He moved close to Garrison and knelt. "This will be very painful. Try not to squeal. I don't want that thing crushing my skull."

"I'm not afraid," Garrison said, his voice rising

three-quarters of an octave.

"Curious," Medvedev said. "You look afraid. I must remove your armor. When we are finished, put it back on and tighten everything above the waist."

Garrison nodded as beads of sweat formed on his forehead.

Medvedev helped him out of his armor.

Opal growled. "Opal crush."

"Not yet, big guy," Garrison said as color drained from his face. "Maybe this isn't a great idea."

Medvedev glared at Opal, then focused on his reluctant patient. "Sit up straight. Face the heating stones. Do not watch me." He shifted his weight on his knees, edging closer to Garrison. "We must start in a neutral position, with your humerus abducted and elbow flexed. I will help you. I am moving your arm. You must relax. Think happy-tree thoughts."

Medvedev held Garrison's upper arm vertical against his body with his forearm bent ninety degrees at the elbow.

"This is easy. Are you going to read my palm next, tell my fortune or something?" Garrison regulated his breathing as he asked the question.

"You know what comes next," Medvedev said.

"Yeah. I do, actually."

Medvedev slowly moved Garrison's hand and forearm away from his body. "I will externally rotate your arm until you say when."

"When?"

"Until you feel resistance and you say when."

"When."

Medvedev continued to apply torque to the arm.

"When! For the love of God! Blessed Saint Kallen and all her gauss bullets, I said when!"

"Sorry. I thought you were acknowledging my instructions," Medvedev said.

Opal growled.

Garrison swayed, eyes rolling around, air squeaking from his nasal passage. He took a sharp breath. "OK, I'm good. Opal, stop making that cry-baby sound. You're freaking me out."

"Opal no cry. Garrison cry. Hurt ears," Opal said.

"I understand, big guy, no shame in it."

"Pathetic," Medvedev said, applying gradual pressure.

Hoffman shifted his stance as he watched the scene, glancing at Masha to be sure she hadn't escaped again.

"When," Garrison said.

"Are you certain? I didn't feel it go back in."

"When!"

"My apologies. Perhaps I did feel it go back in this time," Medvedev said.

"I really hate you," Garrison said.

Medvedev checked the angle of the arm and position of the shoulder. He shook his head. "There must be more external rotation before we move in anteriorly. Brace yourself."

"No, no, no!" Garrison said as Medvedev twisted his hand and forearm away from his body, keeping the upper arm pressed tight to his rib cage. Without waiting to explain what was next, Medvedev seized his shoulder and wrenched it forward.

"Striiiiiiiiiiike Mareeeeeeens," Garrison wailed, then vomited between his feet. King turned away as Hoffman shook his head to clear an unexpected feeling of light-headedness. Masha puffed out her lower lip and made a sad face for Garrison, something between motherly and mocking.

Medvedev stood. "There! It went better than expected. You cried like a little girl, but we did it."

Garrison looked up, his head still between his knees, his face slick with sweat, tears filling his eyes but refusing to fall. He rotated his arm slowly, then raised an elbow gingerly.

"By the Saint!" Garrison exclaimed. "Not bad for a filthy traitor."

"It is better, yes?"

"I wish Booker was here. Better bedside manner and a hell of a lot better-looking than this guy." Garrison hooked his right thumb toward Medvedev.

"Opal no crush." The doughboy sat down, pouting.

****

Hoffman adjusted his suit, loosening everything but the wrists, ankles, and throat cuffs that kept it sealed against the environment. Strike Marine armor regulated body temperature with the helmet and gauntlets off, but there were limits. He didn't want an icicle of Koen air leaking into his sweaty underlayer.

"I'm taking a turn at the cave entrance," King said. "Garrison is too concerned about the cold for a hardened warrior protected by state-of-the-art gear. I almost had him convinced the negative wind chill would speed healing through his armor. I'd like to see how he does without all our fancy tools."

"We'll schedule a training mission in Alaska. Or someplace real miserable like upstate New York in winter. Call it a gut check. Separate the men from the boys."

"Looking forward to it," King said and then strode toward Garrison's sentry position. "Corporal Garrison, you're relieved. Attend to your gear, take in calories and hydration, then get some rest."

"Can I do all that near the heat packs?"

"Is your armor working?"

"Well, yeah. Just saving my energy. Could be a long mission," Garrison said. "I think you should be nicer to someone who just got mauled by the worst medic in the system. Did you break your arm during the crash?"

King put one gauntlet on the forehead of his helmet and squeezed in frustration. "This generation exhausts me. I wish we still made proccies. I'd ask for a tougher batch, less whining and more killing the enemy."

Hoffman didn't think the comment was meant for him to hear, so he ignored it.

Masha rubbed the arms of her environment suit. Standing with her feet close together and her posture closed from ankle to chin, she appeared vulnerable and human. Emotions spilled inside Hoffman. He wondered if her spy craft included deep hormonal and emotional manipulation.

After everything that had happened between them, he should hate her as the enemy. Apparently, his body didn't get that memo. In other circumstances, he would take her hot coffee and ask to sit beside her.

It is what it is, he thought. She was an attractive, strong, intelligent woman. What wasn't to like—other than her traitorous allegiances and nearly getting him killed and costing him his career?

Snow twisted past King at the cave entrance. Opal slept sitting up like an armored car that had been powered down. Medvedev watched everyone, hard eyes looking for weakness in the Strike Marine team.

Hoffman removed two coffees from the remnants of the box from the Mule and pulled the tabs on his way to Masha. He handed her one of the steaming, cup-like bottles. "Drink this. Should help you warm up."

She took it with both hands and held it close to her face, staring at him through the rising tendril of steam. "Are you trying to kill me with bad coffee?"

Hoffman shrugged. "I pretend it's good coffee."

She sipped. "It isn't."

"Best coffee for miles," Garrison said from where he sat near the piled heat packs.

Masha raised one eyebrow and whispered to

Hoffman, "Hot coffee in the cold darkness of certain death. How romantic."

"We've been through worse, and I'd bet Garrison's pay that you have as well."

Masha stepped a half-stride away from Garrison and Medvedev, nodding for Hoffman to join her as she half-turned for a bit of privacy.

"What is this coffee costing me?" she asked.

Hoffman took a sip, turned the cup, stared at it. "I need to know more about the Kesaht. I've never taken my team against them, so I've only been given the need-to-know version—basically nothing. I read the name somewhere. It didn't seem relevant to what I was doing at the time."

"Hmm. You will learn more than you want to know about the Kesaht very soon. But I could speak of them. I know other things of value to you."

"You don't know what's valuable to me."

"Like what happened to Corporal Kate Adams and why she was removed from your team?"

"What? How could you know that?" Hoffman squeezed his coffee cylinder.

"My question is, do you even know why she was reassigned?"

Hoffman's control of the conversation was slipping away. Adams had been removed from his team months ago. King and the rest of the team didn't even see her leave. She never returned from a weekend pass and a transfer notice signed by the division adjutant was the only explanation he received for her sudden absence. There'd been no word from her since, and no answers from the chain of command on where she'd gone or why his team was short a Marine. But Adams was not the immediate issue in the cave.

"The Kesaht," he said.

She took a slow sip of her steaming coffee. "They've attacked other worlds."

Masha set her cup aside and interlaced her fingers over a knee. She looked up at him, and it felt like her spy mask slipped away for a moment. "They always try to take the children alive."

Ice reached into Hoffman's soul. "Why?"

He thought of Dotari children dying of the phage and hoped the cure his team had brought from the lost Dotari fleet was working.

"You remember the Toth?" she asked.

"I'm familiar with them. I didn't enter service until after they attacked Hawaii. They vanished off the galactic scene once the Ember War ended. Did a VR range against

Toth targets once. Heard some stories about them from old timers that fought them on Hawaii."

"Not all of them are gone. There's at least one master left." She sipped her coffee.

"What do the Toth have to do with the Kesaht? And why do I feel like I won't like the answer?" Hoffman asked.

Masha shrugged. "We've seen a lot of Toth tech in the Kesaht fleet. The Kesaht profess a vendetta against humanity—hard to justify as we didn't know who the Kesaht were until they started raiding planets. Given the Toth's history with us…we're pretty certain the Toth are behind the Kesaht's aggression."

"Why are they stealing children?"

"Do you know what a Toth overlord eats? Neurological energy. Back during the Ember War, Ibarra and President Garret sent a kill team to destabilize the Toth after their attack on Earth. The Toth big boss, went by the name of Mentiq, ate a…modified proccie. Didn't go well for either of them."

"The Toth are afraid to eat another human," Hoffman said.

"Take your idea further," she said.

Hoffman didn't want to say the words aloud. "An

adult human could be a proccie. A poison-pill proccie like the one that killed Mentiq. But children…"

"Fair game," she said.

King stiffened. "Jesus. That's why the Toth—and the Kesaht—are attacking us? Because we killed their leader?"

"No," Masha said. "Whatever overlord would've come to power afterward would've sent us a thank-you card. The Toth have a better reason to hate us."

Medvedev spoke something in Basque and Opal slapped him on the back of the head. "English."

Medvedev sneered, then muttered under his breath.

"Nothing wrong with the truth," Masha said. "Terrans don't know it. Might help get their asses in gear if they did."

Medvedev scowled. "You shouldn't be talking so much. This will go in my report."

Masha rolled her eyes. "The Toth are almost extinct, thanks to us."

Hoffman watched Opal, worried about another violent showdown between the doughboy and the legionnaire. He could feel Masha watching him. "The kill team did more than whack their leader?"

"Ha! If only," she said. "Toward the end of the war,

a bargain was made with an...entity. This entity was essential to winning the war with the Xaros. It figured out how to force the Xaros drones to self-destruct."

"Not all of them." A shiver lanced up his spine. From his Strike Marines' expressions, they were having the same flashbacks to the *Kid'ran's Gift* and swarms of banshees.

Masha missed the silent exchange between Hoffman and the others. "In return, the entity demanded...*elikadura*."

Opal reached for Masha, but King put a firm hand on his shoulder to stop him.

"She is trying to say it was given...nourishment. Fuel," Medvedev said.

Masha shook her head slightly. "Strength is a better word. Strength it got from consuming the life energy of every Toth on their home world."

Silence.

"No...that's xenocide," Hoffman said.

"The Xaros drones were an existential threat, even with the Masters dead. A sacrifice had to be paid for victory and the Toth were the lambs, so to speak. Given the Toth's history, I'd call it karma," Masha said.

King grumbled. "Then how did a Toth end up

behind the Kesaht if they were all…eaten."

Masha shrugged and continued. "Best we can piece together is that an overlord was off world with a jump-capable ship before the Qa'Resh disabled all the drives. He skipped out to the Kesaht's system with Crucible tech and took over. Years later, they've got a Crucible gate of their own and now they're using the jump network to attack every human they can find."

Hoffman, sensing a flaw in the logic, locked eyes with her. "The Kesaht think we're the bad guys, xenocidal villains."

"We are. It was war. Problem is we don't know where the Kesaht originate from. Hard to fight an enemy you can't attack," she said.

"This is Ibarra's fault, isn't it? Wiping out the Toth sounds like something he'd do." Hoffman had mixed feelings about Ibarra, the scientist who created him, all the other procedural humans, and the doughboys.

"President Garret was part of that decision-making process. It happened with his consent. Even your pal Valdar and the *Breitenfeld* were there…though he was kept in the dark until it was too late for him to do anything about it," Masha said. She seemed to be waiting on his reaction, wondering which way he would go.

"The Toth were evil," King interjected. "We'd be fighting them directly if they hadn't been taken care of. They wanted the proccie tech when they attacked Earth the first time—so they could raise sentient cattle to feed on. They would never have stopped."

"We gave up that tech," Hoffman said.

Masha smiled dangerously. "Earth did. The Ibarra Nation didn't."

"And now New Bastion is threatening war against Earth because of you," Hoffman said, leaning back from the argument. "Thanks for that."

Masha winked at him. "We live in interesting times. Who knows what tomorrow will bring?"

"What do the Kesaht look like?" Hoffman asked. "Physical weaknesses?"

"Funny thing, the Kesaht are a union of different races," she said. "The Rakka are their foot soldiers, barely intelligent grunts." She raised her cup of coffee to Opal. "The Sanheel are the officer class. Big, centaur-looking monsters. Smart and cunning. There are rumors of a third species, one with better reaction times than the Sanheel are capable of. Those are the ones that pilot their ships."

"Didn't she say something about Adams?" Garrison asked.

"I must have misspoken." Masha sipped her drink.

"You know an awful lot about us," Hoffman said.

"You've been after us for a while," the spy said. "'Know thy enemy' is some tried-and-true advice."

"And what do you know about Adams?" Hoffman asked.

"Adams," she said, a smile tugging at the corner of her lips, "was not *our* enemy. What Earth did to her—and the others—concerns Lady Ibarra. Not that you need the details."

"What? You think Adams was on your side?" Garrison asked. "You two know what *semper fidelis* even means? Always faithful. Adams was a Strike Marine. Loyal to Earth and the Terran Union. I went through basic and selection with her. She never spoke a word about the Ibarras or did anything to make me think she was a traitor."

"She didn't have to," Masha huffed.

Garrison stood up and leveled a finger at the spy. "You just watch your mouth," he said.

"Garrison," Hoffman said, "swap with Gunney and ask him to come over here. He and I need to work out our next steps."

The Marine shuffled off, working his shoulder in small circles.

"Opal, move Medvedev away from the fire," the lieutenant said. "Don't let them speak to each other."

"Sir." The doughboy hooked a hand under Medvedev's shoulder and dragged him to the cave wall.

Masha drained the last of her coffee and lay down next to the heat packs.

Chapter 8

The Mule swooped low over the Teunsaa Valley. Duke glanced through the hell hole, glad he wasn't using it on this mission. Treetops heavy with snow swayed as the pilot circled toward the clearing and landed.

"Out you go," said the warrant officer at the door, giving them the all-clear with a thumbs-up.

"Thanks for the ride," Duke said, then jumped down with all his gear, immediately sinking knee-deep in snow.

Booker landed next to him, frowning at the tactical snowshoes on her feet. "Do these things work?"

Duke shook his head. "Are you neck-deep in snow?"

"Near enough," she said. "I'm starting to think you enjoy winter warfare."

"Better than boarding and clearing a void ship."

"You got me on that one," she said.

Duke trudged into the woods and hunkered down to watch the Mule make several other false landings, then he led the way out of the area. The snowshoes fatigued his legs but kept the weight of his armor from sinking him to his armpits. Once he was moving, he stayed on the surface—his shallow tracks blown away by gusts of wind. Jumping off a Mule ramp had been beyond the design specifications of the snowshoes.

Booker kept pace with him with no complaints, which was one of the things he liked about the medic—she was tough without making a big deal out of it.

"We should take breaks twice an hour unless you think differently. You're the medic," Duke said.

"You're the expert in long-range reconnaissance patrols," she said. "I'll tell you if I need a break. I've got nothing to prove."

"Not to me, you don't," he said.

"Not to anyone."

Duke hiked through snowdrifts, pausing from time to time to check the back trail. The snowshoes continued to minimize evidence of their passage. Field craft still mattered. He set false trails from time to time and used tree branches to further hide their tracks when necessary.

Mountains outlined the horizon, sketched in moonlight and the surprising tranquility between storms.

"We have to stop for the night. Dig a shelter and stay warm," Duke said, trying not to look at her.

"Just you and me, huh?"

"Don't get any ideas," he said.

She laughed. "Your virtue is safe with me. But not your reputation."

"Not sure what you mean by that," he said, looking for a defensible campsite. "Post up by that tree and hold security while I do this."

"You talk about titty bars all the time. Deep down, you're a decent guy," she said.

"Now you *are* going to ruin my reputation." He dug a cave in the snow, then hid evidence of his work. "Mi casa es su casa."

"That's…a tiny hole," she said, staring down into what could have been a snowy grave.

"Think of it as a windbreak with the advantage of being nearly invisible unless you're standing right here. We'll sleep in shifts unless it gets so cold we have to consolidate warmth—which is probably going to happen, so be warned."

"I like warm."

"The wind is picking up," he said, climbing into the shelter behind her, then turning to face the entrance. His field of fire allowed one hundred eighty degrees of visibility. Cut into the side of a packed drift, it also provided an elevated position.

"I should have cross-trained as a comms specialist with Max. No need to freeze my lady bits off."

"Hazards of the job." Duke laughed. "You need to stop washing your uniform."

"I was just about to tell you the opposite."

"Nope. Have to smell neutral, translation…all natural."

"You smell like man funk."

"Let's talk about woman funk."

"I'm already asleep. See you in the morning. Don't forget my breakfast in bed."

"Sweet dreams, baby sister."

"Don't call me that. Makes me wonder about Adams. Why'd she get pulled from the team?" Booker asked, already fading into sleep.

"Just like a woman, start something, then leave me to stew on it half the night."

****

Duke and Booker were out of the shelter and moving before dawn. He signaled her to stop just before the sun came up. "Dangerous time to move. Easy to give away your position. That's why hunters hide in tree blinds when deer come out to feed."

"Good to know. Also explains why I'm not a hunter," Booker said, moving slower today, still recovering from a hatefully cold night. "Easier to get food from a combiner. Comes out all nice and toasty."

Duke adjusted his pace but only for the first half hour. Native animals kept their distance, whisking through trees or into snowy holes. He saw what looked like moose or horse tracks leading to a stream. Closer inspection revealed normal animal behavior.

"Problem?" Booker asked.

"Just checking to make sure the Kesaht aren't using the Sanheel as cavalry. These look like hoof impressions…Quiet…Look there, slowly."

Booker moved as though the winter air were turning her to ice. "Oh my."

A majestic moose covered with white and gray fur stood on a rise, morning light streaming down to set tree branches of ice crystals glowing near it. A second appeared, then two smaller versions. All four of them stared at the snipers.

"Are they afraid of us?" Booker asked.

"Don't know. Have to be careful about projecting Earth-Terran behaviors on local life forms. Something a Pathfinder told me once. For all we know, those things are carnivorous. Or sentient."

"You just gave me a chill. Thanks. That's just what I needed," Booker said.

Duke re-charted his path to avoid the animals wandering out of sight. "The presence of our four-legged friends probably means there aren't a bunch of rampaging Kesaht freaks in the area."

"Good to know."

Hours passed in cold silence as wind blasted snow powder from treetops. Sun glared off the white panorama, forcing their helmet visors to darken protectively.

"Getting close to the top," Duke said.

"Is that why I can barely breathe?"

They crawled to the summit and scanned the next valley with binoculars.

"Contact," Duke said.

Kesaht landing craft swooped in to land near hundreds of others. Rakka and Sanheel poured out to join hundreds of warriors formed into loose packs. Slow-moving landers set down in an adjacent meadow, each deploying a single tank, squat and ugly machines with double-barrel cannons.

"A vanguard force." Duke attached his binos to his belt and pulled his sniper rifle off his back. He took out the two halves of Buffy, his custom weapon, and snapped them together. He fixed an optics set to the top and brought the butt against his shoulder as he scanned over the Kesaht forces.

The twin long vanes of the rifle were matte black, the capacitor port just behind the magazine could take a battery pack or attach to a larger power cell that Booker and Duke each carried. The weapon was a miniature of the rail weapons system used by armor and the Terran Union's naval batteries.

"We going to take a shot?" Booker asked.

"You got a mouse in your pocket?" Duke asked. "This is recon."

"Buffy has a power select option, right? You don't have to break the sound barrier with a shot that'll shoot a hole through the side of a battleship. Maybe we take an officer. Make them nervous…"

"Kill a grunt, kill a general…they'll come for us.

Maybe we can out march the pig boys down there, but they vector aircraft on us and we'll be dead. Dead…and we won't get this intel back to the locals. PDF know what's coming, how many, and from what direction is a lot more valuable than one headshot," Duke said.

"Then why'd you break Buffy out of storage?"

"Because I see better through her," Duke snapped. "Don't dictate my relationship with my girl. Prepare to copy…Tanks analogs. Looks like the front armor will need a full power shot to penetrate…vision slits for commander and driver. Might be able to thread the needle on a lower setting shot. Got some Kesaht engineers fitting chains to tires of their personnel carriers. I count seven tanks and seven-wheeled vehicles."

Booker uncovered her arm screen and typed. "Fascinating. Can I just put 'a shit ton of bad guys'? Joking. Calm down, you grumpy old bastard."

"I'm not old. I'm thirty-seven."

"Uh huh. What about mechanized infantry?"

Duke continued his report.

****

Duke studied the map with the illumination of his

arm screen nearly off as twilight swept through the mountain forest with surprising swiftness.

"Don't see any more aircraft inbound," Duke said. "Looks like the entire Kesaht vanguard deployment is complete. Time?"

"I've been freezing my ass off here for three hours and twenty minutes," Booker said, her teeth chattering.

"Say four hours for them to drop a mechanized infantry battalion-sized force," Duke said. "Our intelligence analysts will want to know that. We figure out their deployment tempo and it'll do wonders for our own plans. Snuggle up close. We need to study the map."

"Lamest line I've ever heard," Booker said.

"You wish. I'd be doing you a favor."

"As a medical professional, I have to warn you the thin air is affecting your powers of observation and reasoning," she said.

"You're telling me you have a lot of experience getting picked up? How many pickup lines have you heard out here at the ass end of the galaxy surrounded by savage aliens and Strike Marine grunts you think of as brothers?"

"Now you made it weird. What did you want to show me?"

"I'll pretend you didn't say that," Duke said and

pointed at a bridge on the map. "Here. They'll cross here. It's a hard line back to the city."

"Long way," she said, her voice sounding tired.

"Not if we cover over this mountain range," he said.

"That'll take—"

"Longer the more time you complain. Let's move."

Chapter 9

Hoffman stretched out his arms, his muscles tight with cold. Garrison cleaned his weapon as Opal looked on, the doughboy seeming almost jealous that the other Marine still had a weapon.

The lieutenant powered up his armor and checked the power reserves. He had almost three days' worth of power at normal activity levels; after that, his suit would become so much dead weight that he'd be as mobile as a knight of old in full plate armor.

"Weather's clearing," King said from the mouth of the cave. His Strike Marine gear was in perfect order. Although he carried an air of exhaustion, his posture was upright and correct, a model of a professional warrior.

Hoffman took a step closer and put one hand on his shoulder. "You're welcome to come, but I want to see for myself." He could feel the silence after the storm. The air in the cave seemed colder and at the same time less threatening. The night had been full of howling wind and whispers of distant Kesaht fighters. What did he really know about Koen? It looked like an Arctic planet, sheathed in ice hundreds of feet deep in most places. Green continents were visible from space, but they were like specks on a blank canvas.

"Garrison, keep an eye on the prisoners. Show Opal the video on your arm screen if he steps out of line. I saw him staring at the legionnaire while he slept," King said.

Garrison laughed shortly. "Does Opal look hungry? Because I'm hungry."

"Focus on the mission, Marine," King said.

Hoffman listened to his team and was thankful for the banter. Teamwork, esprit de corps, and a defined objective could get Strike Marines through most any situation.

He climbed the short internal path to the cave entrance, stepping hip deep into drifts of snow that had accumulated during the night. He paused at the small circle of light leading to the surface and listened. Touching the side of his helmet with one gauntleted hand, he adjusted the tint to resist the harsh glare of morning sunlight from the winter landscape beyond. His IR and infrared filters showed him nothing special.

"You want me to clear that out for you, LT?" King

asked. He held his gauss rifle by the pistol grip with the sling supporting most of the weight. His finger was off trigger and his feet were placed in a ready stance. His left hand was forward of his body and ready to push snow from the obstructed cave entrance.

"I'll get it," Hoffman said. He was always learning from the veteran gunnery sergeant. Sometimes it was a big thing, like a personnel decision, and other times it was how to do something mundane, like brush snow away from a hole. He cleared it out a little bit at a time, pausing to look through first with sensors, then with his eyes to avoid surprises.

"I'm stepping out. Cross behind me to my left and set up security," Hoffman said. They went through the opening as though they were assaulting a door, weapons pulled to their shoulders as they searched over the top of their gun sights for enemies. A tiny adjustment in posture would bring the targeting reticles between their eyes and their selected targets.

He swept his own area of responsibility and saw nothing but wilderness.

"Clear, nothing seen," King said.

Hoffman allowed his gauss rifle to hang but kept his right hand on the vertical handgrip.

He felt like he had seen this landscape before. Something about the snow-covered mountain range and dense forest was primal. Tall, narrow evergreen trees swept across foothills and mountainsides wherever they could grab hold of the soil and grow. In the lowland area, he saw frozen marshes and long legged crane-like birds poking around tufts of tall grass poking out of the snow.

"It almost feels like we're the first ones on this planet," Hoffman said.

"Let's leave the discovery learning to the Pathfinders. Puffies love dropping onto new places and see what'll try and eat them."

Hoffman faced the gunnery sergeant. "Not the adventurous type?"

"Every day in the Strike Marine Corps could be your last. Every tube of nutrient paste as tasty as a last meal. Every alien a chance for target practice and to see how well the lowest bidder made our armor. When do the adventures stop?"

"Right about the time your shuttle crashes in the middle of a mountain range. We seem to be doing better than Masha. So there's that."

"An act, sir," King said, "Everything she does or says is a lie."

"Yeah...we're not at the 'trust but verify' stage with her or the Ibarrans yet."

King scowled. "No, sir. And she's just a little too easy on the eyes and friendly for my taste."

"The Ibarrans grow their own." Hoffman pointed up to a small rocky outcrop. "Doubt they'd train a spy that wasn't a bit charming."

Hoffman moved to a higher position and stood guard as King brought out the rest of the team. Garrison escorted Masha, his visor darkened against the sun just like the rest of the team, and he was moving better than expected. The only pain medication he'd taken from his first-aid kit was anti-inflammatories, which Hoffman thought was strange because the semiprofessional powerlifter had an almost religious abhorrence of anti-inflammatory meds.

"It's freezing," Masha complained over the general comms band.

"She ain't lying about that," Garrison said, shivering visibly despite his powered armor.

"King, you'll have to take point." Staying close to Masha, Hoffman took up a center position to monitor the entire team. The traveling formation wasn't ideal. He wished he had his entire team.

"Do you want me to fall back into the rearguard position?" Garrison asked.

"I'll watch the principal. Don't fall too far back." He muted the comms links to Masha and Medvedev. "We haven't seen any Kesaht fighters or ground troops today. Our biggest threats are internal. Watch the Ibarrans. I trust them about as far as I could throw the big one."

King, Garrison, and Opal acknowledged over the closed channel.

"Do you have an extraction plan, Lieutenant?" Masha asked. "I'm not familiar with the emergency survival suit you issued us. They don't seem to be made for long-term exposure."

"She's trying to say she's cold," Garrison said from several strides back. "Which I totally understand. I feel like my recruiter misrepresented the amount of outdoor time there would be in this profession."

Hoffman ignored the breacher.

"Cold and hungry. That's the stuff they don't talk about in those fancy recruiting videos. Am I right? Gunney, did you ever see a hungry-looking poster boy for the Marine Corps? Those guys probably aren't even in the military. I mean, really, my face camo never looked that perfect," Garrison said.

"Watch your zone," King said over the radio.

"I like to talk when I march through frozen hell. You know that, Gunney."

"If an enemy sneaks up on us, I'm going to make you bunkmates with Opal for a year. He never complains about the weather," King said. A moment passed. "We're moving down a trail to a wide stream bed. Not seeing any footprints or animal markings. It's virgin snow far as I can tell."

"Copy that," Hoffman said. "Start looking for our first rest station."

"There are several good rally points along this route. I'm dropping a couple coded IR markers to collapse on in the event of ambush," King said.

"That's why you're the top," Hoffman said. "Garrison will pick them up as we pass."

Wind gusted across the valley below and through the trees surrounding them. Snow wafted into the sky like disturbed powder. Cold air iced its way into their armor. Birds and other small animals moved in the trees, never coming too close to the invaders. Hoffman figured if they were happy, he was happy. He doubted the animals would show themselves if the wolves were nearby.

"Opal, how you doing?" Garrison asked.

"Opal watch enemy prisoner. Opal look for more enemies to fight. Opal do what Sir says," Opal said.

"How incredibly original," Garrison said. "That's what I like about you, buddy. Always know what to expect. I wonder if you're edible. Don't freak out. I'm not going cannibal yet. It's just that we're lost on an alien planet about to freeze to death and you have to think about these things so you're ready for them."

"Shut up, Garrison," King said.

"Your Strike Marine has a point. That bio-construct might be worth something if we get trapped in a blizzard or another cave," Medvedev said.

"Opal eat."

"Not me, Opie. You'd probably have an allergic reaction or something. Strike Marines like me are notoriously hard to digest. Just ask half the monsters on Barada," Garrison said.

"Tone it down, Garrison. You're going to get him all worked up," Hoffman said. The muscles in his legs and back burned from the hike. His powerful pseudo muscle under his armor chafed him in all the wrong places. Cold leaked through his gear despite the climate-control standards.

"Yes, sir." Garrison checked the back trail, aiming

his rifle in a sweeping arc and scanning with his helmet's and weapon's sensors to be sure he hadn't missed anything. "You heard the boss, Opie. You have to promise not to eat me."

"Opal no promise."

"Hey, hey, hey, Opie. Those were just jokes."

Hoffman saw the crescent fighter in the distance long before he heard its engines.

"Sir, I've spotted a crescent-shaped fighter on heading to ninety-five degrees," King said.

"I see it. Move to cover," Hoffman said.

He grabbed Masha by her left arm and pulled her toward one of the coded IR beacons King had repositioned. Within seconds, his team was set up in a defensive perimeter and hidden from view.

Hoffman watched the crescent fighter through the trees as it hovered over the peak of a mountain and then flew away. From this distance, there was only the suggestion of engine noise.

"I think we're clear to move," King said.

Hoffman gave a hand signal and the team moved out. Masha and Medvedev remained silent through most of the day. King led them up and down trails and along switchback ledges that climbed higher into the rugged terrain.

Hoffman called a rest break. They moved off the trail and sheltered beneath the towering Koen white trees.

****

"We're almost to the pass," King said. "We've made good time, but I think there could be trouble. If these crescent fighters have ground troops looking for us, they've had time to start a grid search and set up ambushes."

"And what better place for an ambush than a mountain pass," Hoffman said, checking his gear and swallowing some nutrient paste. "We have to get to Koensuu City. There's no place else on the route and the enemy can read a satellite photo of the area as well as we can."

"We go through the pass or cut over the mountains to another valley," King said, lowering his voice so the others couldn't hear.

"Is there a natural way through the terrain or are we looking at some mountaineering?"

"Look here." King pointed to a map on his forearm screen. "This is a draw that will lead us out of the pass. There are no artificial structures, mostly because the terrain doesn't allow it."

"You're thinking they won't have armor or fortified positions along this route?" Hoffman said, pulling up his own map. "This way might not be as exciting, but it's even less friendly to whatever kind of armor they have and there's not much room to mass larger forces. Sakkatos tried to get us over the pass."

"But he didn't," King said.

"I appreciate your analysis. I've made my decision," Hoffman said.

"Yes, sir."

"Put Garrison on point for a while. I'm tired of hearing him complain," Hoffman said.

"It's not that cold," King said as he went to give Corporal Garrison the news.

"Without armor, I bet it's really cold. Check on his shoulder and his armor integrity."

"Yes, sir."

Hoffman watched the gunnery sergeant and thanked the Saint, not for the first time, that the hard-faced man was on his team. He'd poached King from a rival officer, Lieutenant Masterson, after the two had a falling out. Masterson hadn't taken well to the ego bruising and had been icy towards Hoffman until the mission to rescue a

Dotari fleet in deep space. Hoffman's last memory of Masterson was the other Marine's body tortured and transformed by the Xaros drone on the *Kid'ran's Gift*. It was a bad way to die and made Hoffman remember Masterson differently than he might have otherwise.

He checked his team's IR pings, noting Garrison was moving forward by the book. He hadn't complained about his broken arm or dislocated shoulder since the legionnaire had reset his shoulder. He saved his complaining for nature and the inherent unfairness of the universe.

King assumed the rearguard position, maintaining visual contact with Hoffman at all times.

Opal led Medvedev and Masha on a carbon-fiber line. Hoffman hung back just far enough that Masha had to turn her head to see exactly where he was walking.

"Got something, sir," Garrison said.

Hoffman moved to join him, crouching behind a cluster of lichen- and snow-covered rocks.

Garrison pointed, moving his hand slowly to avoid attracting attention of diligent countersurveillance.

"What am I looking at?"

"Wait a minute…there…coming out from those trees," Garrison said.

Humanoid shapes with wide shoulders and ice-crusted fur marched parallel to a partially frozen river. He saw weapons—long rifles carried by the barrel—and large packs strapped across their lower backs. Hoffman zoomed in. The aliens had dark-gray skin and blunt muzzles for mouths, red eyes, and upturned noses. Facial hair crowded their faces, giving them an almost simian appearance.

Hoffman took a screen grab and sent it to Masha's and Medvedev's visors. "What kind of Kesaht are these?"

"Rakka," Masha said. "Dumber than a bag of hammers, but they're stronger than they look."

"Uh, no. These yahoos don't look like a crack fighting force. Are those…rifles? Like with rifling in the barrels and smokeless powder?" Garrison asked.

"Slug throwers," Medvedev said. "Chemical propellant. Nowhere as efficient as gauss weapons, but a lucky hit can get through your armor. They're effective when massed against a target." He ran a hand down his side, as if remembering an old wound.

"Looks like the Kesaht made some improvements to old Rakka weaponry," Garrison said. "Lots of nasty-looking knives in their kit, some on long bone handles or poles. Plenty of glyphs drawn onto their armor. Not a lot of uniformity…By the Saint! What is that thing?" Garrison asked as he crouched against a rock and brought his rifle to his shoulder.

Hoffman opened his IR comms. "Take cover. We have hostiles about a thousand meters out. King, make sure our prisoners understand these baddies are not their friends unless they like monsters."

"Received and understood," King said.

"I'm moving closer for a better look," Hoffman said. "Cover me."

He backed away from Garrison's hiding place, crept around it, and continued down the trail to a new observation point. He logged the location in his computer and aimed his rifle scope toward the advancing army moving in and out of the trees.

A new alien towered over the Rakka, its centaur-like body moving through the snow and kicking up puffs of snow with each step. It carried a long rifle tipped with a serrated bayonet. Thick hair was tied into a braid held tight with silver ribbons. Fog wafted from its squat face with each breath, and tusks curved up from the lower lip and jaw.

"Is that thing part horse?" Garrison asked.

"Looks like it," Hoffman answered. "That must be the Sanheel. The officer caste. Fall back to the others. We need to get through this area before they reach it."

"That thing reminds me of Gunney King in a way. Mean and ugly," Garrison said. He lowered his rifle scope, checked his immediate area, and hustled back to King and the others. "Moving."

"Covering," Hoffman said. When he rejoined his team, Opal had packed Medvedev and Masha beneath his large body. King squatted over them as well, hiding their heat signatures.

"Their gear looks like garbage," King said. "On the IR, I don't see any hotspots of battery packs. They're out here in these conditions without heat systems. I thought I was cold…"

"Cold doesn't seem to be slowing them down too much," Hoffman said. "Let's tighten up the order of march and be prepared to hide our principals at a moment's notice. The enemy is moving this way. We need to be through this part of the pass before they get here. King, you're back on point. Let's move."

King set an aggressive pace. Opal let out more line and jogged behind Medvedev and Masha. Hoffman followed. The prisoners kept a decent pace, which told him they definitely did not want to be found by the Kesaht. If there was an Ibarran force out there, he was pretty sure

Masha would have developed all manner of cramps and twisted ankles to slow them all down. Garrison brought up the rear and talked too much on the IR.

"All clear back here. No ice barbarians or centaurs with freakishly deadly spear-swords," Garrison said.

"How's your arm?" Hoffman panted, checking his tactical display as well as the visual position of each team member and his own footing frequently.

"Hurts like hell. Thanks for asking."

They ran, climbed, and hiked in silence for a while. Clouds pushed snow across the sky and threatened to dump it on them. Crescent fighters patrolled distant mountains. Hoffman saw flashes of battle from Koensuu City. He pushed closer to Masha.

"This is an invasion," he said.

"What were you expecting? A snatch-and-grab raid?"

"What are they here for? They can land troops. They could probably smash Koensuu City like they did Pohja Base," he said, nearly slipping on an angled stone in the trail.

"The Kesaht hate all humans. Ibarran and Terran," she said. "They act like we're some sort of xenocidal species bent on galactic extermination. Like we're the same as the Xaros. From the Toth's point of view…I can see how they can make that case."

"You Ibarrans have never tried to reason with them?" Hoffman asked. "Explain who the Toth were and why they were—"

"Annihilated?" Masha asked with a snort. "Just how do we sugarcoat that? A Toth overlord tells a race that knows nothing of the Ember War how humans drove his species to the edge of extinction, and that we're probably coming for them next. What would happen to the galactic opinion of Navarre—and Earth—if word got out about what we did to the Toth at the end of the war? I don't think even the Dotari know all the details of what happened. No, we're not going to throw our hands up and claim this is all some horrible misunderstanding."

"You're saying Earth deserves to fight the Kesaht?"

"Last time I checked, the galaxy isn't fair," she said. "Wasn't fair when the Xaros wiped out the solar system. Now the Kesaht are a problem. I doubt things will be all rainbows and kittens in the future."

Hoffman let the conversation drop as they sprinted across a clearing, on the other side of which were a herd of the moose like the creatures the wolves fed on. They bolted away from Hoffman and his Strike Marines.

"That was subtle," Garrison said.

"Nothing to be done for it," King said. "I'm going to run ahead and make sure the Rakka don't have a scout element ahead of them."

King called back a short time later. "The Rakka vanguard is moving fast. Better start looking for someplace to hide. I'll slip off the trail and try to rejoin you when I can."

"You heard him. Let's make ourselves invisible." Hoffman ran his Marines and the prisoners into the snow disturbed by the native moose, mingling their tracks with the moose tracks, and then directed his team into the snowbanks where the creatures had nuzzled for food frozen to the ground.

Masha raised her tied hands in front of her and clapped her fingertips. "Oh goody! This is where I see the Terran Strike Marine cloaking technology."

Hoffman grunted. "Opal, put her on the ground and cover her. She's the principal. Medvedev doesn't matter except for exposing the rest of us."

He moved to the oversized legionnaire and pointed at the ground. "Get down and get small. Garrison and I will cover you with our suits and try to act as a heat shield." He made adjustments on his arm-sleeve screen. "Match your temperature to the snow."

"You think the Kesaht cannon fodder is equipped with thermal tech?" Medvedev asked.

"I'm not taking chances." Hoffman checked his team to make sure everyone was in place, then dusted himself with snow and activated his suit's cloak. The power drain spiked as the armor cooled itself and threw up a short-range holo field that blended him into the snowbank. His visor cut out all color and he held very still as cold leached into his body.

From somewhere out of view, King whispered over the IR comms. *"They are right on top of you."*

"What's your status?" Hoffman spoke quietly inside his helmet and tried not to breathe. His teeth chattered as the cold from the ground seeped straight through his armor and all the layers of insulation that protected him. "We're short-staffed, Gunney. Don't get seen."

"I'm in a better position than you are. Trust me."

Garrison's voice waved through Hoffman's internal helmet speakers. "I bet Gunney's warm."

Hoffman watched boots stomping across his limited field of vision. After a time, he saw the strange hooves of the Sanheel creature. He assumed it was an officer or some type of battlefield commander, maybe a slave driver of some sort. It stopped, shuffled sideways, then studied the snowy meadow.

Rakka scouts grunted and argued with him.

"They're pointing to where the Koen-moose herd scattered to," King said.

Garrison stage-whispered, trusting his helmet to conceal his words. "I bet you can eat them."

"There is something wrong with your breacher," Masha said.

"Not the Sanheel, the moose," Garrison said.

Garrison and the rest of the team went silent as the column of Rakka foot soldiers stopped. The Sanheel shouted an order. The Rakka unlimbered medium-length pole arms with bone handles and wide blades that curved backwards near the tip. They poked the butt-end of their weapons into snowdrifts and tangles of winter vegetation.

Hoffman bit down hard but couldn't stop his teeth chattering. A pair of Rakka loomed over him, turning this way and that and complaining to their leaders. One jabbed his pole arm violently into the ground in a near-random pattern.

Hoffman felt like every one of the enemy should be staring at him. His body trembled. His teeth wouldn't stop their protestations of the cold weather. He peered through his darkened visor and resisted the temptation to wipe snow away from the lenses. Seen from this vantage point, the Rakka and the Sanheel officer looked like giants from a child's fairytale.

"King…what is our…status?" Hoffman asked.

"Looks like they're on the move again. Hold on a bit longer," King said. "I'll make a note that your tactic for concealing prisoners seemed to work."

"The prisoners are glad not to be caught but ready to get up before they are crushed," Masha said. "And…further abused…with hypothermia…"

Hoffman waited until he hadn't seen any feet or other enemy body parts for a full minute, then five, then ten. "King, report."

A pause.

"They're into the woods and headed up the trail we came down. It won't take them long to figure out which way we went. My recommendation is to haul ass but stay low," King said.

"You heard the man. Let's move out." Hoffman came slowly to his feet, scanned the clearing, then hustled his team toward the trees where King waited.

"Ahhhhh," groaned Garrison. "I think my nipples stuck to the inside of my armor."

"Nipples no stick," Opal said.

"What about you, Lieutenant?" Masha said. "You have anything stick where it shouldn't?"

"Less talk, more evading the enemy," Hoffman said. "King, you got us a hide spot?"

"A little farther and we can take a break. I'm setting up an OP on the next ridgeline. We're above the clearing in the rivers that feed it now," King said.

"We're en route," Hoffman said as he looked around at his team. No one looked happy or comfortable. He could see Masha trembling in her environment suit. Above them, the heavy gray clouds finally let loose and dumped thick curtains of snow on them.

Hoffman once again pointed his rifle scope at the enemy. "There will be more patrols."

"I wish we hadn't blown the crash site," King said. "King for Garrison, could you start an avalanche with your remaining breaching charges?"

"I'm a Strike Marine, Gunney, not an avalanche…planner," Garrison said. "So, I can do nothing or probably bring down the entire mountain on our heads. Your choice."

"Let's hold that in reserve," Hoffman said.

Chapter 10

"I spy with my little eye…PDF scouts," Duke whispered.

"I see another big-ass storm brewing," Booker said, glancing at low-hanging clouds the color of dirty steel. "And a really long drop into an icy river. Have we talked about my fear of heights?"

"You're not afraid of heights," Duke said, still watching the PDF scouts creeping near the bridge. "You're always the first one out when we do high-altitude, low-opening jumps from orbit."

"True. But I'm really tired of being cold. Getting plunged into glacial flow after falling a hundred meters is not a fantasy of mine."

"Not glacial."

"What?"

Duke exhaled, wishing it was time for another dip. "It's just a river with a lot of snow and ice. The first fjord we crossed was cut out of the mountains by a glacier. Closer to sea level. This is just a river."

"What are your new friends doing now?"

"Scouting," Duke said. "Not complete idiots. A little skittish and impatient."

Duke and Booker watched the PDF scouts creep toward the bridge. Sneaking past them in the woods hadn't been much of a challenge. In their defense, the young soldiers had been looking for slavering Rakka and eight-foot-tall tusk-faced centaurs. Something was happening. Duke could see their comms specialist bent over a radio.

"I thought comms were down," Booker said.

"They are. Our PDF friends are freaking out. Probably saw something they didn't like," Duke said. "Yep, here they come."

The young soldiers moved quickly and efficiently. By training standards, their performance was above average. The team leader ordered a bounding overwatch and they moved in pairs. Duke admired their energy, even if it was misplaced.

Booker whispered, "They're going to squat right on top of us."

"That'll make the lesson I'm about to teach them a lot easier," Duke said.

The PDF scout team reformed and concealed themselves within arm's reach of Duke and Booker.

"We have to radio this in. The sooner we get to an IR relay, the better," the squad leader said. "Are you sure you didn't see more than one vehicle?"

"One Kesaht truck, but I'm pretty sure it was a scout vehicle. We—" The team leader froze and looked around. "Never mind. Felt like a shadow just walked over my grave."

Duke's next movement was deceptively quick. Soundless, the motion looked slower than it was. None of the young men reacted in time. He came to his feet like a mound of snow growing from the forest floor and snatched the team leader's camouflage rifle from his hand. Quickly, before things could go bad, he held one hand palm out toward the others.

"Settle down there, folks. I'm from the Terran government and I'm here to help," Duke said.

The squad leader flinched, then recovered. "Shit! You're that Terran Strike Marine dude. Where's the hot chick? You know, the good-looking medic."

Duke flipped open his visor so he could spit.

"You're standing on her."

The man and his companions laughed nervously.

"No, I'm serious. You're standing on my partner. Please step away from the Strike Marine medic," Duke said.

"By the Saint!" The team leader jumped sideways.

Booker came to her feet and sucked in a long breath of air. "Thanks. That was getting uncomfortable. If I'd known he was going to step that direction when you scared the crap out of him, I would've moved sooner."

Duke nodded at the scout leader. "Attend to your team. Tighten up security. It's been a long couple days and we don't feel like doing it for you."

"Yes, sir," the leader said. He redeployed his unit into defensive positions and chastised them. Duke overheard more than one of them point out that the team leader hadn't exactly been on the ball this time either.

"Do you think that taught them a lesson or just humiliated them?" Booker asked.

"Little of both. Did you notice how much denethrite they're carrying?" He watched the PDF soldiers with growing concern. All of them, including the leader, were showing signs of agitation. "What's the problem?"

"The Kesaht are closing in much faster than we

anticipated."

Duke shrugged, then plucked a spare battery from the man's harness. "That's how it normally works." He held up the battery. "For my armor."

The PDF officer shifted nervously, opening his mouth as Booker helped herself to batteries from two other scouts.

She raised an eyebrow and he closed his mouth.

An explosion sounded on the other side of the bridge, suspiciously close to where Duke and Booker had traveled before spotting the PDF scout team. Trees fell. Plumes of snow burst into the air. The young soldiers crouched as low to the ground as was humanly possible.

"What the hell?" one of them said.

"Noise discipline. Get it together," the scout leader said. He looked more carefully at Duke and Booker. "You knew they were coming. Man, you look rough. Don't Strike Marines sleep?"

"Not enough," Duke said.

"What was that explosion? I need to include it in my report."

"We rigged a surprise for the lead vehicle. Should slow the Kesaht down," Duke said. "Booker, get across this bridge and start transmitting our report at the fiber-optic relay. Try not to fall in the icy river."

"Thanks for reminding me." She strode toward a scout vehicle and started talking to the driver.

Duke stepped close to the scout leader. "The Kesaht aren't far behind us. We've been watching them for days. Thousands. A major force that can't be allowed to cross this bridge."

Above them, the clouds opened up and snow fell in thick, lazy columns. Farther away, wind howled through the peaks.

"I don't have authority for that kind of demolition," the young officer said.

"I'll take care of that. Just need a bit of denethrite."

"Sir, I don't think I can do that."

"You're an officer. I'm a sergeant. Don't call me sir."

"I don't think I can surrender explosives to you, sergeant. Not in the ops plan."

Duke rubbed his chin. "Tell them I just took it. They'll believe you."

The scout officer swallowed.

Duke held his gaze as he lifted a pack of denethrite from his armor. "Snipers. What a bunch of cocky prima donnas. That's what you'll say. No one will doubt it for a second."

"The important thing is to stop the Kesaht," the scout officer said.

"Yep." Duke relieved three other scouts of their explosives and walked quickly away. By the time they were able to discuss what just happened, he was climbing under the bridge. Once his eyes adjusted, he searched for a maintenance platform and located a rickety rope catwalk that hadn't seen use since Terrans arrived on Koen and sent out their survey and repair crews.

The scout vehicle with Booker and the PDF soldiers started up and raced toward the other side of the bridge. Duke paused, listening to the sound of wheels on the planks above him as cold wind buffeted his position. Narrow and covered with frost, the access way went from one end of the bridge to the other, hanging underneath the bridge like an embarrassing secret.

Frequent gusts of wind twisted the long, tapering catwalk. Snow whipped around support columns, concentrated through the narrow under-spaces of the bridge. There was barely room for his feet to walk one after the other. The grips, ropes made from local plant fibers, were almost too wide for him to reach at the same time. The alien design and jerry-rigged modifications made navigation more difficult than it should have been. He finally settled on leaning toward the right-hand railing, his kit and his patrol bag hanging awkwardly to one side.

Garrison would've actually proved useful here, he thought. Tactical entries were the breacher's specialty. But he'd been to all the schools and was good at whatever demolition was needed of a Strike Marine team. Just once, Duke would like to have all their resources in one place.

"I'm standing here, missing Garrison," Duke muttered. "Not happening. I need to get some sleep."

Working quickly, aware the Kesaht would arrive at the bridge in minutes—maybe seconds—he located weak points in the main support beams and packed the denethrite charges on one side of each timber. The Terran engineers had bolstered the structure with good steel. Duke studied the puzzle for five seconds and decided his demolition package would work. Might not be pretty, but it would get the job done. The metal bracing had been added to prevent sway, not to support structural weight. Everything would come down once he blew out the ancient wood.

One, two, three, four, five—he inserted the detonators into the soft, malleable denethrite. Rushing now, he removed the time fuses from their safety case, set the countdown for five minutes and stepped away.

A cold shiver ran up his spine.

He glanced down the long underside of the bridge and calculated how long it would take them to get on top and then sprint to safety. "Ten is a good number." He reset the timer for ten minutes and hurried upward.

Machine-gunfire chattered closer and closer to the bridge, explosions rocking the vertical ladder. Climbing up from the swaying catwalk proved far more difficult than he had anticipated. He could feel the seconds counting down.

His breath whistled from his helmet air filters as lactic acid burned through his legs, shoulders, and arms. His kit felt like a hundred extra pounds and his dexterous sniper gloves felt like mittens. He reached the top, burst into the open, and started across the bridge, heedless of enemy fire he could do nothing about.

Rakka sprayed their archaic but deadly machine guns at the scout vehicle smashed halfway through the guard rail and hanging toward the river. "Damn it, Booker. If you fell off this bridge…"

Bullets whipped past his head.

"I don't have time for this."

He ducked around the scout car, using it for cover as bullets punched through the lightweight metal. He ducked in, confirmed Booker wasn't in it, and jumped back. He pulled a smoke grenade off his chest armor, yanked the pin, and lobbed it into the truck. Thick purple smoke billowed out of the shattered windows.

Gauss fire and gunfire zipped back and forth across the bridge, each passing second bringing an increased volume of fire from the Kesaht side. Rounds peppered the arch over the bridge, skipped along the ground, and pinged off the PDF scout car. He raced away, pouring on the speed.

"I'm running, he sees me, I'm down before he shoots," Duke huffed, then belly flopped. Scrambling sideways to further avoid getting shot, he came to his feet and glanced back just as the scout car exploded from a bullet strike. The smoke screen across the bridge grew thicker.

"I'm up, I'm running, he sees me…" Duke charged across the bridge toward the guard tower on the friendly side of the bridge. A bullet slammed into his shoulder, deflecting off his armor but knocking him off-balance. He staggered forward to the ladder and scrambled up.

Duke dragged, kicked, and flopped his way into the large control booth. The modern addition to the ancient bridge was a nexus for lighting, communications, and the planned hydroelectric dam waiting to be built. There was a crossbar that could be lowered to prevent vehicle traffic if travelers weren't being polite.

He looked around and found Booker treating an injured PDF scout. Two of the young soldiers took turns firing from a window, taking advantage of the concrete and steel fortifications up to the windows of the tower. Another scout stood shell-shocked in the middle of the room, fiddling with his rifle as though it needed loading or cleaning. He looked pleadingly at Duke.

Ignoring the young man, Duke went to the windows and yanked down the blast shutters. "These things have gun ports for a reason. Use them."

The PDF scouts who had been returning fire quickly adapted.

Duke took the report chip from Booker and tossed it to the noncombatant in the middle of the room. "Transmit that information back to Captain Pine. Do it now."

"I…should be able to do that. One moment." The man holstered his pistol, then pulled it out again and looked at it. He faced the sound of combat.

Duke crossed the room in three powerful strides, grabbed the man by the front of his armor, and lifted him off the ground. "Function!"

The man's eyes went wide and Duke chucked him

toward the communication station.

"How you doing, Booker?"

"Little busy. Trying to save a life."

Duke considered helping her but disregarded the idea. With Booker in medic mode and his report being transmitted, he felt free to get serious. He slid down the ladder and ran outside. There were no perfect locations, but he found a nice depression between two thorn bushes and tore open his rifle case. He snapped Buffy together and looked through his IR scope and saw a bunch of Rakka foot soldiers hurrying across the bridge. He glanced at the timer on his gauntlet screen: a flashing 0:00.

"Odd. I was expecting more of a boom when denethrite goes off," he muttered.

Wind drove ice and snow across his vision, screaming like banshees through the bridge supports. He spread his feet wider than usual as he knelt to keep his balance and pulled the weapon in tight with his support strap. Heat images advanced toward him. He adjusted his scope for a sharper contrast. At the far edge of the bridge were barely recognizable Kesaht vehicles. More foot soldiers poured across the bridge.

Most of them advanced in combat formations, shooting systematically now that their officer had caught up to discipline them. A small group loitered near the bridge supports where he had placed the explosive charges. He dialed in his scope for greater resolution, sacrificing his peripheral view of the others who were closer and clearly looking for a fight.

It took two tries, but he found what he was looking for. A Rakka grunt held a handful of detonators. The wild-haired, crudely armored soldier looked rather nervous with what he carried. A massive Sanheel officer lashed him with a whip and shouted.

Duke considered the situation. The explosives weren't going to go off. The bridge wasn't going to fall. The lime-faced Sanheel had a good deal of badges and rank symbols on a sash across his chest—probably a senior officer, which probably meant a large force was coming this way.

Rakka scout vehicles edged onto the bridge. Duke charged up his rifle to full power, then aimed at the self-important-looking Sanheel officer. Driving snow would prevent a precision shot, but he had no doubt he could kill the tusk-faced, green-skinned Sanheel thing. From the way he was carrying on, he was a top-tier target.

Additional Kesaht units arrived, both Rakka and junior Sanheel. He didn't see tanks but knew it was just a matter of time. He took a deep breath, held it, then let it ease out as he timed the beats of his heart. He lowered the rifle slightly to aim at the Rakka crouched next to one of the bridge struts.

He knew where he had placed the charges. The unfortunate Rakka holding the detonators couldn't crouch low enough to save himself. Duke felt Buffy vibrate slightly against his shoulder; fully charged and ready to fire a bullet with enough kinetic energy to shatter a boulder or punch through the hull of a destroyer.

Duke fired and the recoil slid him back a foot. The bullet shot through the Rakka, exploding the alien like a popped balloon, and into the bridge below his feet. Duke didn't see if the shot was true, but the ensuing explosion that slapped against his body and knocked him a few inches into the air told him he'd aimed well enough.

Light from the explosion shone through the raging tempest a microsecond before the sound hit Duke. He kept his face down and covered his ears with his hands. Shrapnel winged overhead. Support beams groaned, twisting free of the superstructure. Instinctively, Duke crawled toward the control booth near the PDF scouts.

The collapsing section of the bridge pulled at him like a black hole. Fire plumes reached into the sky, illuminating the storm. Dozens of Rakka and a few Sanheel pinwheeled toward the ice-clogged river a hundred meters below. The senior Sanheel leapt clear of the destruction, three hooves clattering and scraping the far side of the bridge foundation. One foreleg was missing at the knee, spraying blood across the snow.

"Slip backward! Lose your footing, you ugly bastard!" Duke looked for a shot before the snowfall increased, whiting out the canyon. Unknown range, vicious crosswinds, and poor visibility—it was a no-go. Duke slapped a fresh battery into Buffy.

No shot.

****

Bullets shot across the shattered bridge in random bursts as Duke dropped off the ladder attached to the back of the guard tower as it shuddered in the wind. The structure leaned and swayed as Duke jogged toward a cluster of utility trucks with gauss machine guns mounted to the backs and armor bolted to the sides.

The bridge on Duke's side of the river collapsed, the breaking metal sounding like a drawn-out crash of plates broken in a kitchen.

"Don't you duck?" asked one of the PDF soldiers from a pintle-mounted weapon.

Duke rapped his knuckles against the jerry-rigged armor. "They're firing blind. I'd hate to duck into a round. I'd be dead and feel stupid."

He checked for room in any of the vehicles, but all were full of soldiers huddling together for warmth. "You guys really going to make me hoof it out of here?"

"No, sergeant," the scout leader said, pointing to a jeep next to an idling ambulance.

Booker opened the back door of the ambulance and waved Duke over. Two soldiers lay on stretchers as blood dribbled out of the compartment.

"We're waiting on you!" she shouted, pointing at the jeep.

"Moving," Duke said as he opened the back door to the jeep and found a seat open. He unslung his sniper rifle, hopped inside, and looked at an officer in the front right seat.

"Any reason we haven't unassed this place?" the sniper asked.

The officer touched an earphone, then slapped his driver twice on the shoulder.

"Finally got a head count," the officer said.

Duke knew he shouldn't give orders, but there wasn't time and he was out of patience. "All right, what's your name?"

"Lieutenant Travis England."

The jeep skidded against the icy road for a moment, then lurched forward as the sound of incoming artillery pierced the raging storm. Duke smiled.

The driver looked around in alarm. The lieutenant seemed on the edge of panic.

"Relax, sir," Duke said. "That's our arty. I know that sound from Cygnus. General Allan's busy ruining the day of any Kesaht forces near the bridge. Those are ranging shots. In about two minutes, it's going to get ugly."

"But the bridge is out," England said.

"Still plenty of bad guys on the other side of the canyon, dicks in hand, trying to figure out if they can repair the bridge. Nice bunch of targets," Duke said.

"You're awfully sure about that," England said.

"Permission to go faster?" the driver asked.

"I'd really rather not skid off the road and into a tree," Duke said. "I like winning. Die in something stupid like a car crash, it tarnishes the legacy."

"Take it slow," the lieutenant said. "Thanks for the help back there. That was some quick thinking with the bridge."

"Denethrite is like any explosive. It's shock-sensitive," Duke said.

"What about the detonators?"

"Kesaht removed them before the timer hit zero. I didn't have enough time to rig a tamper-proof fuse. Still, got the desired effect when I hit the denethrite with a full power shot." He stuck a finger into an ear and wiggled it. "We're lucky the Rakka didn't drop the explosives into the river."

"Duke," Booker came over the IR, her voice weak in the storm, *"I lost one of the wounded. Second one's holding up better, but we need to get back to base."*

Duke clicked his tongue twice to acknowledge the transmission and debated informing the lieutenant and the driver of the news. The driver didn't seem confident or competent behind the wheel, and giving him bad news that would spur him to drive faster and more recklessly wasn't going to help anyone.

Nothing could be done for the dead.

Duke pulled out his dip can and stuck a wad into his lip.

****

Thran'Ul kicked with one of his rear legs. An almost childish move for a Sanheel who learned to buck soon after their first steps. His hoof slammed a field doctor against a tree, but the doctor shouldn't have mentioned that he was never going to fight as effectively with only one front leg and he shouldn't have been standing behind Thran'Ul when he uttered the offensive words.

The two doctors in front of him were smarter. They kept their eyes down as they worked to fit a prosthetic leg to the bleeding stump at the end of his right forelimb.

"This is a very good unit, Honored Decarian. The very best we can do in the field," one of the doctors said.

His companion was quick to agree. "Very rugged. Only a true war hero could dare have such an augmentation."

Thran'Ul backhanded the man, sending him sliding across the icy gravel of the camp. "It is not an augmentation!"

He stared across the mangled, twisted bridge. Terran artillery had devastated both sides of the bridge abutments. Smoke drifted up from craters. Snow turned into steam in some of them.

Another barrage of artillery fell, splashing into the

river and sending up plumes of water and ice. The bodies of his soldiers had long since been swept away by the current.

He summoned a Rakka thrall chief. "Send your people to the next crossing. Go with them and be sure they capture any human with a rail rifle they encounter. At all costs. Should I learn that you located the sniper and returned without him in chains, it will be your death. Bring me the head of the sniper and the rifle if you cannot take him alive."

"My warriors fear meeting their fate at the hands of this winter demon," the Rakka sergeant said.

"Their fate is their fate. Death to humans. Death to the murdering scourge of the galaxy."

The Rakka grunted acknowledgment and turned away.

Chapter 11

Booker leaned back in the sauna, sweat dribbling down her body and into the towel wrapped around her waist, and tried not to think of Duke and his obsession with titty bars. Garrison was nearly as bad, but somehow less of a creep about it. Maybe it was Duke's near-constant consumption of chewing tobacco when not on a mission. None of the men or women in the steam tent cared about nudity, or if they did, they were orders of magnitude politer than her Strike Marine companions. A woman braided her hair, arms up in a way that accentuated the shape of her breasts, her towel laid carelessly across her legs. Booker was certain the men appreciated the view, but not one of them catcalled or whistled or even let their eyes linger too obviously.

Clouds of steam drifted up to the ceiling, then

spread downward as water was added to the heat source at the center of the tent. Some of the Koen men and women had towels; others didn't. She kept hers around her waist but toyed with the idea of losing it entirely. She wanted all the relaxation she could get while she could get it.

Wood benches lined the walls. Booker thought setting up the tent had to be a regular thing—probably a welcome break from the harsh weather on the planet.

"I didn't even know Benji had been shot until we reached base camp," Lieutenant England said. "Total failure on my part. I should've known he'd taken a bullet through his calf."

"He could've said something. But why? We were fighting. Showing our stuff to the Strike Marines," somebody said in a corner of the room. "Sergeant Booker, how long have you been training with that sniper? The Rakka call him the Ice Claw or something like that. Buddy of mine in Third Platoon heard it from a guy who heard a Rakka was caught and interrogated by Captain Pine's people."

"The Kesaht freak out if they think the Ice Claw is watching them," a soldier said.

"They shit their pants every time a sniper takes one of them out," England said.

"They probably think there's only one sniper on the planet," said another man near the heating element as he poured a cup of water onto the rocks.

Booker shrugged, enjoying the relaxing and sensual feel of finally taking a break. "We've been on the same team for a while. If you think he's scary, you should meet Opal."

"That's a weird name for a sniper."

Booker laughed and it felt outstanding. "Opal isn't a sniper."

"Is that the doughboy? I heard you guys had a doughboy. Didn't they all die after the Ember War?"

Booker's good mood drained away. "I think there are two or three left. Opal's the last one on combat duty."

"If we weren't needed here, half of us would try out for the Pathfinders or the Strike Marines. Our own selection process is pretty tough."

Booker nodded and concentrated on the steam relaxing her muscles. The PDF scouts told her story to several other soldiers, describing the chaos and the physical trials. She'd heard similar talk before, but this seemed almost ritualized.

"Strike Marines know *sisu*," England said. "Booker and the Ice Claw never hesitated to take action. Never complained when the storm hit and bullets flew in our faces."

Booker closed her eyes, listening, hoping they would leave her out of the conversation. She didn't think they were praising her or trying to kiss up to her. Post combat time was a mess of raw emotions, and even thought she was on their side, she felt like an outsider…but a warm, steam-shrouded outsider at least.

One by one, the PDF scouts gave examples of team members overcoming impossible odds. No man or woman talked about his or her own exploits.

"You're familiar with *sisu*, Sergeant Booker?" England finally said.

She opened her eyes. "Grit."

He nodded. "The North Americans call it grit. Similar. I think you and the Ice Claw have both."

"What do you call this field spa?" she joked.

"Hygge," England said without hesitation, pronouncing it hoo-ga. "Coziness."

"It's very nice," she said.

"I heard you were on the *Breitenfeld*," Lieutenant England said.

"It's true," Booker said. "Wasn't on it for that long. Just enough time to get a selfie on the flight deck."

"Where is it? Every rumor I hear about that ship says something different," England said.

Booker had a new appreciation for the PDF scouts but still marveled at how young they seemed. In reality, they weren't much younger than she was, but after several missions with Hoffman's team—the Dotari rescue mission especially—she felt wiser and older. And maybe more damaged.

"Still in deep space. Getting the Dotari home," she said.

"I still can't believe you were part of that. The news channels basically said the entire Dotari home world would've been wiped out by a plague without that mission," England said.

Booker didn't answer. It felt good to keep her eyes closed and be warm.

"What are you doing on Koen?"

Booker's eyes flashed open. She didn't move; she just stared at the ceiling, hoping no one had seen her reaction. "Training mission."

Booker leaned her head back as steam opened every pore in her body. A few of the men and women of the PDF lounging on benches resumed their stories of the desperate fight at the bridge. Their companions murmured appreciation.

Everything was nice until somebody yanked open the tent flap. A familiar Strike Marine stood there wearing his lightweight sniper armor. Booker's arm shot across her chest.

"Felt my ears burning," Duke said. "Get dressed, Booker."

"Never a dull moment," she mumbled as her relaxation faded abruptly away.

She stood up and wrapped a towel over her chest, fully aware that Duke was standing behind her, waiting.

She looked over her shoulder and saw him mostly facing the door, almost like a guard or protective big brother. He put in a dip and shifted foot to foot. She smiled, thinking about his reputation for less than savory establishments in Phoenix…or anywhere he could find them.

When she turned around, he was holding a gun case in one hand and a plastic cup in the other. He spit some of his precious tobacco into the cup and nodded toward the rifle case. "Found a sniper rifle in the arms room. No one signed for it."

"Something happened to Buffy?" She stepped out of the steam tent and onto a sidewalk made of wooden boards. She'd seen plenty of the locals walking from the steam baths to the barracks in just towels and had assumed they carried enough heat with them to get through the open air comfortably. Instead, she felt her pores seize up and chill nip at her toes and earlobes.

"What the hell? Cold, cold!" She hurried to the barracks as Duke laughed.

She got into the next tent and ducked into a small room with a cot and her gear on it. Duke tossed the weapon case around the corner and onto the bunk. Booker huddled next to a heater and finished drying herself off.

"It's for you," Duke said. "PDF is having trouble with Sanheel. That's where you and your newly acquired skills come in," he said.

"Is this one zeroed?"

"Foundry settings. So it would take me a few minutes on a VR range to get it to where I like it. I can probably get it keyed to you before the spring thaw. How's your breath control?"

She snorted. "Never a problem with that."

"Then why can't you hit the broadside of the barn at a mile out?"

"Because the stupid weapons is—you know what? I'm going to get my gear on, then I'll be-be-be knocking a grain of sand off an ant's head at *two* miles! See how you like me then."

"Want to make a bet?"

"No. Just shut up while I change."

Chapter 12

Hoffman took the lead, trudging up the mountain as dusk descended on the pass. The wind died, but the cold blossomed in the darkness, a sensation that shouldn't have been more than a nuisance, but he felt it through his armor.

A squadron of human fighters cut across the sky and crescent fighters engaged them from three directions—right, left, and above. He wondered what Sakkatos would think of their skill now.

Hoffman continued until he found a defensible position, then called up the rest of the team. "Rally on me for rest and recovery. Check gear and consume calories. Run some snow through your water reclamation filters for later."

He waited until the rest of his team was situated, then attended to his own needs. With the Sanheel and

Rakka far behind, the last several hours felt like grunt work. He watched the dogfight and didn't like how it was shaping up. Human ships were faster and more agile, and from what he understood of aerial warfare, the Terran ships fought better and smarter, though the crescent ships were more numerous and aggressive.

A salvo of missiles fired from the Eagles and mauled the Kesaht. Hoffman pumped a fist in the air, then his spirits fell. Two dozen Kesaht fighters dropped out of the clouds and shot through the Terran battle formations. Bits of flaming wreckage rained down on the mountain tops as the tide turned for the worse.

"We call for an evac now, we might as well hang big ol' 'kick me' signs from our necks," King said as he watched the one-sided dogfight play out. "We don't have air superiority to protect a Mule coming in and out. If we send a radio blip and the Kesaht detect it…"

"They'll be all over us." Hoffman looked back at the prisoners. "I don't even know if they're worth that risk. They're high-value targets, but there's no value in them unless they talk and give up intelligence on the Ibarras' spy network."

"There are ways to make people talk," King said. "Ways I don't think we'd ever use against other humans.

You think we should cut them loose?"

"Hell no. You know what a pain in the ass it was to even catch them. And Medvedev will pay for what he did to Max, one way or another. They're our prisoners and we still have a duty to keep them safe until we can pass them on to intelligence."

An Eagle fighter exploded, casting a sharp yellow light across the dogfight.

"I used to envy the flyboys," King said. "All hot meals, bunks…crew rest. Now they're in the shit with the rest of us and getting the worst of it."

"King and Garrison, help me look for parachutes, anyone that managed to bail out," Hoffman said.

"There are too many Kesaht fighters," Masha said. "And they make no distinction between a pilot that can or can't fight back. They see someone bailed out, they'll be dead before they hit the ground."

"They take no prisoners?" Hoffman asked.

"They do…but those they take are never seen again," she said.

"Kesaht fight to the death," Medvedev said. "None have ever surrendered. Remember that."

Ships went down on the other side of the mountain pass while others disintegrated from direct hits. Hoffman moved the team farther through the pass and took up another position to watch the end of the battle.

He saw a ship go down but couldn't identify it. "Anyone see if that was one of ours?"

"Not sure," King said. "Lot of smoke and debris in the air."

"Garrison, you have command while we're gone. King, come with me. Let's have a look," Hoffman said.

They moved quickly, then slowed their pace as they neared the smoking wreckage.

"Kesaht fighter," Hoffman said.

"That's probably best. All we need is more walking wounded. Maybe this pilot can give us some information," King said.

Hoffman didn't respond as he shouldered his gauss rifle and moved forward. Gunney advanced on the left flank.

The crescent fighter was wedged into the earth with both wings broken off and the cockpit smashed.

"Sakkatos was right about their landing skill at least," Hoffman said.

"Doesn't look much different from our Mule at this point. Sorry, not trying to be a dick." King advanced beside Hoffman, both aiming their rifles from two separate angles into the cockpit, whose glass was shattered. The cover buckled as small explosive bolts blew the hinges and the top slid off to one side. The pilot was slender, with an oval-shaped head concealed by a smooth helmet. Neither Sanheel nor Rakka at first glance.

Hoffman shouted, "Terran Strike Marines, don't move!"

The alien pilot lay huddled against one side of the unpowered cockpit, purple blood dribbling down a cut across one shoulder.

"We don't have their language in our translation gear, do we?" Hoffman asked his gunnery sergeant.

King shook his head.

"I am Lieutenant Thomas Hoffman, Terran Strike Marines. Keep your hands where I can see them," he said, motioning up with his rifle.

The alien pilot unsnapped its helmet and pulled it free, staring at Hoffman with huge deep-blue eyes that dominated its slender features. Long-limbed, its tin arms moved with grace, despite the injuries. The humanoid looked better-suited for the cockpit of a combat fighter than other members of the Kesaht coalition. The flight suit concealed most of the pilot's body and was pressed tight to the alien's left side. Blood soaked through the tightened section, and Hoffman was sure the flight suit had compressed to combat injury. The lieutenant locked eyes with it as he aimed his rifle at the pilot's chest.

"I speak your foul language," it said. "You are abominations and will be destroyed. Murderers!"

Hoffman stepped back and leaned close to King. "I don't think they like us."

"Us or the Ibarrans? We're not all on the same side. You Kesaht know this?" King asked.

Hoffman stepped onto the sheared-off wing base as the pilot struggled to release himself from the cockpit. Hoffman aimed his gauss rifle at the alien's chest and watched. "I think this one is what Masha described as an Ixio."

"I don't like it. Just like I don't like poisonous jungle frogs. We should blow it in the ship. Only way to be sure." King reached into his pouch as though looking for a breaching charge.

"You are all tainted," the Ixio said as it struggled to get up, then fell back into the cockpit, panting. "There will be no mercy…only redemption by fire for…you all!"

"This thing talks about mercy?" King asked.

"How badly are you hurt?" Hoffman asked the alien.

The Ixio shook its head, and the lieutenant saw a thin sheen of crystals against the base of the alien's head.

"Just kill me," it said. "Prove what you are. That your kind is beyond all hope. I know what you've done!"

King shook his head. "That blood loss isn't stopping. You move him, you kill him. Might as well blow the ship and be done with it."

The pilot spat dark blood. "I took down five of your fighters! I will go to *stovasha* with honor. I will spill more human blood in the next fight."

"Your war's over." King stepped onto the rim of the cockpit, aiming his gauss rifle at the Ixio's face.

"Hold," Hoffman said. "There's no such thing as a mercy killing in war. Only murder."

"I was at New Caledonia after the massacre," said King. "The entire colony was wiped out by an attack…I don't know…just like this one. Can I personally prove the Kesaht did it?" He hit himself in the gut. "I know they did it. How many xenocidal alien forces have we encountered since the Ember War? We fight wars for territory, resources, and tactical advantage—for survival, not mass murder."

Hoffman lowered his voice. "I understand."

"Look at the way they assaulted this planet. You

know they hit NC."

"Calm down and think. A prisoner of war is worth more than this," Hoffman said.

"They killed every man, woman, and child!"

"Not…the children…" The Ixio laughed painfully.

Hoffman and King whirled on the man.

"What about the children? Where are they? What did you do with them?" Hoffman demanded.

The Ixio shrieked in pain, then assaulted Hoffman and King with alien words.

Hoffman raised his gauss rifle. "There's no redemption for murdering children."

"The Kesaht never murder children."

"Tell us where they are. We will trade prisoners for recovered children."

"Kesaht never kill the children. We take them to the…" The Ixio coughed blood, then reverted to swearing at them in its native language.

"Where do you take them?"

"And now I go to my reward." The Ixio reached up to its neck and pulled a ring dangling from one side. The Ixio's flight suit loosened and the pilot let out a groan as blood gushed out of its mouth and seeped through its chest. It slumped over, its last breath gurgling in its throat.

Hoffman reached for the dead alien, then pulled his hand back. As he studied the body, he saw an intricate jeweled bracelet wrapped around the wrist of the wounded arm. He wondered what kind of family charm it might be or what it meant, then moved away from the cockpit.

"Do we have time to pull him out and ransack this thing?" King asked.

"I don't like the look of the lights. Might self-destruct or start sending out an electronic beacon if it hasn't already," Hoffman said. He climbed down and backed away from the wrecked fighter.

"I'll call Garrison over here to booby-trap it," King said.

"No. If a trap goes off, the Kesaht will know we were here. Best to leave him to the wolves."

"Yes, sir."

Chapter 13

Hoffman's team, still unable to contact the base or the garrison in the city, moved higher into the pass, and he saw evidence of ancient civilization—trail markers and the occasional handrail near what could have been steps. On the switchback trail, he lost sight of his team. "Let's tighten it up. We've dodged enough Rakka over the last two nights. No need to spread out here."

"Received and understood," King responded by IR comms.

"Thousands of years ago, the entire mountainside was a city," Masha said.

"I can see that in places," Hoffman said.

"It will become more obvious."

"You've been this way before?"

Masha looked up the mountain. "This is the first

place we examined when we came to this palatial ice ball of a world."

"Let's talk about the objective."

"Skiing. Some hiking. Medvedev wishes to paint a landscape for his portfolio," she said.

"You don't strike me as a nature girl," Hoffman said, smiling at her disgusted reaction.

"You should give me a weapon so I can fight when they catch us," Medvedev said.

Walking beside Masha, Hoffman ignored the legionnaire. "On a scale of one to ten, how are these slopes for potential ski resorts?"

"Double black diamonds," she said.

"Skiing," Hoffman said. "A little of this, a little of that. Taking in the sights and doing some skiing here on Koen. I'm surprised Ibarra doesn't give all his best spies a vacation pass here."

She glared at him. "You say that like there is only one Ibarra."

Hoffman hid his confusion by studying the details of her face, trying to pick up on any change of expression that might indicate she was lying.

"We're not as bad as you think we are," she said. "The Ibarra Nation would be quite content to be left to our own devices."

"That's what you were doing here?" Hoffman asked. "And on Nouveau Marsellie? And New Bastion? Minding to your 'own devices.'"

Masha winked at him.

They walked for a while, leaning up the steep parts of the trail. King and Garrison chatted back and forth about the terrain and argued about when Garrison would get a turn on point. Hoffman listen to the IR radio communications in one ear but focused most of his attention on the spy. There was no way to maintain visual contact with everyone on his team, but glimpses of individuals appeared between the narrow white trees below him.

"I've been this way before," she said. "I know the way through the mountains. Through the ruins. Tunnels and mazes. Shouldn't be dangerous, but a person could get lost."

"I had a buddy who went into the Pathfinders, looking for archaeotech. Stuff like that."

"Everyone is looking for archaeotech." She paused. "And here we are."

Hoffman pinged King's IR link, signaling him to listen in, then spoke casually. "Doesn't look like much. The earthen mounds in the valleys and foothills remind me of Koensuu City. Every planet has something similar. That doesn't mean the secret to galactic survival is here," Hoffman said.

"That doesn't mean it isn't," she said. "You should know from your briefing that I don't get sent random places."

"You're too good for that."

"Damn straight." She stopped walking. "How long are you going to keep our hands zip-tied? Med has a point. He could be useful in a fight."

"No doubt," Hoffman said, crossing his arms.

"No matter what you think of us, we're not friends of the Kesaht. They make no distinction between Ibarran humans and Terran humans. Give my legionnaire a weapon. Something small. Otherwise, he is a liability you must protect."

"Rather than a traitor who will shoot me in the back," he said.

"We're beyond that now. Look around, Hoffman. One mistake and we're dead."

"Welcome to the glamorous life of the Strike Marines," he said. "Enemies on my left and traitors on my right."

****

"I can lead you through the mountains, through a maze of ruins the Kesaht don't know about," said Masha.

"Sounds completely safe. Not at all like a trap," Hoffman said.

"I had one other friend on this plant," she said, "and your sniper shot him in the face. Rude, but that's neither here nor there. I know a little shortcut back to the city that's nearby. You want to give me a smidgen of trust or you want to stay out here until frostbite nibbles away at your favorite body parts?"

"She's got a point," Garrison said.

King slapped the Marine on the back of his head.

"What were you looking for out here, Masha?" Hoffman asked.

She crossed her arms and worked her jaw side to side as they stared at each other.

"Don't say I didn't offer. Put that in your mission log: team froze to death out of spite."

Hoffman waited for Gunney's response via the IR comms.

"I've heard worse ideas," King said. "If the

legionnaire steps out of line, Opal can just crush his head. Or I'll take him. Either way works."

Hoffman looked at another storm system creeping over the mountain range, then at Masha. "What does Medvedev mean to you?"

"That's an interesting question."

Hoffman waited for her answer.

"He is loyal and skilled. I respect him," she said.

"He dies first if you betray our mission. And don't flatter yourself. I'll take him out first because he's the greater threat."

"Agreed, Lieutenant Hoffman." She pushed her bound hands forward. "You're an officer and a gentleman."

Hoffman opened the team link. "We're moving in five. I'm taking the principal on point to check for an alternate route. King, handle that matter we discussed with the other prisoner."

Looking up the mountain, Hoffman was skeptical there was a way through the direction she wanted to go. "Lead the way."

"I've got my eyes open," King replied.

The path grew so steep that he wondered what type of animal could climb it, probably goats or something equally reclusive. The way split off from the valley and seemed to be leading straight into a wall of granite. Tendrils of ice covered the vista. A frozen waterfall stained the stone green and light blue.

"Is this the maze of ancient ruins you're talking about?" Hoffman asked.

"Are you worried, Lieutenant?"

He shook his head. "No. One thing's certain. There's no place here for a secret squad of Ibarran legionnaires to set an ambush."

"You'll learn to trust me," she said.

Once they arrived, the tunnel was hard to miss, but from the trail or from aerial surveillance, it would be invisible. From the miserable little streambed he stood upon, it looked like the open front doors to an alien cathedral. The support beams were carved with symbols and bold lines. Precious metals and gemstones remained where time hadn't eroded them away.

That a landslide had buried the tunnel entrance was not the bit of operational friction that Hoffman had anticipated.

"We can get us to the city, but you have to trust me," Masha said. "This is the best way through the mountain pass—unless you want to call in reinforcements and duke it out with the Kesaht."

"We?"

"I can't make this climb by myself. It took Med and me nearly a day to set all the anchor points. You're going to tell me Strike Marines are trained for climbing, but that's not why I need him. Med knows the way better than I do."

"You climb with me and Medvedev climbs with Opal and Garrison. Not open to negotiation." Hoffman motioned for the rest of his team to get ready.

"This would be a lot easier if you weren't so stubborn," Masha said.

"Get used to it." Hoffman followed her up. She climbed well, rarely slowing to check for handholds or reevaluate her route. Before long, they had located the anchor points from their previous visit to the ruins.

"These would be really useful if we had climbing kits," Garrison said. "You know, a couple hundred meters of graphenium rope. How you doing there, Opie?"

"Opal climb."

"Not much for conversation, is it?" Medvedev said.

"Use what you have," King said, ignoring the Ibarran legionnaire.

"We have nothing," Medvedev said. "The enviro suits you put us in fit poorly and do little more than keep us dry. We have no ropes, climbing kit, or weapons if the

Kesaht ambush us."

"Pray they don't," Hoffman said.

"I have. Many times," Medvedev said.

"Our Strike Marine gear has carbon line. Use it but don't rely on it. It's made to drop into windows, not scale mountains," Hoffman said, focusing on Masha. Her graceful movements propelled her upward at a pace he found difficult to match, especially while talking to his team.

The rest of the team came next, followed by King. He grabbed one of the anchor points with his left gauntlet and leaned out to look at the rest of the team. "Opal, stay close to Medvedev."

"Yes, sir." The doughboy moved methodically, always maintaining three points of contact before reaching to the next handhold.

Medvedev, slightly ahead of Opal, looked down at him. "Is it afraid of heights?"

"He isn't afraid of anything," Garrison said.

"Opal climb," Opal said and then his foot slipped. He replanted it seconds later and continued without hesitation.

"Careful, Opal," Garrison said, moving on a parallel course to the giants and watching their every move on the difficult ascent.

Opal hesitated. "Fingers don't fit." The muscles of his arms and upper back strained as his fingers clenched the vertical outcropping. He started to slip. "Opal should have brought longer rope."

"Opal!" Hoffman shouted just as the doughboy fell. Garrison lunged for him but didn't have the leverage or the reach.

Medvedev's hand shot out like a snake and seized Opal by the wrist. He strained as the doughboy swung from his grasp, Opal's feet dangling over a very long drop.

"Let go of him before you bring us all down!" Masha shouted.

"Don't let go! I'm reeling out my tactical cord!" Garrison grunted. "Piece of…"

Hoffman stared past Medvedev into Opal's eyes. Two Strike Marines with powered armor might've been able to save the doughboy. Medvedev was strong, but the struggle to hold Opal was writ across his pained face and strained neck.

"I can't…hold him…forever," Medvedev said.

"Screw it! Piece-of-crap latch." Garrison climbed horizontally and seized one of the anchor points. With his other hand, he pushed up on Opal as King scrambled upward to add his strength to the maneuver. Several tense moments passed before Opal found better handholds.

"You got a grip, big guy?" Garrison asked, his voice an octave higher than it should have been as he gasped for air. "Don't mind me. I've been skimping on my training runs. Little out of breath here. My bad. And this arm is somewhat less than a hundred percent."

King grunted and cursed as he levered Opal toward a better position. "Note to self, doughboys aren't made for mountaineering."

Masha spoke quietly to Hoffman as they watched the Strike Marines and the legionnaire work together. "Your men are brave. Mine is just stupid."

"Why? Because he'll have to fight Opal later? How many of us did you hope to take out during this climb?" Hoffman asked.

She hung by one of the anchor points and stared at him. "None, Lieutenant. You Terrans have all the guns. Gravity is a harsh mistress, but I'm not ready to discard you all just yet. There is a place to rest soon if your walking steak doesn't try and kill us all again."

****

"I hope you brought us here for more than the view," Hoffman said.

"Don't get too attached," Masha said. "Beauty always comes at a price. In this case, the price is misery." She hugged herself and shivered in the cold wind of the mountaintop. "Mother Nature is overrated. Sleet and snow will hide us from the Kesaht. And rescue. And the mercy of the Saint."

"Gunney King promised our Arctic training was so hard reality would be a vacation. I would like to note for the record that the assertion was a gross exaggeration," Garrison said.

"Watch your zone, Garrison," King said.

"What zone, Gunney? Pretty lonely up here on the top of the world."

As Gunney King and Opal did a sweep of the escarpment, King slipped and fell to one knee near the top of the trail. Opal snatched his wrist and heaved him back to his feet before his butt hit the snow.

"You were gonna die," Garrison said. "Good thing we have Opie."

"Watch it, Garrison," King said. "And we're all gonna die one way or another. Just not until we complete the mission."

"I love NCO mirth. Makes all this fun." Garrison indicated the cliffs they had climbed for hours and the contrails of distant air-to-air battles, the sound of explosions booming out of sync with the action.

"Opal never complains," King said. "He's a good Marine."

"Best in the corps. Who's second-best, Gunney? Don't say it. We all know how you feel. I'm hungry."

Hoffman turned away from their banter and found Masha staring at him. She shivered constantly, and although her complaints were politer than Garrison's constant griping, her expressive eyes sent mixed messages. *Help me, Thomas Hoffman. Keep me warm. Take me away from all this.*

He blinked the thoughts away.

"Come with me, Lieutenant. Med packed away our extra food and water." She led him to a rock and started to dig. "Would you be so kind?"

Hoffman scraped frozen gravel away from a narrow depression with his gauntleted hands.

She stood too close. "Our second supply drop was right here. Med made the command decision to leave half what we brought rather than slog it where we are going now."

Hoffman studied the escarpment. "Nice place for an air drop. Must have been harrowing. What made it worth the risk?"

"We had a well-planned time schedule until a bunch of Strike Marines spoiled it."

Hoffman cracked open a small cache of supplies.

Medvedev, his hands once again tied in front of him, sat solemnly and watched. "Good thing I didn't rig up those grenades."

Inside were a pair of battery-powered thermal liners, climbing gear, and ration bars with non-English writing on them.

"Ooo, bacalao." Masha held a hand out to Hoffman. "Salted cod. Tastes better than the nutrient mush you've forced down our throats."

Hoffman tossed the salted fish right past her to Opal, who ripped it open and stuffed the whole thing into his mouth.

"Really?" she deadpanned.

Hoffman tossed the rest of the food to his team.

"At least let her put on the heat lining," Medvedev said. "It would be the humane thing to do. Look at her. She's freezing to death."

Hoffman tossed gear and the last ration bar to

Masha. "Take a load off. Check your gear. Take in calories. Hydrate."

"Nature's calling me," Masha said. "Now that we're out of the freezing cold and there's a minor degree of privacy behind that rock over there…"

King shook his head. "Your enviro-suit recycles your—"

"Filter pockets are full," Masha snapped. "And you think we're going to run out of water? If I never see snow again, it won't be too soon."

"Search the area," Hoffman said to King.

Masha rolled her eyes as King went behind the rock and emerged a few moments later and flashed a thumbs-up.

"We start trusting them to do class three downloads and we might as well give them pistols," King mumbled.

Hoffman didn't respond.

Masha came back and flicked her hair before she sat down next to Medvedev and tore into an Ibarran ration pack.

Later, at midday, the sky cleared completely and a battle for air superiority raged closer. Hoffman heard the Eagles firing rail guns in the upper atmosphere, the sound reaching his position well after they had lived or died fighting.

"The Kesaht are really bringing it to Koen," Garrison said as he cleaned his gear and repacked it in his kit.

"Are they always like this?" Hoffman asked. "Berserkers? Mad dogs? Tireless warriors?"

"They are zealots. The Toth convinced them humans are evil. You can expect everything from swarm tactics to suicide attacks. I've watched them plunge their fighters into the hulls of our gunships," Masha said.

Explosions ripped through the distant clouds like rolling thunder as two waves of crescent fighters sliced over the horizon in pursuit of Terran Eagles.

Chapter 14

"Guess what I'm thinking," Booker said, barely moving her lips as she lay next to Duke in the sniper perch, her rifle covered with strips of burlap cloth and branches as she stared through binoculars. The two of them were nestled in a tangle of underbrush where two ridgelines converged. The position was high enough to see, but not high enough to silhouette them against the silver skyline.

"Wondering what kind of field meds you've got that can ward off cold? Maybe some brandy in an IV," Duke said, adjusting the focus on his own binoculars and gazing across the mouth of the mountain pass.

"Survey says…wrong. I was fantasizing about the steam tent," Booker said.

"Me too," he said. "Or what you and the fine laddies of Koen were doing in there."

"Creep."

"You started it."

"Because I'm freezing to death. Need something else to think about."

Duke exhaled slowly, wishing for nicotine, caffeine…or anything ending with "ine." Snow fell heavily between the sparse trees as another storm loomed on the horizon. When it hit, visibility would be crap. "First rule of sniper school. No whining about the cold."

"That is the twentieth 'first rule' you've told me."

"You're right. We should start from the beginning. Rule one, no whining about the weather. Rule two, everything I say is law. Rule three, no more steam tents."

"Doesn't have to be this cold," Booker said.

"Our armor stays turned off. We'll stick out like a doughboy in a buffet line if we power up. Anyone with infrared optics will be calling down artillery strikes on our position as soon as they see us," Duke said.

"You may have a point."

"Refer to rule number two." He paused. "Looks like Kesaht vehicles coming out of the pass. Must have found a way around the river or this is another division from another valley."

Duke and Booker counted in silence as a long line

of vehicles came into view and maneuvered down the switchback road.

"Most of those are lightly armored. That one, right there, is open-topped. What the hell is wrong with these Rakka dudes? Do they enjoy freezing their balls off?"

"Mountain clansmen before being assimilated into the Kesaht hegemony," Duke said.

"How do you know all this shit?"

"I read the briefings."

Booker lowered her binoculars. "That wasn't in our brief, not for this mission."

"I read all the briefings. Every non-classified document on the enemy I can find. Thought everyone did that," Duke said.

"I can make a shot from here."

"No."

"Give me a chance. I need to start logging shots," she said.

Duke raised one finger. It was a small motion, barely noticeable. "Patience. We're hunting."

"What makes you think this'll work?"

"Kesaht are using Toth tech. Reminds me of an after-action report I read from the Ember War. A sniper named Bailey had to make a shield penetration on a high-value target."

"Toth? I thought they were gone," Booker said.

Duke spit into his bottle, a highly technical sniper skill learned only through experience.

"Wait, you read old sniper files too? Like for fun?"

"Do you read medical journals?"

"Of course."

Duke studied the landscape for a moment. "Do you think I read that crap?" Three birds flew up from a copse of trees between their positions in the road. "Here we go."

An explosion sent a vehicle straight into the air, the sound reaching Duke and Booker a moment later. Smoke and flames trailed the vehicle during its upward progress. Rakka scrambled to each side of the road and went prone, weapons thrust out before them as they fired blindly.

"Fourth truck. One thousand eight hundred ninety meters," Duke said.

"Got it," Booker said. She took up the slack on her trigger and waited.

Gauss bullets from the PDF ambush team bounced off the shield protecting the Sanheel officer. The half-humanoid, half-horse creature aimed its oversize weapon into the woods and placed accurate fire on the PDF position.

"Three, two, one." Duke and Booker fired simultaneously.

The Sanheel's power shield wavered but held.

"You missed."

"I...might have."

Duke slapped in a new power pack, then kicked his boot against hers. "Get ready."

She was already recharging her rifle when he spoke.

"Three, two, one." They fired.

A snap-crack later, the Sanheel's head exploded in dark mist.

Rakka infantry saw where their officer had been firing on the PDF and opened up with everything in their arsenal.

Another Sanheel rushed forward, bypassing the bottleneck of armored vehicles. The galloping officer skidded to a halt and opened fire on the ambushers. The Rakka used his accurate fire to direct their bullets and shoulder rockets.

Gusting wind blew snow and smoke across the battlefield.

"Aim nine degrees left," Duke said.

"I can make the shot."

"Don't argue," he said. "Three, two...bang."

Both sniper rounds blasted through the Sanheel. It twisted and reared as it crumpled to the ground.

A ripple of visible fear swept through the Rakka line. One moment they were brutalizing the PDF ambush team, the next they were huddling around an armored personnel carrier. The Rakka equivalent of a sergeant or small-team leader yelled and screamed and shook his fists but changed nothing.

"Load and hold fire. Be ready," Duke said to Booker as he took aim at the armored personnel carrier that had yet to open. He put a round through it and watched ammunition cook off. Seconds later, an Ixio officer escaped out the back. Long and gangly, even less physically suited to this environment than humans, the Ixio ran into a snow-covered field.

"He wants to die tired," Duke said. "Time to fill up your logbook. Range, nineteen hundred seventy-nine meters. Target moving at consistent speed. Lead by two meters and watch your breath control."

Booker drew back the trigger of her sniper rifle until the weapon sent out a powerful gauss round. A moment later, the top half of the Ixio splattered across a snowdrift.

"All right. Class is over. Time for the teacher to

play," Duke said. "Switch to low-power shots and make them count." He began dropping Rakka in quick succession and could feel Booker watching him.

"That's a lot of kills," she said. "I wish I could acquire targets that fast and hit most of the time."

"Every time," Duke corrected. "You must decide to hit every time, not most of the time. Get to work. Take your time and focus on your breath control and range."

He shot three more as they emerged from cover and made a break for the tree line. Before long, the Rakka were in full retreat. Some tried to recover vehicles while others sprinted in panic.

Duke reloaded, then looked at the storm.

Booker followed his gaze. "We should head back to camp. This position is pretty hot right now and I don't like the look of that storm."

Duke shook his head. "No. Got an idea."

"Uh…I thought only officers got visited by the bad-idea fairy."

"Snipers only have good ideas."

Booker stifled a slightly hysterical laugh. "You want to go looking for an army of Kesaht?"

"Got it in one."

"I'm down like a clown," she said. "I think I've

reached level one sniper crazy."

"Only eleven more levels to go," Duke said. "If this works, we can really put a hurting on the Kesaht."

Chapter 15

Tell me again," Hoffman said.

Masha repeated her description of the route through the high-altitude maze. Across from Hoffman and Masha, King listened attentively while Garrison and Opal waited just out of earshot with Medvedev.

"It is not something to go through, but over. Like walking rooftop to rooftop," she said.

"Except we'll be traversing stone spires and vertical escarpments instead of buildings." King opened and closed a fist, then held it flexed for a moment—clearly restraining his temper. "With no cover or concealment. If you're wrong, we fall thousands of feet to our deaths—and that's assuming you don't have confederates waiting to ambush us."

"There is no one to help me but Medvedev. As for

the route we must take, my bodyguard might remember details I have forgotten."

"I doubt that," Hoffman said. "Ibarran spies aren't known for poor memory or insensitivity to details."

"Touché," Masha said. "It doesn't matter if you believe me or not. The way down from here is deceptive. Take the obvious way, you will find yourself on an exposed ledge as the storm moves in." She nodded toward clouds stacking across the horizon.

"This route doesn't make sense," King said. "Whoever these ancients were, they made it harder to get up here, not easier."

"You must be tired, Gunney," she said.

King clenched his jaw, holding her gaze as though they were prize fighters squaring off.

"The maze work was a defensive measure. Threats to their civilization always came from that side of the mountains," she said.

"You assume," Hoffman said.

"My assumptions are frequently correct. This is my area of expertise," she said.

"Of course. I forgot you were sent here to look for alien artifacts. Let's talk about that," Hoffman said.

"Oh, right, guess this is the time I should see if the

Terran Union wants me as a double agent," Masha said with a sniff.

"What was that?" Medvedev asked.

"We're a package deal," the spy said. "But good luck convincing him to flip. He's like a damn stump."

"I cannot wait to be done with you two," Hoffman said. "Let's figure out how we're getting through this mess."

He waited for King to chime in, but his top NCO kept his eyes on the horizon.

"I might have made a different decision if you had described this secret path of yours. Rope bridges and rock spires would be more inviting if the ropes hadn't disintegrated a thousand years ago," Hoffman said.

"Have courage, Strike Marine," she said.

"Garrison, watch her." Hoffman moved away to speak with King. "What do you think?"

King stared at his feet, then raised his gaze. "Not much choice at this point. We use what safety lines we have. Go down ten feet at a time. Recover the lines and repeat. It'll take forever."

"Speed is essential in this. Move without the safety lines?"

"Risky. Opal's proven to be a weak climber," King

said.

"No choice." Hoffman assembled the team and the prisoners.

"Masha and I will lead. Garrison will follow, holding security over the entire team. I'd rather none of us have to shoot you, Masha, but we'll wound you and carry you if necessary. If Medvedev steps out of line, my men will shoot to kill." He looked at the big Ibarran legionnaire. "Are we clear?"

Medvedev nodded. "Yes, Lieutenant Hoffman. We are very clear. This is what I assumed from the beginning."

"Good," Hoffman said. "Opal, your primary job is to watch Medvedev. Keep him alive if possible. Kill him if necessary."

"Yes, sir," Opal said.

"King, you're also with Opal and Medvedev, adjusting your position as necessary. You're responsible for guarding the rear of our formation."

"Yes, sir," King said.

Masha led them down a steep trail to the first footbridge. Hoffman wasn't sure how it was still swinging but saw clearly that the hand ropes had rotted away long ago. He hesitated at the edge of the platform, finding it flexible and intricate by design. "This bridge looks like archaeotech. Simple, but amazingly well-engineered."

"You probably made the same assumptions that I did, that there *were* handrails or ropes that have degraded over time. Medvedev and I decided during our first trip here this is not the case. These causeways were made for creatures who didn't fear heights, or perhaps didn't walk on two feet as we do," Masha said.

Hoffman followed her across the bridge, keeping his knees bent and controlling his breathing as the surface moved left and right under their weight.

"You could crawl on your belly. Hold on to the platform with your arms and legs. It would be like climbing a rope horizontally," Masha said. "The problem we found with this approach last time was that your packs tend to pull you around to the underside of the structure. Hanging from this footbridge with all my gear tugging me downward is not one of my fondest memories."

Hoffman looked at the rest of his team waiting to step onto the footbridge. The simple act of turning his head to face Masha nearly tipped him over the side. "Let's just get across and take a break."

She smiled, then walked confidently to the end of the bridge. He looked down, seeing the chasm below his feet as wind buffeted him. The bridge became less stable without her weight.

Cautiously, he raised his gaze to hers. She watched him, arms crossed over her chest.

Step-by-step, he reached the ledge. "Hoffman for King, copy?"

"King for Hoffman, receiving clearly."

"Allow the bridge to come to a complete stop, then come across with Garrison. The bridge needs a certain amount of weight to remain stable. Medvedev won't do anything with Masha on this side, and if he does, my money's on Opal."

"Understood. Coming across with Garrison."

Hoffman and Masha watched until the entire team was on the ledge together, then he looked down at the next phase of the high-altitude maze. The course they needed to travel cut back upon itself and was invisible from this angle. It irked him that he had the high ground but couldn't see the route.

"All right, Masha, let's go," Hoffman said.

As they descended toward the bottom of the canyon, level by painfully slow level, he looked up. Attacking in that direction would be suicidal. He wondered what kind of creatures were this adept at mountain climbing.

"Are you starting to trust me?" Masha asked.

"No."

"I could have killed you ten times during the last few hours," she said.

"My team would continue the mission. King would make your life miserable, right after he killed your bodyguard," Hoffman said.

"That would be unfortunate," she said.

"Which part?"

She didn't answer.

Chapter 16

A pair of Rakka huddled near a fire, its yellow light illuminating hairy faces and scraggly uniforms. Frost and mystery stains covered their body armor. Weapons were invisible beneath layers of improvised clothing—bedrolls and blankets wrapped on top of combat gear.

A gauntlet grabbed one around the mouth from behind as a blade protruded from the Rakka's throat. His eyes went wide but probably never saw the exact same thing happen to his companion.

Duke lowered his victim to the ground, then wiped the bloody blade on the Kesaht battle kit. Booker, behind the other dead Rakka, did likewise.

"Told you this is where they are," Duke said.

"Nice of these assholes to shine a beacon for us," she said as she kicked snow toward the fire.

Duke grabbed her arm. "Don't do that."

They backed away as though they'd never been there. Snow was already covering the bodies, leaving them as growing mounds. When Duke looked back a short time later, he could see the glow but few details. Gray clouds raced low over the mountains, often skimming the ground. Snow fell so hard he couldn't tell the precipitation from the storm system that produced it. He could hear a groaning sound and thought the wind might be angry enough to rid Koen of humans and Kesaht.

Booker held his gaze, obviously wanting to say something.

"Go ahead and break the first rule. Tell me how freaking cold you are," Duke said.

"I really didn't think it could get worse. My fingertips feel like I've been pounding them with hammers. This is like an out-of-body experience," she said.

"Worst I've been in."

Booker perked up. "Really? An old bastard like you has probably been in thousands of storms."

"Watch it, spring buck." He swallowed chewing tobacco inside his helmet. "I'm thirty-seven. Not old."

Booker made some kind of grunting snarl in response. "All right, maybe I deserved that." A crosswind knocked her sideways. Duke slipped and went to one knee.

"Yep, worst storm I've ever seen. Let's go kill someone."

They moved down a steep animal trail, slow and steady all the way to a low ridge about one hundred meters from a large Kesaht camp. Duke went prone, the cold ground soaking through his insulated armor as though he were wearing a T-shirt and shorts. Booker snuggled in next to him with her sniper kit at her side and no more words of complaint. Freezing and exhausted, Duke didn't feel like a conversation either.

He spied on the camp for several minutes before either of them bothered to whisper in their IR mics.

"Might be a full division. Not sure about their table of organization and equipment, but it's something close to that. Four squadrons of tanks. Reconnaissance vehicles. Armored transports. What am I missing?" Duke asked.

"I'm just checking your numbers against my numbers," Booker said.

Duke's first indication that this was the cream of the Kesaht crop was the frequent patrols, one of which was headed their way. "Get ready for company. They'll have to come really close to spot us."

"Standing by to stand by," Booker whispered into

her helmet chin mic. "Have I told you prone is my least favorite position? Hurts my neck."

"Sucks to be you. Good thing you're not a real sniper." He paused. "But if you were, you could roll up your poncho and put it under your chest. Elevate your thoracic spine and take pressure off your neck."

"You couldn't tell me this an hour ago?"

"Don't. Move. At all," Duke whispered.

The Rakka patrol stomped through the miserable weather, closer and closer to Duke and Booker. Gusts of wind pelted ice against Duke's helmet loud enough he could barely hear Booker when she talked, as infrequent as that was now that the Rakka were dangerously close.

The first Rakka passed over Duke, nearly stepping on him. The aliens were bigger than he expected up close, the Rakka's hair and armor and demeanor as wild as any xenotype Duke had ever faced. The patrol had a heavy musk somewhere between a wet dog and old straw. Seeing them in battle led him to believe they were always on edge berserkers. What he saw now was a suffering soldier. The Rakka point man would likely welcome combat rather than endure night after night of this bitter storm.

The main body of the patrol passed. The rearguard was almost as large as the main body, which Duke found interesting.

"Booker whispered over the IR commlink once they were passed. "Do you think they're worried about ambush? With that rearguard?"

"I'm not sure. So far, we've been on the money predicting what they'll do in any given situation. The first mistake we make will probably be our last," Duke said. "Pathfinders deal with this type of stuff a lot. I read their reports too."

"I skim, looking for info on new and interesting diseases."

Duke aimed his binoculars at the camp and went over it section by section, looking for any detail he had missed.

"Lot of good it does us to find this place," Booker said. "There's no way PDF arty can range this far out. What exactly is the point? I mean, we can take out a couple officers before they find us. You gave me the impression we were going to strike a major blow."

"O ye of little faith. I'm going to kill them all."

"How?" Booker's fatigue was starting to show in the tone of her voice, just as Duke knew he would be less than pleasant in any conversation not relevant to ending this mission and getting warm. "We've got maybe two dozen rounds between us."

"Nineteen, but I only need one."

"The cold's frozen your brain," Booker said.

Duke exhaled slowly, wishing for the hundredth time since they started down from the summit that he had another can of dip. What he did have in his kit was carefully rationed and he had gone a bit over already. "What did you notice about those Rakka? Other than them being deader than usual?" Duke turned far enough toward her to give her the look.

Booker shivered. "They were colder than I am."

Duke wagged his finger at her. "Their armor is just dead weight. Unpowered."

"No heat layer," Booker said.

"What else? How is our field of fire?" Duke asked.

"Damn good. They've been cutting down trees. Burning them for firewood, looks like."

Duke nodded, liking his plan more than ever. "There...center of the camp. See that heat plume? That's their generator."

"So?" Booker asked, studying the scene for tactical options.

Duke moved his binoculars along power lines that ran from the generator to tents and vehicles and saw a stack of power packs covered with tarpaulins next to the generator. The big Sanheel officer from the bridge battle came into view, walking slightly off-kilter with his cybernetic front leg.

"There you are," Duke said. "That's a senior officer, whatever rank structure they use. Look how they all jumped when he said boo."

"Take them out?" Booker asked.

Duke shook his head. "I'd like to. I think this one is trouble. Probably holding a grudge after I blew off his hoof. But take a look at those lines on the ground near the generator."

"Yeah?"

"Shields. Which are off-line to save power in the storm. We hit ugly down there, they'll pop the energy walls and ugly's the only thing we'll hit." Duke pulled his gauss rifle to his shoulder. "But you see that battery stack? The one with all the wires running to it from the heaters?"

"What about it?" Booker's question was lost on the wind as Duke slipped into concentration.

The wind died down. Booker's tension mounted as she thought conditions were right for a long-range shot, but Duke held perfectly still. Down in the valley, antennae on the back of Kesaht vehicles waved slowly in the breeze.

Loose snow gusted across the camp, then settled to the ground.

Duke pulled the last tiny bit of pressure on the trigger and sent a gauss round downrange.

The battery stacks popped and fizzled. Sparks arced into the air. Rakka ran around like in a panic. The metal-legged Sanheel shouted and beat any Rakka he could reach about the head and shoulders.

Shields hummed to life, distorting the air.

"Great," Booker said.

Duke lifted his head from his weapon sights.

The shields flickered and went out as battery stacks melted down one by one in quick succession. The load transferred until the generator exploded and slagged the other power packs. Lights went off across the camp, swallowed by the blowing snow and approaching dusk.

Duke smiled. "Mission accomplished. Time to displace."

For the first time since they began this mission, Booker finished packing her gear first. She was getting better than Duke was willing to admit. He liked working with her. She led the way up the goat trail, or whatever animal came this way frequently enough to scar the landscape. As soon as they were at the summit, they descended into a parallel valley and stopped to check their gear and drink from helmet tubes.

"Think it'll work?" Booker asked.

"If they run their vehicles for heat, they'll drain them in hours. The storm will last another day, at least. They've already used up most of their firewood. There's going to be a lot of dying of exposure down there," he said.

He looked through his visor into hers. They were close enough to see each other despite the tempests devouring the mountains. He smiled and pushed one of his power-up buttons. Heat seeped into his extremities.

Booker laughed. "Oh yeah, that's what I'm talking about. Warm armor is good armor."

"Let's blow this popsicle stand." Duke led the way into the storm that swallowed them and all evidence of their passage.

****

Two hours later, they were well away from the Kesaht camp enveloped in a storm Duke couldn't quite describe, even to himself. It felt like three or four storms stacked on top of each other.

"Right here. I'll dig first. You hold security, then

we'll trade," Duke said.

Booker gave him a brief thumbs-up. Even with the heating elements at full strength, she was bouncing up and down on her toes to stay warm.

"Honestly," she said, "if they can find us in this mess, we should let them kill us out of respect."

Duke looked up at her and froze.

"Kidding. Kidding," she said.

Duke covered his weapons, set them beside his work area, then popped loose an entrenching tool and started to dig. He made the shelter long enough for both of them to fit inside and almost deep enough to crawl into. Then he signaled her and she took her turn. He stared into the night with his patrol rifle held close to his body to keep it out of the driving ice and snow as best he could.

"That should do it," she said. "Let's get toasty." She climbed in and pulled her gear after her.

Duke checked their tiny perimeter one last time and then crawled in with his gear. Inside, he pulled the tarpaulin even tighter and fastened it down with small stakes from his kit.

Booker put down a heat pack and turned it all the way up. "My favorite part. Love my armor, but a girl needs downtime."

Duke broke apart his sniper rifle and cleaned it. Booker cracked her armor and leaned back with an instant cup of soup.

"Surprisingly quiet in here. Or I'm going deaf from all these explosions."

Duke continued to clean.

"It's not bad," she said.

"What's not bad?"

"Shooting aliens. Not like putting crosshairs on a human, I mean. That seems like it would be a hell of a lot harder," she said.

"Have you ever shot a human?" Duke asked.

"Nope." She hesitated, busying herself with her soup. "I've been wondering about that. You have any trouble shooting that Ibarra sniper back in the city?"

"Yeah, but only because he tagged me first." Duke touched a welt on his hairline. "There was a moment when I debated beating feet out of my hide, but then the sniper would've picked you all off one by one. Besides. He caught me square in the dome and couldn't kill me. Figured his next shot wouldn't get me either. Saw him re-aiming to the park and took him. Easy shot. Things got a little fuzzy after that." Duke finished his sniper rifle and put it away, then took out his patrol carbine and started working on it.

"So it was easy to kill him?"

"It's never easy. I just got through the resistance quick—which is easy when your life, or your squaddie's, is on the line."

"Never thought of that. All my training was against Xaros. Vish. Kroar. Not humans."

"So?" He pushed a brush through a port on his patrol rifle but looked at her as he raised one eyebrow.

"Do you think we're going to fight the Ibarrans? They're all proccies, but they're human."

He finished his rifle in several quick motions, put it away, and took out his pistol. "I'm worried about the Kesaht right now. You should be too."

Wind tugged at the tarpaulin, straining the eyebolts buried deep into the ice walls of their shelter. The howling sound grew louder and Booker shifted closer to the heat pack. Duke finished cleaning his pistol, decided the hell with the tough-guy routine, and moved as close to the warmth as he could get.

****

Trace amounts of heat came with the dawn.

"This planet is a harsher mistress than the

irradiated steppes of Santarra," Thran'Ul thought.

The Ice Claw had turned Koen itself into a weapon against the Kesaht. Rakka and Sanheel bodies lay strewn across the valley. The lesser Rakka had crawled to freshly dead Sanheel and burrowed under them for warmth. The bizarre tangle of bodies was obscene and Thran'Ul wished he could burn the nightmare away, which brought on a fantasy about warming himself near a fire.

Some of the corpses had blood iced to their faces—from clawing themselves in a ritual to retain lost honor before death. He would never understand the Rakka. They were good only for fighting and dying.

He came across Shin'lon, an old officer, one Thran'Ul remembered seeing in a parade before he was old enough to join the martial service of the Kesaht. The old officer had burned Rakka for warmth before he died with a Rakka half-spear in his back.

Thran'Ul scratched at frostbite on his face until dead tissue peeled up. He picked it off. All around him were dead Rakka. None of the frozen bodies had died with honor. He hated the Rakka scum. Their bravery came only in large groups, and only when they were driven to a battle frenzy. Not one of the lesser race could take honor from a universe ravaged by human murderers.

Something changed in the air. A pinpoint of light appeared in the upper atmosphere and descended toward his position. A Kesaht lander, he thought, more appealing to look at than the Terran Mules but less durable and slower. He didn't know what a "mule" was but sensed it was a mundane creature. One of the Ibarran humans he had captured and then stomped to death had called him a mule and laughed. But not for long. None of the human murderers were brave under the hooves of a Sanheel.

The lander did nothing correctly. If his people could fly the machines, they would sweep grandly around the area and see enemies or other threats before touching down to the surface. The Ixio pilots were often foolish, but their skills and reaction time made them superior to the Sanheel as pilots, and the Ixio served the Kesaht union in that role well.

A ramp lowered from the back of the lander and the Ixio named Dorsaria emerged, his face covered with contempt and disrespect for the warriors who had died here.

Dorsaria walked to a pile of Rakka and contemplated the bodies. Folding his hands behind his back, he pretended to ignore the biting cold and Thran'Ul

Thran'Ul didn't like his expression of disdain or his posture.

"I must inquire as to the delay," the Ixio said. "Some manner of equipment failure, perhaps?"

"A sniper. One of unfortunate talent."

"The ones the Rakka called the Ice Claw? Curious the sniper manages to thwart each of your advances. The Risen grow impatient with your lack of results."

Thran'Ul listened but was distracted by how his own junior officer had called the sniper Ice Claw. He had even found himself thinking of the human murderer in such terms. It was a disgusting weakness to give his enemies such honor.

"The war in the void has stalemated. We desire the human city to surrender as the fleet must follow suit. The threat of mass execution has that effect on humans," Dorsaria said.

Thran'Ul stomped one hoof. "Then we move on the city now."

"The casualties will be—"

Thran'Ul kicked a frozen corpse, breaking its arm off at the shoulder. "They serve the Kesaht. Their sacrifice will be remembered."

"Lord Bale does not measure success by the trail of our dead. If becoming Risen and joining the ranks of the immortals is your goal, this is not how to do it."

"If I fail to capture the city, then I will never be Risen."

The Ixio evaluated him in silence for several moments. "Your choice."

Thran'Ul shifted his weight from hoof to hoof as the energy for combat grew too intense to resist. "Take me to the forward division. The time of caution is over."

Chapter 17

Wind howled up the narrow canyon and down from the summit. Swirling blackness reached up from hell. Snow and ice pelted Hoffman's visor, screaming like banshees all around him, slamming his team with gale-force winds focused in the narrow spaces of the Koen Mountain Ruins.

"Reel out your entry cords and tie off with the person in front of you! We have to stay together!" King yelled. "If one person falls, we all fall!"

"I volunteer not to fall!" Garrison shouted. "Still can't get my cord latch to unfreeze. Tired of junk armor and crap equipment. Stupid utility belt."

"You have the best gear in the Terran military, except for the Armor Corps maybe," King said. "Grab on to Medvedev. Opal, tie on to Medvedev."

Hoffman clipped the carbon-fiber cord normally

used to swing from rooftops into windows on to the back of Masha's belt. Her environmental suit felt thin; it was just a temporary covering meant to augment a breathing apparatus while the wearer sat near a crash site and waited for rescue.

His body ached with fatigue. His mind felt like it was under water with a hurricane booming above the surface. "We need to find a place to rest. There isn't room for mistakes up here."

"Agreed," King said.

"Masha. Find a place to stop," Hoffman said.

"OK, Lieutenant. Just don't let me fall." She paused, looking at her route. "We need to go upward for a bit. Find a spot to rest, then start down the next section."

He pushed her onto a ledge, then released her so he could climb steps so old he wasn't sure they were artificial. She thrust her hand down and he took it. She pulled, and he clambered over a difficult section.

"Opal can't see! Opal hate mountains!" He turned to Medvedev, tying a thick cord from his belt to the Ibarran's enviro suit. "Don't fall."

"I'm not the one who fell last time."

"Opal didn't forget," Opal said.

"How much farther?" Hoffman asked.

"Almost there," Masha said.

Hoffman shivered as though he'd been dunked in a river of ice and hung up to dry in the harsh wind. It wasn't the first time the cold of Koen had touched him. He waited for heat to radiate from tubing inside his armor. Nothing happened. "Hoffman for team, check your battery reserves."

They sounded off one by one and the news wasn't good.

"The armor plating will be useless once we're down to trace power. I'd rather not wait too long and lose comms," King said. "Short-range, line of sight is better than nothing."

"Even that will be gone before we make the city," Hoffman said.

Cold seeped into the joints of his armor and through linings around his neck and underarms. His elbows stiffened and his fingertips ached as though struck by hammers. A shiver ran up his spine, causing him to tremble head to toe. For a minute or an hour, the discomfort would be bearable. He didn't want to think of all the miles yet to travel before they reached Koen City.

As Masha climbed downward, wind caught her and yanked her sideways. Hoffman wrapped both of his arms around her waist and pulled her back, and the storm swallowed them both for a moment. His only connection with reality was his numb feet touching the hard surface below his boots.

"King for Hoffman, are you good?"

"Hoffman, here. We didn't fall."

"I've got maybe two minutes of battery assist left. Will need to keep moving to maintain body heat. In the short-term, I think we'll be OK."

"It's climbing down the mountain and then fighting our way through hordes of Rakka to get into the city that will be the problem," Medvedev said. "You should give me a weapon. I can help you."

"I'm sure there's some just lying around here. While you're at it, can you grab some heat packs for the team?" Hoffman said. "I understand your argument, Medvedev. No need to belabor the point."

"I hear you," Medvedev said. "And I will continue to ask. It is my duty."

"At least I'll know you haven't died." Hoffman signaled a halt. "All right. King, you have security while we ditch the armor plating."

"Yes, sir." King stood with his weapon ready, head on a swivel as he scanned the cramped area. Visibility remained poor. Sheer cliffs loomed around the ladder-like trail they had been navigating for hours.

"Let me help you, Opal," Garrison said.

The doughboy complied, his expression tense and slightly confused. "Opal wants to keep armor."

"It's not as dumb as it looks," Medvedev said. "We all want armor."

"I'd settle for a stack of blankets and a fire," Masha said.

Hoffman didn't disagree with her. He carefully removed the plates to his armor, stacking them off to the side of the trail. The pseudo-muscle layer against Hoffman's body would keep him warm even with a trace charge and would recycle his body's kinetic energy into heat as he moved. So long as he was walking, he wouldn't freeze to death. Without the plates and without power to the strength-assist systems, his capabilities became distressfully average.

Garrison finished helping Opal and quickly removed his own plates, balancing them on a rock. "I'm going to miss you. Good times, bad times—you were always there for me."

"It's only armor," King said. "Take security. It's my turn." The gunnery sergeant removed the heavy plates and stacked them, then stared at them in private communion.

"Isn't so easy, is it, Gunney?"

"I've worn this gear for a long time," King said. "I'm ready when you are, Lieutenant."

Hoffman moved as he issued the command. "Let's get this over with. Masha, how much farther?"

"The maze will take time to navigate, but we are near the bottom," she said.

"Stay together. Keep moving. The wind should die down once we emerge from the maze into the foothills," Hoffman said.

Masha hesitated at a fork in the path. One way led out onto a rock causeway, the other down into a deep crack less than a meter wide. "Neither of these looks familiar. It's hard to see in this weather."

"Pick one and let's move," Hoffman said. He followed her without broadcasting the decision to the rest of the team. The weather didn't improve, but they found their way onto more level ground. When he looked up, he was amazed by how far they'd descended from the summit.

****

Hoffman sheltered his team in a cave barely deep

enough to hold them. Huddled together, they were marginally warmer than walking into the endless gale. The darkness of night transformed into a murky tempest.

"Check your gear. Check your partner. We're moving," Hoffman said.

"Sir, can I say this has been my least favorite mission since the *Kid'ran's Gift*?" Garrison said.

"Every mission is your least favorite mission," Hoffman said. "Let's move."

"It's not just the weather. I haven't blown anything up on this planet. How will I show my face at the EOD school at Twentynine Palms?"

"I'm sure we'll find something needing explosive deconstruction. Team, move out," Hoffman said.

The complexity of the maze intensified when they reached the bottom. Instead of navigating dangerous heights, they marched between towers of stone. "I think all the storms on the planet must come through this canyon," Hoffman said.

Masha didn't react to his shouted words. Snow caked on the front of his under-armor. He looked back at his team and saw them shambling forward. Heads down, bodies leaning into the wind; none of them looked ready to fight.

He couldn't feel his fingers or his toes. He fantasized about standing in front of a campfire, the snow popping and hissing as it melted. Instead of warmth, he found a patch of ice. One foot shot forward and sideways. Masha grabbed him as he fell.

"We've got to get out of the wind," he said from one knee. "It blasts into this canyon like a weapon."

"We continue," she said. "The end of the maze will be abrupt."

"If you get us through this, I'll make it up to you," he said, not sure exactly what he meant. "Forget I said that. Not thinking clearly."

"Never admit weakness to an Ibarran, Thomas Hoffman," she said, then turned in to the wind. Walls of rock stood to her right and left as she advanced with her head down and arms hugging her body. "You may need to push me. I'm too small to make much headway in the wind."

He pushed her through a narrow passage that didn't seem to end. "Count off from King."

"King, moving in rearguard."

"Garrison with Opal and the second prisoner." Static scrambled the IR link. *"Also freezing to actual death."*

"Opal hungry."

"Hey, Gunney? Why is Opal looking at me like that? He promised not to eat me."

"Can it," King said.

"Medvedev, sound off."

Neither of the Ibarrans responded.

"Medvedev, I need to know if your communication hardware is working," Hoffman said.

"I am here. Without a weapon or proper equipment for this death march."

"No radio check for me, Lieutenant?" Masha said without looking back.

"I know your helmet is working, and I can see you most of the time."

King cursed. "Comms won't last forever on residual power. We'll be using hand signals soon, which means Garrison will be useless."

"I know my hand signals, Gunney. The ox, though…and I don't mean Opal."

Medvedev held up his middle digit.

Hoffman beat snow from his under-armor. "No more unnecessary chatter. Keep moving. Tighten up the formation and try to maintain visual contact down the line."

"We are near the end of the maze. Beyond this

point, there will be no cover or concealment for miles—only rocky foothills crisscrossed by the erosion of landslides and nearly forgotten glaciers. There are thousands of lakes and frozen marshlands humans have yet to explore."

Hoffman chopped his hand forward twice. "Let's move. Clock's ticking."

She led the way, picking up the pace to a fast walk in places. The wind died almost immediately. Foothills spread toward the horizon. Creek beds and sinkholes scarred the landscape.

Comms chatter stopped, but he sensed something was wrong. "Hoffman for King, radio check."

No answer.

He held up one fist to freeze his team in place and the Strike Marines covered their fire zones and waited for orders. Hoffman suspected they were trying their IR comms.

Facing Masha, he tapped his ear, made eye contact with her through their visors, and all but shouted, "I'm going back to talk to my NCO. Don't go anywhere."

"And miss this delightful chance to escape?"

Dense mist lowered from the darkening sky. His Strike Marine boots gripped the treacherous rock trail better than tactical footwear of old, but it was nothing like the mag-plate enhanced functionality they could expect during shipboard fighting.

"Garrison, how are your comms?" he said as he touched the Strike Marine's shoulder.

Garrison's helmet muted his voice and was starting to fog up without trace power to work the air filters. "No comms. I think I'm getting even colder, if that's possible. Now we have freezing mist."

"Keep an eye on Masha." Hoffman checked on Opal and Medvedev, meeting King halfway.

"We need to tighten up our column," King said. "Not ideal in this terrain, but it is what it is."

"Back to basic infantry tactics. Roll back war-fighting tactics hundreds of years."

"Oorah," King said dryly.

Hoffman warmed up his command voice as he moved forward. "Garrison, take point."

"Moving to point, sending back the prisoner," Garrison shouted.

"Look sharp. Use hand signals. We're going to march to Koensuu City and link up with the rest of our team," Hoffman said.

"I can't wait to see Booker so she can fix me right,"

said Garrison.

"Ungrateful Terran," Medvedev grunted. *"Kakamutiko."*

"English!" Opal swiped at Medvedev's helmet but missed when the man ducked.

Garrison pushed his left palm forward urgently. "Enemy contact."

"Get behind me and stay down." Hoffman stood over Masha, searching for enemies through the sights of his gauss rifle.

Flashes of booming muzzle fire snapped into existence on their left flank from slightly higher ground and the top of a gravel slope. "Contact left! Get on line! Get on line!" Hoffman shoved Masha on her stomach and lay across her as he returned fire, his lack of armor plates making him feel especially vulnerable.

The rest of his team adjusted their positions, responding to the ambush with accurate counterfire. Several ice-crusted Rakka tumbled out of their hiding places with fatal wounds to heads and upper torsos.

"Stay down," he said, pushing Masha against the ground. He sprang to his feet and charged. "Assault through. Assault through the ambush!"

King repeated his orders as Garrison and Opal

rushed at the shallow Rakka trenches the ambushers had dug just deep enough for concealment. Strike Marine boots churned up frozen gravel as they advanced, firing on the move, working as a team.

Rakka fell back to a secondary trench that was deeper than the first.

Hoffman and his team hit the ground. He looked back from the ambush trench at Masha and Medvedev. They were still taking fire but were curled up behind what cover they could find.

"I feel naked," Garrison said.

"Opal want armor."

"What else does Opal want?" Hoffman asked as he switched a fresh magazine into place.

"Kill enemy!"

"Then let's get 'em," Hoffman said, bursting from the trench and rushing the Rakka before they could solidify their position.

"Assault! Assault! Assault!" King shouted.

"Oorah!" Garrison shouted as he reached the enemy position first, engaging them with his gauss rifle at close range.

"Kill enemy!" Opal jumped into the trench, swinging his hammer into a crushing blow against a

Rakka's chest, then kicking another Rakka in the face.

King, at the end of Hoffman's team, dropped into the trench and fired down its length, enfilading the Rakka as they scrambled to escape. Hoffman did the same toward the other end of the line as Kesaht bullets snapped past his helmet, the familiar sound of gauss rifles raging all around him.

"I don't like fighting this close without real armor!" Gunney King shouted.

Garrison reloaded, his movements honed by hours of practice. "You're telling me! I think the lieutenant might have shot me in the ass."

"Counter assault! Fall back," King said, retreating from a swarm of Rakka. "This will be…a problem without our…armor."

Hoffman's team fell back two by two, covering each other with volumes of gauss fire. They reached the first trench—the ambush trench—and weren't given time to establish their position. He didn't see any Sanheel officers but the Kesaht grunts knew how to fight once it started.

"Moving!" Garrison said, falling back with Opal at his side.

"Covering and suppressing!" Hoffman and King fired into what looked like a sloppy squad of charging

Rakka. Shaggy hair danced from the violence of their movements and they handled the crude firearms with aggressive confidence. More than once, he saw a Rakka drop a magazine from a weapon with no attempt to recover it. The Kesaht grunt merely slammed a new one into the receiver well and continued to spray ballistic projectiles at Hoffman's team. More than a dozen of the brutes charged with bone-handled pole arms, wide blades reflecting explosions like mirrors.

"Set! For the record, I'm not a huge fan of the trench-warfare thing we're doing," Garrison said.

Hoffman and King fell back. As soon as they reached their original position, Hoffman looked for Masha and Medvedev and couldn't find them.

"Here they come!" Garrison shouted.

Rakka swarmed down from the heights in waves. The moment felt surreal and Hoffman missed the sound of radio chatter in his ear. There was less crosstalk and fewer jokes than he was accustomed to when things got tough. Bullets snapped by him, grazing his arm and leaving a bloody wound. He dropped to the ground and moved sideways.

"You don't have armor," King shouted at him. "This is exactly why I hammered movement tactics into the team during training."

Hoffman fired a controlled burst from his gauss rifle, then turned on his side to look at his team. He did a quick headcount, marked their positions in his memory, then faced the fight. Enemies piled up before him with holes punched through their inadequate armor. He wondered if they were poorly equipped or just refused to wear the gear that was issued them.

"The barbarians are at the gate now! You should give me a weapon!" Medvedev said.

Hoffman shifted to his left, popped up onto one knee to aim over a rock, and fired three more bursts. He wanted to move again, but there was no time. He fired over and over, reloading frequently.

"There are a lot of these guys," King grunted as he fired single rounds at single targets.

Hoffman looked at Garrison and noted with approval the breacher was making his shots count as well. Opal fought as he always fought, undaunted by danger and frighteningly proficient in all things involving combat.

"Fall back, tighten it up, and watch each other's backs," Hoffman said.

Rakka leapt forward with melee weapons—pole arms, wicked clubs, and weapons that could be a cross between a trenching tool and an axe.

Opal hurled a rock at a Rakka and crushed its skull, then shoulder-charged forward and stopped the oncoming Rakka. The two masses ground to a halt in the middle of the trench and Opal shot his right elbow forward, the blow taking a second attacker across the bridge of his nose and knocking him off his feet. The doughboy aimed a front kick at the third enemy and sent him flying all the way back to the original trench line.

Garrison slung his rifle over his back and tightened the strap in a fluid series of movements. A moment later, he had his breaching prybar in both hands. The heavy lever wasn't meant for fighting, but he put his hours of strength training to use, slamming the omnium-forged bar into one face after another.

King fought with a pistol in his left hand and his Ka-Bar extended from his right gauntlet. He moved with methodical proficiency, frequently glancing toward Hoffman to make sure the team commander wasn't issuing him new orders. Somehow, he worked this into the frantic pace of battle.

Hoffman moved through the chaos, firing his pistol at close range. When enemies came too close, he kicked them or simply sidestepped their advance. He looked around for Masha and found her crouched behind a rock near her bodyguard. Medvedev had joined the fight.

The heavily muscled legionnaire lifted a Rakka into the air, holding the creature by his waist before slamming it down onto its head. The pair wrestled around on the ground until Medvedev rolled away victorious and a new attacker knee-kicked him in the face. He fell backward and the Rakka advanced.

Opal grabbed Medvedev's attacker from behind by its long hair and yanked it off its feet. Without hesitation, Medvedev launched himself at another of the Kesaht grunts and wrestled the primitive rifle out of his hands. No sooner did he have the weapon than a cluster of the enemies tackled him to the ground and pummeled him.

"Masha! Stay close to Opal and he will protect you!"

The beautiful Ibarran spy hesitated, seemingly torn between Medvedev and Opal.

Hoffman heard hooves and turned just in time to see a Sanheel bound over a line of ice-covered rocks. It carried a short shotgun in one hand and a spear in the other. Hoffman ran to help and screamed at King, but the gunnery sergeant was too far away.

Garrison broke free from his attackers and rushed

between Masha and the Sanheel, slamming his breaching tool against the Sanheel officer where the horse body and humanoid body met.

The Sanheel shouted a curse, then screamed at the Rakka to come defend him. Garrison ignored everything but swinging his breaching tool, driving the massive, eight-foot-tall creature back, blow after blow. Then, almost at random, he stepped back, drew his pistol, and emptied it into the strange enemy.

Sanheel death throes—flailing hooves and thousands of pounds of muscle—lashed the air. Garrison retreated, eyes wide.

Rakka stared at the dead officer, then fled the way they had come.

Hoffman searched for Masha and saw her crouching defensively. Medvedev staggered toward her, then stopped when he spotted a Rakka assault rifle lying at his feet. He bent down for it.

Opal lunged forward and stepped on the weapon. "No weapon."

"Lieutenant Hoffman, he's a better fighter than any of you!" Masha shouted.

Hoffman stared at the heavily muscled legionnaire, a man so thick through his chest and torso that he rivaled

Opal. Armed, the man was a formidable enemy.

"I swear by Saint Kallen that I will do all in my power to defend you and your team so long as you keep Masha safe from these Kesaht scumbags," Medvedev said.

King and Garrison stared at Medvedev. Hoffman moved closer. "I'm not one for religion."

"You know enough Marines that are to know I'm true to my word," Medvedev said.

Hoffman looked to Masha. Her expression was tired and worried. She nodded and he thought she was sincere.

"Opal, let him have the gun." Hoffman walked forward, then leaned close to the legionnaire. "If you violate your oath, you'll never make it to a trial. My people are going home alive and we will complete our mission."

"By the Saint." Medvedev crossed himself.

Hoffman turned to Masha for confirmation. "I have his oath. Don't make him betray it and get killed."

"What purpose would that serve? While we are talking about weapons…" She glanced at a pistol on the ground.

"Not you. Not a chance. I haven't forgotten New Bastion," Hoffman said.

She sighed and rolled her eyes. "You are going to hold that against me forever."

****

Hoffman's depleted, battered team arrived at the outskirts of Koensuu City, where smoke drifted into the air from explosions in and beyond the city. The sky was crisscrossed with contrails of Terran and Kesaht fighter craft. He spotted fortified positions manned by tanks and other heavy vehicles. Mules dropped down from orbit with reinforcements and materials. If not for the imminent danger, it would have been impressive to watch.

Outside the city were Rakka—on foot, in vehicles, marching to the orders of Sanheel, milling forward in unorganized masses of brewing violence.

"I never thought I'd be so happy to see an alien city as cold as this one," Garrison said, cleaning his weapon as he sat on a mound of rocks and stared at the enemy units between them and the city defenses. "Too bad there's absolutely no way inside. I mean, there's a gap in their line, but what good does it do?"

Masha rocked forward and back where she sat on another primitive rock hedge. "I can get us inside. Sneaking into places is what I do for a living."

"Soon as we're inside, we'll find a nice warm cell

for you," Hoffman said.

Masha trembled from head to toe, hugging herself and stuttering as she spoke. "I'm really…tired…of being cold. Sick of winter…and sick of living outdoors."

"She's right," Garrison said. "Spies know how to sneak into places. I vote aye."

"Aye, what?" King asked.

"Aye. As in yes. As in, can we please let the Ibarran super-spook show us her secret way in?" Garrison said.

"For once, I think the meathead is right," Masha said.

"You're going to have to narrow that down a bit," King said.

"Where?" Hoffman asked.

Masha moved to the edge of their small camp and pointed to a location in the distance where the Rakka had set up a small camp of hide tents. "They are parked there for a reason. We can get past their sentries, then to the wall where that tower has two flames burning on top of it instead of one, then into a passage that will take us inside the city."

"I'll think about it. King, let's have a conference. Everyone else rest, recover, and get ready to run and fight," Hoffman said.

****

"King, I'm putting you up front with Masha this time," Hoffman said.

"Is it my turn to get hit on?"

"Need fresh eyes on point. I don't like getting stuck in a rut. I'll trust that you'll keep to the long, illustrious line of professionals who wore the bloodstripe before you if she bats those big blues at you."

King frowned but held his comment. "You know they're blue?"

Hoffman's cheeks flushed.

"I bet she's up to something. She's been working me—not you—since we caught her. You're with her in there and it'll throw a monkey wrench into her plan. Keep her from trying anything that'll force us to shoot her and the ox."

King studied him carefully. "I hate spies. The 'I know you know that I know that you know' game is a pain in the ass. I miss when we could just shoot things to solve our problems. Easier and more honest."

"That's why you're taking a turn up front. Once we're inside, you'll take Garrison and escort them all the way to the local police station. We need to lock them up someplace stronger than a field base. Nothing changes once we're inside. The mission is still the mission, and I have a feeling she'll make a break for one our safe houses if we give her a chance."

"Shouldn't we stick together in that case?" King rubbed the back of his neck. "Call back the rest of the team, get Duke and Booker to help us out a bit? Maybe even Max if he's recovered?"

"Of course. I just want you to know that you're carrying the ball if things start to go sideways. Complete the mission no matter what," Hoffman said.

"Yes, sir."

"Then let's get moving." Hoffman signaled Garrison and Opal, then spoke to the Ibarrans. "Medvedev, I don't want to see you more than ten feet away from Opal. I'll be watching you. Garrison will be on overwatch. Masha, you're going to show King the way."

She glared at him. He ignored her and ordered the team to move.

Darkness and freezing mist helped them for once. He felt exposed and noisy without his armor. His team had spent so much time training in the gear and maximizing all its technological benefits that going in their under-armor pseudo-muscle suits felt strange.

Not all the Rakka slept, though many did, and once night fell, he didn't see any Sanheel officers. They seemed to congregate in a large longhouse-style tent that smelled like cooking food. Strange music came from behind the oversized tent flaps. Whenever a group of wandering Rakka approached, Hoffman and his team stepped back into the shadows until they passed.

"Barn door's open," Garrison said. "Sorry, couldn't resist."

Hoffman, too tired to laugh, continued.

Masha understood her business. She didn't take them straight through the camp, but through the areas that were little used. Feeding lines and equipment repair centers were clustered with enemy fighters at all hours of the day and night. The perimeters were guarded by patrols. Areas closer to the wall were dominated by masses of Rakka ready to deploy at a moment's notice.

After about an hour, they worked their way into the lightly populated area that Masha had pointed out before they began the stealth mission.

King tapped what would have been the collar of his uniform if not in the pseudo-muscle gear—the signal to summon the unit commander forward. Hoffman moved up silently.

"She wants to talk to you," King said.

"Go ahead," Hoffman said.

She hesitated, then spoke. "This last part is tricky. It's an open area and I'm not sure how good their night vision is. If we can get to the wall, I can find a doorway—almost a hatch, really. The only good thing about it is that the Sanheel will be too big to chase us into it if something goes wrong."

"This section of the wall has a fraction of the Kesaht facing it, still far too many for us to fight through if someone sounds the alarm," Hoffman said.

"I suggest being really quiet."

"Let's get moving," Hoffman said.

"At least you're not a coward," she said.

Hoffman resisted the urge to tell her that was exactly what she had called him when they first met on New Bastion.

They left the relative concealment of the mostly sleeping Kesaht camp. Hoffman guided them with hand signals, encouraging them to stay close enough to communicate without bunching up to become easy targets if the alarm went up. The journey across the short distance seemed to take forever. When they reached the door tucked into the base of the city wall, Hoffman wondered if he had held his breath for the last several hundred meters.

"All right, Masha, it's the moment of truth," Hoffman said.

"Horse-man coming," Opal said.

Hoffman looked around, unable to hear anything unusual. The mist was sliding away on a breeze and stars twinkled above. He felt exposed.

"Your doughboy has good ears," Medvedev said. "Kesaht stealth patrol, with a Sanheel officer. Probably probing the defenses. That's why it was so easy to get through their line. The active part of the camp on the other side of the city is a distraction."

"Get ready," Hoffman said. "Stealth weapons if you can. Garrison, stand on Masha if you have to. Medvedev, I expect you're fighting on our side right now."

"I'll fight. Watch and learn," Medvedev said. "The legion knows how to kill these things."

"What crawled up your ass?" Garrison asked.

"I'm tired of working with amateurs."

"Med, buddy, we're going to go a few rounds when this is over," Garrison said.

"Looking forward to it."

Garrison took Masha by the arm. "Don't run off.

I've got an evaluation coming up."

Hoffman, King, Opal, and Medvedev moved around the curve of the wall to approach the Sanheel probe.

"Opal, jump on that officer and break his neck. Quietly."

"Opal kill enemy."

"Not gonna work," King said as they met a half-dozen Rakka ahead of the Sanheel officer.

The Rakka stepped back, startled, then charged forward, screaming war cries.

"Get that door open!" Hoffman shouted as he lunged forward with his Ka-Bar extended.

A gauss round slipped by his head, taking his first opponent directly between the eyes. Two more enemy fell on top of the first.

"Kill enemy!" Opal yanked his hammer off his back and rushed the Sanheel, who reared up and flailed at the doughboy with steel-shod hooves.

Opal ducked sideways and swung the crude weapon in a looping, horizontal arc. One of the Sanheel's rear legs exploded and his entire mass plummeted on top of Opal.

The doughboy rolled sideways but too slowly and the eight-foot-tall alien crashed down and rolled over him.

"Opal mad!" The doughboy twisted free of the

horse-flesh avalanche, ducking away from flailing hooves. He came up covered in frozen dirt and muck, swinging his hammer downward on the Sanheel officer's exposed neck.

Medvedev slipped aside from a Rakka spear thrust, palm-striking the passing elbow a fraction of a second later, hyperextending the joint and driving the damaged arm across the Rakka's body. In virtually the same instant, he pulled the Rakka's belt knife with his right hand, stabbed it in the throat, dropped to one knee, and stabbed it twice in the femoral artery inside the thigh.

Medvedev stood as the Rakka's partner jumped at him, head-butting his new opponent hard enough to knock him off his feet. "Now I fight for the legion and the Lady!"

Hoffman retracted his Ka-Bar, unslung his gauss riffle, and opened fire on a half-dozen charging Rakka. The warriors had bayonets fixed to their machine guns and seemed desperate to draw blood.

"If they weren't so stupid, we'd be dead already!" King shouted, dropping another pair of the berserkers with well-placed shots.

Another round flashed between Hoffman and King, visible only because it struck a particularly large Rakka in the throat. Both men hesitated.

"Where the hell did that come from?" King asked.

"Masha, get that door open!" Hoffman said.

"Yes," Masha said. "We're inside. There's a second door that will be more difficult. Hold them off a little longer."

"Running out of time. Get it open or we're leaving," Hoffman said.

She disappeared into the shadows of a short, low-ceilinged tunnel and Hoffman ducked halfway into the doorway to watch her, the darkness giving her movements a surreal unevenness. With muzzle flashes dancing in his vision, it was hard to see exactly what she was doing.

She looked over her shoulder, paused, then held up a hand for him to stay back. "It is trickier than I remember. Sixty seconds and we'll be inside the wall."

"That's a long time right now." Rakka bullets ricocheted near Hoffman's head. He turned, fired, and turned back to make sure Masha wasn't betraying his team.

She knelt near the bottom of the door.

"What are you doing?" Hoffman asked.

"The door won't open. I'm sorry."

"Did you try to pick the lock?" Hoffman said, gesturing toward the metal box more than two feet above the bottom of the door.

She looked at the box, her manner distracted—

almost stunned.

Hoffman moved farther into the passage, furious at leaving the battle. "Tell me what you're doing, or by the Saint, I'll show you what we do to traitors in the field."

Her eyes were moist, slightly unfocused. "I thought I saw a piece of archaeotech. That was the real reason I came here. We can eventually get in this way, but it isn't the best. I hoped to recover the alien technology and escape the Kesaht."

"Are you crying?" he asked.

"No, Lieutenant Hoffman. I'm tired of failure," she said. "It is ungallant of you to mock me."

"I'm not mocking you," he said as a bullet bounced into the low-ceilinged hallway. "We need to go. No more secret quests. If you think there's an artifact, you better tell me about it."

Eyes downcast, she nodded. "Just leave me here. I've no reason to continue."

He hauled her to her feet and marched her outside, shielding her body with his when they emerged. "Change of plans," he announced to the team.

An incoming gauss round flashed over Garrison, killing two lined-up Rakka.

"I love that guy." Garrison half-laughed as he fired

his weapon into an increasingly dense swarm of Rakka.

"What'd I miss?" Hoffman saw more enemies falling than seemed possible and realized what was happening. Only one person he knew could execute that kind of precision shooting.

One of the Rakka staggered backward, staring into the mist as though seeing a demon. "*Iasta sivu!*"

One Rakka, then two, then all of them repeated the curse. They fell over each other in a panic.

"They're retreating!" Garrison shouted.

"It won't last. We've got to abort," King said. "There's a gap in the enemy line, but Lady Luck isn't going to wait forever."

Hoffman saw a glint off a mirror from a line of trees beyond the Kesaht camp—two signal flashes, followed by one, followed by three.

"That's code for clear to move," King said.

"Strike Marine code," Garrison said. "You think that's Duke?"

"Who else can shoot like that? Look sharp and move out. Can't let Duke do all the work." Hoffman dragged Masha by her arm.

"No, no, no!" Masha yelled. "We must get into the city!"

Snow fell from the windless sky.

"Not more snow! I was going to take a hot bath in there," Masha said.

Chapter 18

The sky was actually blue by the time Duke and Booker reached the small town at the end of the valley. They were no less cold, but not tortured by a blizzard.

"Looks like they have some pretty high-speed lookouts," Duke said, pointing at a group of kids darting between the trees.

"Colonist kids. Wonder if they were born here," Booker said. She walked backward for a few steps to observe their rear. A few strides later, Duke did the same thing while she faced forward. It was a relaxed order of march, something they had been doing since they broke camp this morning.

The next picket of youngsters they came to had more kids, but they held their distance.

"And now we're surrounded," Duke said. With Booker at his side, they strode into the small town of

Terran colonists. Adults came out to greet them, a few armed with militia weapons.

"It's the Ice Claw!" said one of the young men, pointing at Duke and his rifle. "Who's the other one?"

Booker snorted. "Wait. Why aren't they pointing at me?"

"You can be my trusty sidekick. I'll give you a good name, like Doc the Whiny…"

"I'm not your sidekick. You can get side kicked…"

None of the buildings in the town were old. Duke guessed there had been several expansions. The first people to come here had used prefabricated dwellings. After a while, they started building out of natural materials. What he didn't see were any of the elaborate buildings or exotic walking lanes of the ancient Koen civilization.

"No danger of finding artifacts here," Duke said.

"It never seemed like it worked out in the *Last Stand on Takeni* movie. The original *Breitenfeld* Strike Marines were always finding something bad. I like this place. It's homey. We haven't had to kill anybody today, which is nice."

Duke patted his side patch for his chewing tobacco, then drew his hand back. "You're getting soft."

The crowd grew and surrounded them.

"I'm getting tired of playing second fiddle to a long-in-the-tooth prima donna with delusions of grandeur," Booker said. "What am I, chopped liver?"

"You carry my ammo. You're the ammo bearer. AB."

"I know what AB really stands for. Dick."

One of the town elders, or some type of official, approached and shook Duke's hand. "Anything you need, Sergeant Duke. I apologize for the kids. They think the idea of the Ice Claw very romantic. I just want you to know we are informed out here in the backwoods. My cousin is an aide to Captain Pine. He sent me a note to watch out for you and your assistant."

"'Ice Claw'?" Duke asked and spat tobacco juice into the snow.

"You haven't heard?" the older man took a data slate from his jacket and tapped it quickly. He handed it over to Duke. On the screen was a paused video of alien writing on a wrecked building. Duke hit the play icon and the screen panned to dead Rakka and burning vehicles.

"Intelligence officials say the words translate as 'Fear the Ice Claw's reach'," came from the screen, the tone of the words matching a newscast. "The message has been found written on the invaders armor and vehicles, and is a direct reference to the actions of one Strike Marine sniper's efforts to waylay the alien advance. The Strike Marine, identified as one Staff Sergeant Duke, is currently operating outside Koen City."

Duke grunted and handed the slate back.

He jerked a thumb at his rifle.

"Her name's Buffy," Duke said.

"They didn't even mention me?" Booker tossed her hands up. "Not even as the ammo bearer? Executive assistant? Better looking half of the duo?"

"This is Bluehill, head of our militia," the elder said as an older man hurried over, his breath fogging in the cold air.

Bluehill half saluted, then brought his hand back to his side. Salutes were a mortal sin in a combat environment. Signaling who was important was like asking a sniper to kill someone.

"Major Michael Bluehill. Formerly of the 90th Ranger Regiment. Been on Koen since the beginning. Helped put down these prefabs. Didn't know then we'd be defending them from aliens. So that's why the layout is less than ideal."

Duke was prepared to comment, but doubted he was needed in this conversation. The man talked. Booker shot him annoyed looks. He tried not to laugh.

"...So you see, Duke—I can call you Duke, right—that ridge is a perfect sniper perch. Good concealment, only one way up to it, and even if they know you're there, what could they do about it? No bumbling Kesaht countersniper can match your skill," Bluehill said.

"I'd be more worried about artillery and crescent fighters," Duke said.

"Well, sure. But what's the chance of that happening?" Bluehill asked. He shouted at one of his militia men to cover the perch with more camouflage.

Duke hammer-fisted Booker in the shoulder when the townsmen were distracted. "Stop kicking me. Just stand there and be a medic. I'm the sniper here."

"That's better. Pull the net across," Major Bluehill said, looking up at his very young, totally confused private. It didn't seem the young man had any more faith in the position than Duke had.

"I'll work my way around from another direction," Duke said. "Rule of mine. Never be seen."

"Never be seen going to your perch?"

"Never be seen. Anywhere."

"Ah, gotcha," Bluehill said.

"We could use a couple of those IRRs," Booker

pointed to a pallet with Infrared Guided Rockets the size of a forearm. "They can punch through Kesaht armor."

Bluehill looked at her as though just realizing she was there. "You have to hit through the top armor, warheads are about fifty/fifty on a frontal attack. You're with Sergeant Duke?"

"Maybe he's with me."

"I just thought…How do you determine seniority when you're both…I mean, you look so young."

"I am young compared to that old boot."

"Thank you, Major," Duke said, taking rocket tubes from the major's men. "We should get set up. You should evacuate. Especially the children and old folks."

"Evacuate?" Bluehill and the town elder asked at the same time.

"There are about three divisions of Kesaht coming this way. They will overrun this town. All I'm going to do is slow them down. Captain Pine has a PDF blocking force in route, but it won't be much. I suggest, Major, that you start digging trenches there, and there, and there." He pointed at several terrain features in the narrow, ascending valley. "Interlock defensive fields of fire. Set up a fallback point there and evacuate all nonessential personnel."

Major Bluehill swallowed, staring wide-eyed.

"It's not a bad location, Major. Perfect for a delaying action."

"OK. Thank you, Sergeant."

The people of the town and their militia sprang into action, ringing a church bell to summon everyone for work.

"That went well," Booker said.

"Fun while it lasted. Thanks for ruining my moment of glory."

They climbed past the over-camouflaged sniper perch and kept going. Duke found an animal trail, followed it around the town, and discovered several possible perches.

"Here? Good cover and concealment. Three escape routes. Two natural cave bunkers close by in the event of artillery strikes," Booker asked.

"No. Back to town, I think. Building top. The depth of the valley has the town in shadow for a few more hours. Good concealment and good escape routes for afterward," Duke said.

"I think we should go back to Bluehill's spot. They went through all that trouble to set it up for us," Booker said. When she saw the look on Duke's face, she added, "Kidding."

A lone artillery shell, probably a ranging shot, whistled down and exploded on the amateur sniper hide.

Duke and Booker stared for several seconds, then made their way to a dark, three-story building. Kesaht countersnipers and artillery fired blindly into most of the potential overwatch positions.

Duke rolled out his sniper kit on a roof with a good view of the Kesaht advance up the valley. "You're up, Doc."

"Oh, yay. I'm the opening act." Booker went prone behind her gauss sniper rifle, pulling it in tight to her shoulder as she pointed her toes out. "Give me range on the Sanheel officer with the red sash."

"1997 meters. Crosswind gusting twenty-five. Barometric pressure 22.9."

"Shot away." Booker emptied the air from her lungs, paused, fired. The top of the Sanheel officer's head blew off.

"Next target," Duke said, "1990 meters."

"Wait."

"Get to work, Doc."

"Got 'em. Shot away." A second later, she drilled her second, long-range shot.

She missed the third and fourth but hit the fifth Sanheel in the throat as he rode in a panicked circle.

"Duke, I think they have Doppler devices."

"I saw them as well. Triangulation technology is a countersniper's wet dream. My turn. Don't call my ranges, just stay on your rifle and take your time with follow-on shots." He lined up six shots and took all six targets down with smooth efficiency. "We won't be able to stay much longer."

He put a round through the engine block of the lead vehicle, forcing crews to drag it off the narrow road.

"Duke…" Booker said.

"I know. They're pointing at us. Time to go." He led the way across the building top and down the back way.

Crescent fighters dropped out of the overcast sky, strafing the building seconds after they left it. Kesaht landers raced over the town, flaring their engines to a sudden stop, and descended to release airborne assault troops in several locations.

"What a shit sandwich!" Booker said as they ran for the corner of a low building and Koen unleashed another storm.

"Just start eating it by the corner!" Duke yelled. He slid to one knee while raising his sniper rifle to fire a single round at a stack of enemy Rakka bulldogging their way around the corner. Five of the Kesaht grunts flopped onto their backs, their blood spurting through the falling snow.

The point-blank round continued through a building behind them.

"Moving!" Duke said. Jumping to his feet, he darted forward.

"Covering." Booker switched to her patrol rifle, using three-round bursts where necessary. "These guys are tough."

"Set," Duke said, slinging his sniper rifle and pulling his close-quarters battle weapon around front.

"Moving," Booker said.

More Kesaht landers passed overhead. Duke and Booker raced from strongpoint to strongpoint, killing on the move or from stationary positions.

"Kind of miss the team right now!" Booker shouted. She snapped her bayonet forward on her right arm sleeve, stabbed a charging Rakka in the throat, and kept moving. "Need to reload."

"Then do it." Duke transitioned to his pistol and cleared out a dense knot of assaulting Rakka. "Sorry, dudes. You're in my way." He front-kicked one who wasn't quite dead and ran over him as Booker followed, reloading on the run.

Sniper rifle and kit tight on his back, carbine held in his left hand against the strap and pistol in his right, he found his best speed and hustled forward. "I need to reload my primary when you're done."

"Do it." Booker turned, assassinating a squad of Rakka trying to catch up with them. Return fire grazed her left shoulder and helmet.

"The PDF is pulling back, taking the local militia with them," Duke said when they reached the edge of town. Farther up the valley, near a bridge, the PDF launched rockets and mortars at the Kesaht entering the other side of the town in force. A company of tough infantrymen led by veterans advanced through their ranks and took up a strong position ahead of the bridge. Soldiers teamed up behind rock formations and disabled vehicles.

Duke and Booker ran to them, then past them.

"Ice Claw!" they cheered.

Duke hesitated. These men were digging in to hold the line against an irresistible enemy advance.

"Get moving, Sergeant," an officer said. "That's an order. We'll need you to cover us during the tactical retreat."

"Yes, sir," Duke said.

Booker ran at his side. "They're not going anywhere."

"I know."

Chapter 19

Two platoon-sized detachments of Rakka warriors and one Sanheel officer pursued them to the edge of the forest as Duke's sniper rifle snapped rounds over the Strike Marine's heads, taking a Sanheel in the chest and dropping him face-first into the snow. Rakka fired wildly from behind the Marines, kicking up tufts of snow and sending hissing rounds past Hoffman's head. He pointed at a line of rocks just beyond the tree line and slid around the cover just as Duke fired again.

Hoffman swung his rifle around a rock and opened fire on the charging aliens while Opal covered Masha with his bulk as she huddled against the rocks. Garrison and King joined Hoffman as they cut down the attackers. Medvedev held his pistol close to his chest, his eyes on Opal.

Incoming bullets impacted trees, sending bark and leaves flying. Gouts of snow and dirt blossomed into the air with no rhyme or reason. The Rakka charged forward until one with a bone necklace was shot by Garrison and pitched forward. In one heartbeat, the Rakka abandoned their charge and turned tail back to their camp. None of them stopped to check on the fallen Sanheel officer.

Duke ceased firing.

Hoffman faced Masha, who wasn't breathing as hard as he had expected she would be after running for her life. "What were they yelling?" he asked.

"I think it's…cold claw, or something like that," she said.

Hoffman smiled wryly and looked toward the trees, wondering where his sniper was positioned.

Masha moved closer and he was drawn to her presence. Cold, filthy, and exhausted down to his core, he still felt a thrill for the woman who was his worst enemy.

She spoke softly. "He *is* very good."

"You keep your hands off my sniper."

"He shot my asset in the face. I will hold a grudge."

"You want to get on Duke's bad side?" Hoffman asked.

Masha walked ahead of them into the forest. "Now

if we can only find this mysterious savior of ours."

Hoffman tried to activate his radio inside his helmet to contact the sniper before he remembered that he was completely without power. Not even a residual current generated by his movements existed at this point. He adjusted the sound baffles that he had ratcheted up to maximum during the running gun battle from the wall and was rewarded moments later by a lonely whistle in the darkness.

He turned to face the sound of a distant bird. "You hear that?"

Masha cocked her head. "So?"

"Ain't no blue jays on this ice ball," King said.

"Exactly." Hoffman listened carefully.

"I'd recognize that pathetic squeaking anywhere," Garrison said. "And I'm pretty sure that's a cardinal, maybe one who dips tobacco."

"Let's go." Hoffman checked to make sure Opal and King were watching Medvedev, then fell in beside Masha. She really was cold. At times, he had thought her complaining was an act, and maybe it was up to a point. Right now, she looked small, miserable, and ready to be done with this misadventure.

A familiar voice greeted them long before Garrison

arrived at the point where he had assumed the sniper was hiding.

"You're just going to stomp through the forest now? I step away from the team for a couple days and you're worse than a bunch of boots from basic training. And what was that panicked flight from the wall?" said Sergeant Duke from somewhere in the darkness.

"I see you, you old dinosaur," King said. "Get your lone-wolf ass out here so I can address your failure to help us sooner."

Duke stood up a few feet from King, who was facing the wrong direction. He held his sniper rifle on one hip so that it pointed at the sky, breaking the outline of his nature-enhanced camouflage. "I brought Booker."

"Don't try to bullshit a bullshitter," Hoffman said. "Booker's got the concealment talents of a potato."

Booker stood from the next stand of bushes. "I'm getting better."

"You're not," Duke said.

Garrison strode forward, arms spread wide, and embraced the sniper in a hug that lifted the branch-covered man off the ground. "I never doubted you! Can you please, please loan me some of those modified heat packs snipers are always bragging about?"

"Heat packs?" Masha nearly jumped into the air after Garrison's question.

"Why are you touching me?" Duke asked.

Garrison backed away, apologizing with every step. "Hey, sorry, Duke. Just wanted you to know you're still my favorite sniper. Even if you let me freeze, you didn't let me die out there."

Booker moved awkwardly forward in the cumbersome camouflage. She had pieces of Koen bushes tied onto parts of her armor. "I have a few extra heat packs."

Garrison beamed, completely abandoning Duke in favor of the medic. "Hey, you look good in shrubbery. I ever tell you you're my favorite medic? Really could've used you back there when that ox was 'fixing' my arm and shoulder."

Booker handed him a heat pack, then passed the rest of the bundle off to King. She faced Garrison with a frown. "I can see it."

Medvedev stiffened. "You can see a field-splinted arm and reset shoulder under his pseudo-muscle layer? I doubt it."

Booker faced him and tried disarm the legionnaire with a casual swipe of her hand. She got a firm grip on the weapon and used her armor to pull again. Medvedev held firm until she gave up.

"You're letting him do combat medicine *and* carry a weapon?" she asked. "Duke's right. This unit has really gone downhill since we left it."

"What about us?" Masha asked. "Medvedev and I need heat packs."

"Fresh out, sister," Booker said.

"Bitch."

"Better check your girl, Med. She's about to get choked," Booker said.

"Masha, don't piss her off. She's got a chip on her shoulder," Medvedev growled.

Booker jabbed a finger at the Ibarran legionnaire. "Have you forgotten about Max? I'll show you a chip up your…"

"Booker!" King grunted.

"I haven't forgotten," Medvedev said.

Hoffman stared down his team, then took one of the heat packs and zipped it into his pseudo-muscle layer. "Let's move out. Duke, fill me in while Booker checks on Garrison. We can do this on the move unless you think we need to stop, Booker."

"He's made it this far. I'm not going to work on him

until we're safely inside the Delta FOB," Booker said. "What's your pain level, Garrison?"

"The blue pills with the white stripes," the breacher said. "Unless you've got the red ones? Then it hurts extra."

"Motrin and water? Fine," Booker said. "Let's hoof it to the FOB and everyone can get warm and eat. Then we take ground transport into the city. The Kesaht haven't been able to fully surround it yet. We can get in with a lot less fuss than with the spy girl's plan."

"My way should have worked," Masha said.

Duke looked over the Ibarran spy with something less than a professional eye. "I'd be interested in this little secret passage our lady of treachery was taking you through. Might be safer for someone stealthier than a team dragged down by two prisoners and a doughboy."

"This is why we keep you on overwatch," Booker said.

"You could get through the tunnel, Duke. The rest of your team, especially her," Masha made a face at Booker, "lack necessary skills."

"No tunnel," Hoffman said. "We're done with that. Tell me what you've got, Booker."

"We'll have to run a gauntlet to get inside, but we have armored ground cars that are pretty fast," Booker said.

"Let's get to Delta and recover," Hoffman said. "I'm exhausted from certain team members' constant whining." He looked at Garrison.

"Sorry, s-s-s-sir." Garrison made his teeth chatter as he answered, then inserted a battery into his armor, clipped it down, and shuddered like a cat. "Oh. Oohhhhh, yeah."

King smiled broadly as his armor heated up. "You brought a battery to activate said NCO's heating element. Sergeant Madilyn Booker performs better than her peers in areas of planning, equipment maintenance, and getting along with others. Top marks. Promotion recommended."

"That's all it takes?" Booker asked.

"Your performance evaluation writes itself," King said.

"Gunney smiled!" Garrison said. "We'll call it the Miracle of Koensuu Field."

Duke watched the team impassively.

"What's the situation inside the city?" Hoffman asked Duke and Booker while they hiked.

"Bad," Duke said. "That wall doesn't do much. More decorative than functional—and incomplete. Looks neat, but the Kesaht sent in raids. Their last serious assault was barely stopped. The air battle's been particularly fierce, looks like."

"I have some firsthand testimony of that," Hoffman said. "It's good to see you, Duke. How's Max?"

"Could be worse. Not dead yet."

They came through a tree line and the medic motioned to a ring of small tents and a pair of armored cars covered by active-camo netting. Hoffman saw motion in foxholes dotting the perimeter.

"And here we are. Delta," Booker said, pointing at the encampment. "In all its glory."

"Forward operating base," Duke said. "I told them I didn't need it, but they plunked down a QRF team full of untried but over-trained PDF Rangers. Best they have on planet."

"They assigned you a PDF Ranger team for support?" Hoffman asked.

"There have been some incidents. Regulars and militia are doing as good as expected with no experience under their belt. Captain Pine asked me what I needed. I told him my Strike Marine team or some Rangers," Duke said. "I was half joking, but here we are."

Hoffman noted well-placed pickets with alert soldiers improving their foxholes. "Let's get warm."

Garrison and Masha ran to the tent, ducking inside well before the others.

Chapter 20

Hoffman held a cup of hot cocoa near his lips as steam curled upward and heat radiated onto his face. The FOB warming tent served more than just Duke's sniper mission. Patrol and reconnaissance units stopped in to strip out of their armor and warm up.

"No need for this. I can tell you my temperature, Sarge," Garrison muttered around a thermometer as Booker prodded at his arm and shoulder. "Damn cold. Bottom-of-a-frozen-lake cold. Void-space cold."

Booker pulled back far enough to look him in the eyes. "I only put that thermometer in your mouth to shut you up. I'll check it off my list of effective remedies for chatter-box-annoy-ia." She slid another device under Garrison's armpit and pushed his arm down to keep it in place. "Hold still. I need to look at your extremities."

"So why do I have this thermometer in my mouth? You could just ask me to shut up."

"It's an old rectal thermometer I found lying around. Couldn't resist."

Garrison spat the instrument across the room.

Hoffman watched the medic methodically check each team member and a few members of the Planetary Defense Forces reconnaissance teams as needed. She was without a doubt the most popular medic within a hundred kilometers of the Koensuu City sector.

"She can set your broken arm or kill you from a thousand meters," one of the young PDF admirers said to his buddy.

None of Hoffman's team had spoken much since arriving at the warming tent. Exhaustion crashed down on them like a swarm of Rakka.

"Wrap your feet and hands," Booker said, distributing warm, damp towels as she talked. "Best we can do right now. A little bit of warming goes a long way when it comes to frostbite. Slow and steady. No more freezing today."

"That's why you're the best medic in the Corps," Garrison said. "Do you know what they let that Ibarran ox do to me out there?"

"Funny you should mention it." Booker placed both hands on her thighs, smiling at him with all her charm.

"You're gonna hurt me, aren't you, doc?" Garrison made puppy-dog eyes at her, pleading for mercy.

"Sorry, tough guy."

"It's OK. I kinda like it when you hurt me."

"Remember that. I'm giving you a local anesthetic," she said as she unzipped the pseudo-muscle layer off his broken arm, then sprayed the ugly blue flesh with an aerosol.

Garrison looked at his bruises and turned his head away.

"Lidocaine? Really? How about the good stuff before we get to the ouchy parts?"

"Shhhh. Think happy thoughts. Play Opal's tree-painter video," Booker said.

"I'm not a doughboy," Garrison said, relaxing under the touch of Booker's calloused hands and confident voice. "It probably doesn't work on me."

"This isn't so bad," Booker said. "Easy cheesy. You have a closed-wound, linear fracture of the ulna. Non-displaced. All good things. Your armor has arrested any worsening of the problem. And now you have me to the rescue."

"Hey, Gunney. On second thought, can I get the happy guy? Any video but when he paints a mountain. Pretty please."

King pulled his Mil-II Ubi from his kit and turned it on. Opal wandered closer to watch the video.

"Everyone should have a tree friend. Maybe more than one. See, just keeping the brush moving. No mistakes, just happy accidents..."

"I'm going to make a small incision here and take a look with my medical field scope, then a little minor surgery to introduce stem-cell osteoblast into the wound area."

"Will...that hurt?" Garrison said, still watching the video.

"About ten times as bad as what Medvedev did to you. He should have laid you supine and weighted the arm. You would've had instant relief."

"Instant?" Garrison squeaked. He cleared his throat and continued in his usual, gruff voice. "He turned my arm on purpose. That jagoff was trying to hurt me!"

Duke came in the tent carrying ruggedized cases in either hand. A gaggle of starry-eyed junior enlisted soldiers from the PDF followed him in, all hefting cases.

"Who wants power armor?" Duke asked as he

dropped the boxes and rolled his shoulders back and forth. "It's not Strike Marine standard, but it matches the local gear. Helps to be dressed like everyone else. Keeps the enemy from thinking you're important and friendlies from thinking you're a baddie just because you ain't dressed right."

"Finally." King popped open a case and removed a shoulder pauldron. "Felt like I've been fighting in my skivvies since three mountains ago."

The gunney frowned and wiped a thumb along the edge. It came back with a smudge of blood.

"Sorry, sir," one of the PDF said. "This is all repurposed gear. There's a rush to get replacement parts into the fields and—"

"I'll try not to add to it for the next guy," King said.

"Opal." Duke dragged a long case over to the doughboy. "You remember what Christmas is?"

"Shinies?" Opal asked.

Duke kicked the weapon case open and Opal removed a heavy gauss rifle. He hefted it against his shoulder and looked down the barrel, then brought it to a table and began to field strip it. The doughboy's expression didn't change as he detached the firing chamber and looked into the breach.

"Need—" The doughboy looked at Duke and took a cleaning kit offered by the sniper.

"That's the happiest I've seen Opal since he strangled two Rakka to death at the same time," Garrison said.

"It's the little things," Booker said. "Warmth. Caffeine. Heavy caliber gauss rifles firing on full cyclic."

"Gear up," Hoffman said. "War's not going to stop just because we need a break."

Duke dragged an armor case over to the lieutenant and helped Hoffman into the plates.

"What's it like on the front lines?" Hoffman asked the sniper.

"Situation isn't good. No one was expecting this kind of attack. The Kesaht don't do anything like they should. Like a normal enemy would. Mass waves attack in some sectors. Pinpoint raids behind our lines in others. Quality of their operations varies. We drop enough Sanheel and an entire attack will grind to a halt. The Sanheel stay back and concentrate on running their fight and the Rakka are more effective. The centaurs seem awful eager for glory, which is fine by me. Makes them easy targets."

Hoffman plugged a breastplate into the ports on his pseudoarmor and felt his suit contract and expand as it adjusted to the weight. The local gear had a forest camo pattern. He made a mental note to find a stencil and rank insignia later.

"The city doesn't have standardized defenses," Duke said. "It's improving, but it's hard to get reinforcements to the surface with the air and space battle above it so hot and heavy. Our Eagle pilots outclass the enemy, but they're outnumbered. More than a few Mules have gone down on various missions," Duke said. "I've been able to take the initiative, knocking off commanders when I can find them, citing you as my commander and basically refusing to be shoved into the line to sit in a hide with my thumb up my fourth point of contact."

Hoffman looked down at his sleeve display, which felt heavy and bulky minus the armor he had left in the mountains. The powered parts of his under-armor layer functioned. He had requisitioned a battery for each member of his team so they could communicate and record reports.

Alerts vibrated through the display. He glanced around and saw his team receiving similar messages. "All right, that's it. We've got orders to collapse defenses. That means back to the city."

Masha slurped down her soup as she stood. Medvedev took her by the elbow and hurried her toward the front of the tent.

"No. Wait. Stop pulling me. This is the best, hottest soup I've ever tasted," she complained.

"We must go. I think we have already stayed too long. These Terrans don't do things as we do in the legion," Medvedev said.

"You heard the boss," King said. "Let's move it, people. Garrison, help our prisoners back into their zip ties."

Masha swore. Medvedev glowered at Garrison as the restraints tightened.

Hoffman and the others packed their gear and rushed to the armored ground transports. The commander of the FOB pointed at one and told him to get in. "You might not believe it, but right now it's better than a Mule."

PDF Rangers held their defensive positions around the Delta Forward Operating Base until the last moment. Through the view port, Hoffman saw them running to their own armored cars. Moments later, the column sped away from the Kesaht camps and toward a lightly defended route to the northern section of Koensuu City. Mangled buildings and cratered walking paths stretched away from his limited point of view. The armored car ignored the subtleties of the twisting lanes, cutting straight across delicate landscapes thousands of years old.

Hoffman's vehicle was in the middle of the line, driven by a Planetary Defense transportation specialist. He listened to the man's radio but kept his mouth shut. The driver knew what he was doing.

The column sped into the city, swerving down the winding streets and flashing electronic credentials ahead of them to checkpoints. Guards made them stop, but only briefly.

Broken buildings, scorched pavement, and bloodstains demonstrated the intensity of previous battles. Hoffman barely recognized the city. Street intersections flew by as fighting intensified behind them.

Chapter 21

"Got a call from my boss. Have to dump you here and take a priority medical evac," the driver said.

"Understood." Hoffman gave the dismount hand signal to his team. "Everyone out, including the prisoners."

"HQ says I can keep the prisoners and drop them off with security," the driver said.

"Our mission, our problem. Thanks anyway."

The driver tapped his earphones.

"HQ wants all your firepower at Valkyrie Tower. The PDF are holding on by their fingernails and you Strike Marine types are supposed to be the best of the best." He jerked a thumb at Duke. "I can handle two prisoners in restraints."

"These aren't a pair of drunks that violated curfew," Hoffman said. "These are agents of a foreign power.

Slippery ones."

The snap of gauss rifles echoed through the street, mingling with explosions. Hoffman looked over the side of the cargo truck, then at the two prisoners.

"Something fishy about this," King said over the team's internal IR.

"Yep. Didn't like that at all," Hoffman said, sweeping his rifle sights along the street. "But there are men and women dying over there. None of us became Strike Marines to shirk out when the fighting starts."

"You think the Ibarrans would pull something in the middle of a siege? With no way off world?" King asked.

"You think the whole team needs to drop them off at a police station and eat donuts?"

"Negative, sir. Give me Garrison and I'll take the prisoners downtown. I'll make sure they're secured, then we'll find our way back to you. You go shed some blood for the Corps. Just save some aliens for me," King said.

"That works. This city falls, it won't much matter where the prisoners are." Hoffman switched off the IR channel and stomped his foot twice. "Driver. Take the prisoners and two of my Marines to the police station. Rest of us will hoof it to the front."

"I'll send up that you're on the way," the driver

said.

Hoffman leveled a finger at Masha. "See you soon."

"Is this cell heated?" Masha asked.

"Fight well," Medvedev said. "For her sake."

Hoffman and his team jumped off the back of the truck and Garrison waved goodbye as the truck sped away. His team was just as under strength as before. Now he'd swapped in two sniper-armed Marines for a close-in urban fight.

"Let's move in case there's a traitor broadcasting our position as we stand here chitchatting." He opened the squad link. "Team move, heading 285 degrees. Traveling security. Assume the area is hostile."

Rockets leapt outward from the city defenses. Hoffman quickly identified them as M-37 Gremlin barrage munitions, designed to saturate an area with shrapnel.

"Gremlins," Duke said, "those are last-ditch munitions. Final protective fire."

"Enemy's pushing. Step it out, Marines," Hoffman said and ran toward the sound of gunfire.

****

Duke sprinted up the stairs, unrolled his kit near one

of the banisters, and aimed his sniper rifle across the room and out a tall window. Booker, not looking happy, dropped beside him and aimed her sniper rifle as well.

"What targets do you want?" Booker asked.

"Officers."

"My favorite," Booker said.

"The windows are thirty feet tall and thirty feet away. We're practically invisible this deep in the room." Duke relaxed against his rifle.

Booker imitated him.

Opal took a defensive position on the first floor, blasting Rakka that came too close to the front of the building with his heavy gauss rifle.

Hoffman cleared the other rooms, already missing King and Garrison each time he went around a corner. Going solo on this was as tactically wrong and bad field craft as it could get, but he didn't want surprises.

Something snapped through an exterior window as he crossed a hallway to reach another room. He looked down at his left arm. Blood leaked from a graze wound. The pseudo-muscle sleeve peeked open and closed when he moved.

Once he finished his fast-and-dirty clearing mission, he dropped to the floor near Opal and removed a compression bandage from his kit. Folding it in half, he shoved it into the hole.

Duke fired again and again.

With wounds and the perimeter addressed, Hoffman checked Duke's progress. For the second time, the Rakka advance had stalled. Sanheel officers rode in tight circles at the end of the street, shouting at the Rakka infantry.

Duke fired and a Sanheel tumbled over dead, landing on a pair of Rakka.

"Kill enemy!" Opal cut down a rush of Rakka, ending their lives fifty meters from the front door of the Koensuu City mansion.

Rockets streamed down on the building, blowing out walls around Hoffman and Opal. Debris exploded across the ballroom, spraying Duke and Booker's elevated position above the dance floor. The sniper and his observer ducked their heads for several seconds, then started firing—first Duke, then Booker.

"Take your time, Booker. Make every shot count," Duke grunted.

"Screw you. I'm killing the hell out of these things."

Duke fired three times. Two Sanheel and a Rakka countersniper died.

Hoffman moved to a different window on the main floor, ducked out, then stepped out on a ruined balcony with one foot. He retreated seconds later. "Duke! Another air strike's inbound. One crescent fighter moving low and slow."

"I see the evil bastard," Duke said.

"Rooftops are the only way out of here," Hoffman said. "Rakka have the building surrounded and seem to be getting paid by bullets expended," he shouted over the roar of the incoming crescent engines.

Duke paused, then fired three quick shots.

"Good hits," Booker said. "I think you brained the pilot with the last one."

Duke pulled back from his rifle, paused, then scrambled to his feet. "Clear out!"

Hoffman saw what was happening at the same time. "Dive for the corners! Move!" He grabbed Opal by one arm and manhandled him forward, a tactic that worked surprisingly well, considering their size disparity. The doughboy yielded to him instinctively.

The crescent fighter hit the windows Duke had been firing through and would have killed him if his position wasn't on the opposite side of the room. The windows towered almost three stories high with smoke billowing outward now. Debris rained down from the ceiling, walls, and balconies. Hoffman and Opal charged through it.

Burning jet fuel dripped from above and ran down the stairs to spread across the ballroom floor. Rakka scrambled over what had been the front wall. A banister railing slipped out of place and reached into the smoke and dust twenty feet above the floor.

"Duke, we're leaving!" Hoffman led Opal up the stairs, jumping the streaming fire and ducking bullets zipping in from the streets surrounding the building.

Hoffman raced past his snipers. Duke packed up his primary rifle, slinging it across his back before switching to a smaller patrol carbine. He held the top of the stairs as Rakka splashed through the burning fuel. The first balked, but a Sanheel rode into the ballroom from hell, reared up like a warhorse, and slammed his hooves down on the reluctant assaulters.

After that, Rakka were berserk to attack.

Duke fired one, two, three times on as many targets.

Hoffman stepped onto a narrow side balcony and pointed to a similar building across the alley. "That balcony is lower than this one!"

"By five inches!" Booker shouted.

"Let's go, Opal."

"Opal help sir!" The doughboy grabbed Hoffman by his neck and his belt, swung him back once, then hurled him over the gap.

Booker retreated, holding one hand forward and one hand on her patrol rifle. "Opal, no!"

"Opal help Booker!" He flung the medic over to Hoffman's new location on the neighboring balcony.

"Opal help Duke!"

Duke slapped his grasping hands aside. "Don't you touch me. I know how to jump between buildings."

"Opal help?"

"No."

Opal pouted, then looked up. "Opal jump last."

"Fine, you big dummy. Opal can be the last man."

"Last doughboy," Opal said.

"Whatever." Duke leapt the gap, hit the target balcony, and rolled to one side to keep from tumbling over the sniper kit on his back.

Opal turned to face a trio of rampaging Rakka. He kicked the first one in the pelvis, sending it flying into the others. "Opal kill enemy later." He jumped the gap. The balcony shook when he hit without rolling, absorbing the impact by dropping into a low squat.

"By the Saint, you're a big dumb bastard," Duke

said, then started picking off the Rakka firing down on them.

****

Hoffman could barely speak; his throat was so dry. There was nothing he wanted more than water. No amount of adrenaline or caffeine could keep him going another step, which made him unreasonably glad to see the PDF retaking the area.

The local militia did double takes as Duke passed them by; the long vanes of his sniper rifle made him easy to spot.

"These boys are green but earnest," Duke said. "They do all right with the proper leadership."

"I told you that was him," one of the privates said to his buddy.

"I knew it was. Wasn't doubting you. I just said it was amazing we're fighting beside him," another private said.

Booker rolled her eyes. "They really like Duke."

"Greatness is its own reward," Duke said.

"Such humility." Hoffman grumbled.

The team arrived at a frozen water fountain and a

PDF lieutenant hurried over.

"Wait here ten minutes. I'm being told they're sending your gear. And…oh…the battalion CO has a message for Duke. He says stay frosty. Sorry, he's a bit of a corny dude."

"It's OK," Duke said. "Not everyone can be stone-cold killers like you and your platoon."

The young lieutenant beamed and went back to his men.

Chapter 22

King stood on one side of the booking desk while Garrison held his position on the other, his gauss rifle ready. A young, clean-cut, eager-to-please Koensuu City police officer checked his Ubi data slate for orders.

"It's too late to cause trouble, Medvedev," King said. "You missed your chance."

"Good thing you finally learned your lesson," Garrison said.

The legionnaire appeared bigger without Opal standing there to dwarf him. He looked more menacing despite a room full of police officers and a future surrounded by simple but uncompromising security measures.

King pointed at Masha. "You get your own room. There won't be any need for a bodyguard here."

"This isn't necessary. Haven't you figured out by now the Kesaht are here to kill all of us?" Masha asked.

"I don't see your point. What could one spy do to stop an invasion? Even if I trusted you to fight on our side, urban combat isn't in your wheelhouse," King said and then indicated the police officer. "This fine gentleman and his friends will keep you safe until we can arrange proper transport."

"Or you could just take my word we won't try to escape," Masha said. She leaned forward to see the officer's name plate. "I'm sure Officer Stevens could keep an eye on me while I have a hot cup of *Izara* cocoa in the cafeteria."

King blocked her movement toward the cop. "Got cuffs?"

The young cop swallowed, reached behind his back, and came forward with two pairs of old-style handcuffs, which King snapped on to each of his prisoners. A pair of cops then placed the Ibarrans in adjacent cells facing the booking area.

King high-fived Garrison.

"She's the best-looking mission target I've ever seen, but I'm glad we're done with her. I wonder if we get extra leave due to the hardships she caused us," Garrison said, unfastening his armor with a sigh of relief.

"Don't hold your breath. I've got a call for transport back to the front." As King removed his helmet and armor from the waist up, sweat squished out of his pseudo-muscle layer. "You guys have any hot chow around while we wait on our ride? Don't mind if it's room temperature white bread and bologna."

"Sure thing. Let me check my Ubi to see what's on the menu."

King's mouth started to water.

"You guys know the sniper? The one they call 'Ice Claw'? He really scares the piss out of the Kesaht. Sure wish we had a whole battalion of Strike Marines like you down here."

The young cop kept talking and talking until King grew bored. Garrison rolled his eyes in annoyance as King looked behind the booking desk, noticing a distinct lack of clerical staff.

Two police officers entered through a door marked "vehicle bay." They seemed to have just left their patrol duties because they were fully armed and wearing ballistic vests.

Four officers from the detention area walked into the room. Three additional officers stepped out of the locker room, strapping on gun belts without a word.

"Well, this sucks," King said, reaching for his weapon. "Garrison…"

"Ez itzazu hil. Baina minik egin ditzakezu," Masha said.

"Well, answer her, big guy," Garrison said to the bodyguard, leaning one elbow on the booking desk near Medvedev.

Masha's expression turned to ice. "I wasn't talking to him."

The young cop, the one who had looked wet behind the ears and about as dangerous as a choir boy two seconds ago, smoothly drew a weapon from his belt opposite his sidearm. For a moment, King thought it was a second pistol.

Garrison stepped back and threw up his left hand defensively, still holding his gauss rifle on its sling with his right hand but pointed at the floor. "What the hell are you doing?"

King felt cool metal against the back of his neck and pain lanced down his back as a taser arced electricity through his body. He heard a crackle as the ground rushed toward his face. Pain blossomed from the bridge of his nose as he went into convulsions, unable to blink voluntarily.

Garrison fell beside him, electrodes with dangling wires embedded in his cheek.

The two biggest guards grabbed Garrison by his heels and dragged him roughly across the floor. The tasers had fired tiny flechettes that embedded in his skin to link wires to the device. Electric current coursed between the two connection points. One of the flesh hooks came loose as they dragged him and the circuit was broken.

Garrison immediately twisted like a wrestler, grabbing one of them by the wrist. At the same time, he kicked the other away with his feet, taking out a knee.

The angelic-faced kid-cop attached a fresh cartridge to his taser and fired again.

King, able to see but unable to act, felt sorry for Garrison as electrodes bit into his forehead. Garrison went down with a spasming groan through gritted teeth.

A pair of cops yanked the battery packs on Garrison's armor, slapped a muzzle across his mouth and chin, then cuffed his hands behind his back with practiced efficiency. They dragged him into Masha's cell and dumped him in a puddle. King was disabled and restrained the same way and then dropped unceremoniously against the bars, his body still twitching.

Masha ran her fingers down King's face as his

cheeks ticked with the last of the taser assault. The spy rolled her palm over with a bit of sleight of hand and a thin metal disc, held between two fingers, glowed dimly.

"We did find artifacts here," she said. "But when we realized that you devil dogs had our scent, we stashed it in our mountain cache site with the intent to send locals to pick this up after Medvedev and I had made it off world. Thank you *so* much for taking us back to pick it up." She tapped King on the nose. "And thank you extra for doing a less than thorough inspection of where I had to pee in that cave. This little gem was hidden in a fake rock."

She patted him on the cheek twice and made the third touch almost as hard as a slap. Then, with pistol in hand, she pushed Garrison down on his back and straddled him. She thrust the muzzle under his chin. "How long have you been chasing me?"

"Mrrrumnmrrm…" Garrison said through his gag.

Masha twisted the pistol barrel deeper into the soft tissue under his jaw. "I see. I also see that the geo-political events may change your next assignment. Seems to me that if I kill you two, it'll be personal between me and your hunky lieutenant. So I'll let you two live. You tell the lieutenant he gets this close to me again, he'll be too competent for me not to kill. Oh, and thanks for the escort back to the city."

Garrison mumbled as Masha kissed him on the forehead.

King glared at Garrison.

Garrison shrugged. "Mrrrummerrrmsnns."

Masha strutted out of the room. Medvedev stripped King of his weapons and unsnapped the gauntlets off his forearms. He slipped the gauntlet with the Ka-Bar over his hand and flexed his fingers in the glove.

"You'd steal a Marine's blade?" King asked.

"And your rifle." Medvedev hefted King's gauss rifle and gave it a quick pat.

"We have a shuttle to catch, my strong bear," Masha said, already striding toward the front door.

Medvedev gave King a nod, then followed her out the door.

The clean-cut kid checked the locks. "Sorry about this. I really am a huge fan. This is for the greater good. Someday we'll all laugh and drink a beer over it." He made a fist, held it to his heart. "For the Lady!"

Garrison grunted out expletives as best he could through the gag. King rapped the back of his head against the bars, wondering just how he'd explain all this to Lieutenant Hoffman.

Chapter 23

"Duke for Hoffman, we're in position," Duke said. "Any word on our next move?"

"Hold and update me with real-time info. I'm checking something here. Might be a good route to the police station." Hoffman's voice echoed in the scratchy, half-scrambled IR radio.

Duke popped a stim tab and put in a dip.

"Do you think that's safe?" Booker asked. "Adding nicotine to combat meds?"

Duke rolled back to his rifle and snuggled up behind the scope. Flattening himself to the ground, he spread his feet wide and turned his toes outward for greater stability. Booker sighed in resignation, then imitated his pose.

"How do you spit that stuff while you're lying on

your stomach?"

"Spit or swallow, depends."

"Disgusting."

"That's why you'll never be a great sniper. You might be good, but never a master," Duke said.

"That's such bullshit," she said. "If anything, it probably jacks up your heart rate and increases your ocular nystagmus."

"Can't outshoot me, so you're going to bore me to death with science," Duke said.

"I'll show you how I can shoot."

"Really?"

"I'll put my next shot right between the eyes."

"You've always been obsessed with that shot. Not necessary in combat. Hostage rescue? Sure. Out here, throat, lungs, or pelvis disable the enemy just fine."

"No shit," she said as her fatigue started to show. "All I'm saying is chewing tobacco doesn't make you a better sniper. And if I wanted to dip, I'd dip. What's the big deal?"

He turned his eyes on her, barely moving his head. "All right." He snaked his arm down the side of his body to a utility pocket. "You have to move slow, keep your arm close to your centerline. Avoid showing movement to the enemy. Retrieve the can. Move it near your helmet but go slow. Savor the moment. Wait for the reward."

"This isn't happening," she said.

"Open the can. Don't spill. This stuff is worth more than your life right now. You can't pack it without violently snapping your wrist—so plan ahead. Do that part before you slip into your hiding place. Or just give it a few gentle taps. Gentle movements. Peace, love, and harmony with the planet so the enemy won't see you trying to kill them."

"This isn't necessary."

"Savor the moment, my young apprentice. Open, pinch, pack the dip into your lower lip—unless you've got bleeding, then move to your upper lip—which actually makes it easier to spit while lying prone," Duke said.

Booker shook her head slowly, rolled her eyes, and exhaled in defiant frustration. She took the can, tapped it, pinched a tiny portion of tobacco, and slipped it in between her lower lip and gums. Her eyes went wide, then squished shut as her face wrinkled in horror. "Soooo disgusting, blehh."

Duke held the open can near her face. "Don't waste it. Put it back. Five-second rule."

Booker covered her mouth with one hand, fighting

the urge to vomit.

"Back in the can, Booker. I can't exactly run down to the PX for resupply."

She closed her eyes, pushing her forehead to the ground.

"Booker?" Duke asked, an edge in his voice.

"I swallowed it when you put that can in my face," she said. "I hate you."

"Rule number one. Don't waste dip. Fail."

"It burns."

"You'd get used to it if you were a real sniper."

"Good thing I'm a medic."

"Fail. Complete fail."

"Little dizzy."

Duke chuckled.

"Gonna puke."

"No, you're not." He went back to searching for Sanheel officers and troop movements.

Booker recovered, took the can, and put in another dip. "Momma didn't raise a quitter."

"I admire your spirit, Doc. But when you stand up, you'll be dizzy. Plan for it," Duke said.

"This is so disgusting."

Duke gave a short whistle to silence her. "There's

that big, peg-legged Sanheel bastard from earlier," he said.

"Are you sure?" Booker asked. "Not really a peg leg. Decent prosthetic from what I've seen of their tech level."

"That guy has to be something special in their officer corps. He just won't die. *Until now*," Duke said. He emptied his lungs and settled every part of his body against the ground, then drew the trigger back to its breaking point and held it.

"Wait. I think this is a bad shot," Booker said.

Duke broke the trigger tension in one smooth motion, drawing it straight back through the trigger housing. The weapon thumped against his shoulder. The gauss round went exactly where he wanted it.

The Sanheel, somehow bigger and more menacing than all the others despite its prosthetic front leg, continued to pace back and forth like a good target.

"What…the…actual…" Duke raised his head a fraction of an inch as though it would allow him to see better. "Sons a bitches! You clever assholes."

Booker didn't move. "Hologram."

"Not. Good."

"I bet you're glad Hoffman isn't here to see this." Her voice went up half an octave. "Oh shit! Artillery!"

"It'll go in my report," Duke grunted, searching through his optics for the real target.

"You're not worried about getting shelled?"

"Of course I'm worried. Let's collapse back to the boss and the dummy before they drop an artillery barrage on us," Duke said.

"I'll lead," she said.

"Smooth is fast. Don't draw attention…"

Booker didn't wait for the lesson. Moving slowly to avoid attracting the eye of enemy countersnipers, she backed away from the edge of the rooftop, pausing to pull her weapon after her every few inches.

Duke held his position. There were plenty of targets now, all of them looking for the Ice Claw or however they said it in their language. Squads of Rakka rushed from building to building and destroyed vehicle to destroyed vehicle as others covered them. He saw several Sanheel and at least one Ixio searching the area with oversized binoculars. They stayed behind cover, barely exposing their heads as they looked for him.

"They're across the isthmus, entering the outer ring of the city. This is about to get real if we don't do something," Duke said.

"Set," Booker said from the threshold of the service

door behind and to one side of him. She aimed her rifle. "Covering."

"Moving." Duke slipped backward like a snake, his movements smoother and more practiced than Booker's but essentially the same. Once he had retreated ten meters, he took a knee, closed all the ports on his rifle, slipped a field sheath over it, and slung it across his back. Seconds later, he pulled the sling of his short patrol carbine to the front and looked through the sights.

Booker swept her sights right to left, then left to right, both hands on her patrol rifle, her elbows tucked in tight to create a more stable shooting platform.

"This should cheer you up. Boost your growing ego," she said. "Tanks. Headed our way."

Duke saw one armored vehicle after another emerge from the wooded area on the north side of the isthmus. The war machines were vaguely like old Terran versions. The enormous armored vehicles had one track down the middle with bulbous pontoon skis off each side for balance.

Booker snorted. "I know they're dangerous, but it's hard to get worked up after seeing our Armor Corps fight."

The first tank turned with surprising agility, elevating its main gun as it continued to move. Four others followed, vibrating the snow on the ground around them.

Duke wondered if they could fire while moving as he recorded details through his helmet microphone. "Kesaht armor. Five big guns in the forward echelon with two companies of light infantry in close support. Unknown if these vehicles are operated by Rakka or Ixio." He paused. "Tanks are some big sons of bitches…doubt the skinnies would get in them."

The five tanks veered to the left, smashing through snowdrifts and shattered buildings on the fringes of Koensuu City. A second tank platoon emerged from the same tree line and shifted to the right. When both squadrons were a kilometer from Duke's position, they reduced speed and approached methodically.

"They're looking for you, *Ice Claw*," Booker said.

"If you're trying to get under my skin, it isn't working."

Booker huffed and recorded her own report.

A third group of tanks arrived.

"Duke for Hoffman. We have fifteen tanks with a lot of infantry following behind. Looks like a 'sweep and clear' mission," Duke said. "I think they may be arriving at your bridge uncomfortably soon."

"Received," Hoffman said, the IR comm link crackling with interference. *"Get prepped to move. This*

bridge isn't high enough to blow. No water in the canal to slow them. Snowdrifts could be two inches deep for all I know."

"Unfortunate," Duke said. "I like blowing bridges."

"So I hear," Hoffman said. *"Plotting our next move. Do you have additional high-value targets?"*

Booker stared at the advancing tanks and infantry units. "They really don't like you."

Duke finished his notes, then radioed Hoffman. "I don't like any of these targets. Recommend we work our way back to HQ."

"Once bitten, twice shy," Booker said just loud enough for Duke to hear.

"Received and understood," Hoffman said. *"Holding strongpoints at the bridge abutment. Rally on my position for exfiltration."*

"I heard that, Booker," Duke said, then keyed his mic. "On our way."

Duke and Booker descended an external stairway on the back of the building. He thought it might have been a fire escape if not for the ornate railings. On the ground, they moved through the alley and down the street to join Hoffman and Opal.

"I'll be honest, sir. If we wait for this battlefield to

stabilize, there'll never be a good time to transport the targets off planet," Duke said.

"I don't see a clear way downtown to the police station. This mission gets more complicated every time I see you," Hoffman said.

"I started helping the PDF while you were stomping through mountain ruins. This is war. Only going to get worse."

"We have to survive to complete the mission. King and Garrison have our precious cargo locked down," Hoffman said. "The PDF are trying to envelop a force five times their size and pick them apart with guerrilla raids in combination with decisive battle tactics. I wonder who put the first idea in their heads."

"What did you want me to do while you were off hiking the scenic highways and byways of the Koen Mountains? Some of us work for a living," Duke said.

"I don't disagree. This is full-scale invasion war." Hoffman paused. "Defeating it is more than our team can handle."

Duke patted his vest, didn't find what he was looking for. "Can't take our precious cargo into orbit with Kesaht in control of the ground, air—and space, for all we know."

"You can't win the war all by yourself, Duke," Hoffman said.

"Air assault ships," Opal said, pointing toward the sky.

"Would you look at that?" Duke spat to one side. "These Kesaht ground pounders don't quit."

Rakka crowded the open doors of airships, ready to hit the ground running. Duke couldn't see the intended landing site, which was behind the Strike Marines. "The PDF knows better than to let them land there. That's deep inside the city."

"Between us and the PDF spaceport downtown," Hoffman said. "We need to go defensive. Call in support."

Duke cursed.

"Can't we have one mission go according to plan?" Hoffman asked.

"The PDF need help," Duke said.

"We need to slap a bandage on this mess, secure a Mule that can get past the Kesaht fighters, and deliver the Ibarran agents to the *Falstaff*. Enough war games."

Air defense missiles whooshed away from PDF batteries, slamming into Rakka troop transports and exploding two with direct hits. Others broke apart as they spiraled to the ground, throwing Rakka assault troops in all directions.

"They waited long enough. Might be enough to stop them if they could do it twenty more times," Hoffman said, stalking toward what looked like a boathouse built into the side of the dry canal. "This building has thick, stone walls and it's right next to a possible exfiltration route across the bridge. If we're going to get enveloped, we might as well choose the location."

Duke and the others rushed inside the building and up the stairs to the roof, where sweeping handrails and elaborate stone benches spoke of ancient parties and special events. He spread out his sniper kit—a white and gray camouflaged mat with extra magazine pouches sewn into it—and checked his range.

"Commanding view of the waterways and the parks," Duke said. "I think these walking trails are actually some kind of race course—*were* some kind of race course."

"There's a balanced logic to everything when viewed from here," said Booker. "With my scope on maximum magnification, I can see to the end of the causeway. They had to move their tanks and other equipment that way or come from the mountains…and I've good reason to believe they don't like that route as much as they once did. If the PDF could get through the forest or around the lakes with a large enough force, they might repel these Kesaht jerk-offs."

"Opal, watch for the air assault troops," Hoffman said, then crawled nearer to Duke. "The airborne shock troops are attacking everything, which means they're concentrating on nothing."

"You're trying to tell me they aren't coming this way," Duke said without looking at his team leader. "Yet."

"Getting through them to HQ downtown is officially miracle territory," Hoffman said.

"Better pray," Booker said.

"Tanks are stalled. Sanheel-led Rakka are bounding forward in large groups," Duke said. "One moment." He fired. "That's one less Sanheel officer."

Hoffman retreated to the center of the roof and attempted radio contact with C&C on the ship or anyone at PDF HQ. Duke heard his broken conversation with staff-level officers. He tuned it out and scanned the battlefield for the best targets.

"We can drop a lot of the officers but not all of them," Booker said just before she fired. "I think I got one. Shit, he's limping back to their tank line. Why are there so many Sanheel out front?"

"They're going to charge," Duke said.

"You've been fighting them longer than I have. What the hell is this?" Hoffman asked.

"I don't know, sir. Almost seems like a personal thing," Duke said.

"They really don't like Duke," Booker added.

"Hoffman for King, respond." Hoffman drummed his fingers on his knee as he attempted radio contact several times. "We should be able to get through. I can contact HQ for updates and PDF commanders keep sending me requests for sniper missions. Why doesn't King answer?"

"Maybe something happened to them," Booker said.

"It's not like them to ignore radio protocols. They should've reported in," Hoffman said as he studied the advancing enemy. "They're coming fast. Their artillery will be attempting to soften us up about now."

All of a sudden, Kesaht air space cleared of fighters and troop transports and shells screamed down from high-angle shots, shattering buildings, streets, parks, and walking bridges at random. Five or ten shells hit the scattered, undermanned PDF defenses. Moments later, the Kesaht artillery teams began marching explosions three hundred yards ahead of the charging Sanheel.

"Not good," Booker said.

Duke caught a glimpse of Hoffman running toward

the other side of the roof and thought he was most likely looking for the airborne Rakka units.

"Booker, we have a target-rich environment," Duke said, firing three times. "All this for one little old sniper."

"Two snipers, Duke. We're a team, remember?" Booker said.

Duke selected a Sanheel officer ahead of the others and shot him in the throat from almost three hundred yards. The horse-like legs gave out, tumbling the alien and two others following him. Again and again, he fired, pausing to check the temperature of his barrel and his ammunition levels. "No art in this kill fest. Just shooting fish in a barrel."

"Until they reach us. Then it'll feel a lot less artsy-fartsy." Booker fired.

"Give 'em hell, Booker. I need to check something," Duke said.

Booker didn't respond and continued to fire on Sanheel officers as Duke twisted onto his side. Dragging the rifle around to use its scope would take too long so he pulled out his binoculars with one hand and searched up and down the canal. What he saw was a street leading into a cul-de-sac, a route than looked like an escape route but wasn't. The right flank of the Sanheel charge would reach it soon and right behind them, Rakka infantry and tanks.

If the most wanted enemy of the Kesaht were to flee that direction, the Sanheel would pursue him. He might slip between buildings and cross the dried-up canal before they reached him, unless the snow filling it was deeper than it looked. An image of sinking to his neck during the middle of his escape plagued him, but he knew what he had to do.

"Duke for Hoffman, I have an idea. A way to get us out of this mess and back to HQ," Duke said.

"Tell me," Hoffman said.

"There are a series of streets looping around a lot like the park boulevards. A big tangle of dead ends. I can draw them in. The Sanheel and the tanks will clog it up. Won't be able to turn around or make half the corners. They might bust through, but that's a risk we have to take. My not-so-humble opinion."

"How do you know the Rakka airborne units will chase you? They're on the other side of the canal. We'll have to move in the canal or take the bridge by the boathouse."

"I'll give them a reason."

"Fine. Let's do it. We're right behind you," Hoffman said. "Opal. Get ready to rappel."

"Opal no fall this time."

Duke packed his gear in record time and spooled out his rappelling line, hoping it was long enough to get him to the ground. "Do you have ropes?"

"Used what we had in the mountains. Wasn't included in the resupply," Hoffman said.

"Why am I suddenly the sniper, the senior team member, and the quartermaster?"

The artillery barrage ceased.

Booker fired a final round and gathered her own equipment. "I have rappelling line."

"Leave it in your kit. We won't have time to police it up and you might need it somewhere else after I'm on the ground," Duke said.

Booker stared at him in horror. "No, Duke, don't be stupid."

"Complete the mission, Booker."

"What's he talking about?" Hoffman asked.

Duke backed off the rooftop and rappelled to the ground in two bounces along the wall. The moment he was down, he gave the rope a twist and a pull to bring it down.

"Duke!" Hoffman cursed. "What the hell was that?"

"He's like this sometimes," Booker said. "He's taught me *so* much."

Duke sprinted toward the advancing right flank of

the Sanheel. The half-horse aliens picked up speed, some of them firing wildly as they galloped ahead of the Kesaht force. Snarling and cursing, their mangy hair and tusks made them look like demons seeking revenge.

He stood tall, shot a leading Sanheel in the chest, then pivoted to search for the rampaging Rakka airborne on the other side of the snow-filled canal. Five or fifty feet deep, there was no way to tell. Getting the Rakka's full attention took nearly twenty rapid-fire rounds requiring three magazine changes done at speed.

Jumping to his feet, he sprinted into the maze of streets and walking paths he had seen from the top of the ancient boathouse. Sanheel clustered together, their advance slowing when they shouldered each other sideways to reach Duke first.

Rakka shock troops plunged across the canal, half of them sinking over their heads in the snowbank. Others walk-swam through the snow and reached Duke's side of the canal. They climbed over buildings, daggering their claws into the walls, screaming war cries, racing ahead of the ranks of Sanheel coming up behind them, their hooves striking the frozen ground in an eerie rhythm.

He reached a covered structure that reminded him of a picnic complex along I-70 before the Ember War, except the trim was artistic, the short support pillars were enshrined with ruins, and ice accented all the hard lines and corners. The snow canal ran under it, wider here than in other parts of the city. Narrow trees lined a dozen roads leading to the open-air building.

The best thing would be to keep moving—fast—but he stopped, fished one of Garrison's premade charges out of his kit, and connected it to the entryway. A trio of Sanheel rushed into view, charging up the main access road to the building.

Duke aimed a two-hundred-yard shot from a standing position, drilling the leader in his mouth right between his bent tusks. "This is going to hurt my reputation, but here goes nothing." He shot one in the shoulder and the other in the arm, just to keep them properly motivated. Seconds later, he was running through the picnic hall and out the other side.

Ignoring the switchback road before him, he dropped on his left hip, sliding down the steep hill with his patrol rifle held high. The sniper kit on his back caught the ground several times, nearly flipping him around as snow blasted against his visor. At the bottom of the shortcut, he came to his feet and sprinted to the next structure—a mirror of the one he'd just left but on the other side of the canal.

His booby trap exploded and a brace of Sanheel officers screamed in pain. Others charged around the structure, lined the bank of the canal, and fired rifles and handguns at him. He looked back once. The entire facade of the structure collapsed on his pursuers. Gasping for air and trying to ignore the burning in his legs, he rushed into the city.

Rakka shock troops were everywhere—in the streets and buildings and swarming from alleyways. Duke rushed into a dark doorway, gunfire rippling from the end of the street as he disappeared. Bullets shattered against the wall and pain seared through his left cheek. Blood spattered down from his lightweight sniper helmet. The fingertips of his right hand came away bloody before he realized he had touched the wound. Cursing the distraction, he settled into a steady jog.

Catching his breath seemed more important that getting shot in the face. He could run. No Strike Marine made it through selection without maintaining their physical conditioning, although that didn't mean he was winning any races against the kids he served with these days.

"Great idea, Duke. Good job. What kind of sniper gets himself shot by a bunch of alien grunts?" He berated himself as he fished a compression bandage from his blowout kit without stopping. He dropped the bandage, caught it, nearly dropped it again, and finally slowed to a walk.

The front of his gear was slick to the waist with blood. "Looks like more than it is," he muttered. Checking his arms and hands, he found more blood. "I must be a sight. It's gotta look worse than it is. Only a flesh wound. No…big…deal."

He pressed the square of fabric into his face wound, clenching his teeth in anticipation. The compression bandage was treated with quick-clot chemicals. They worked great but always felt like fire in an open wound. "Ahhh…that doesn't feel good."

He closed his emergency medical kit and ran. Buildings were taller this far from the ancient park system and the maze of canals and sounds of battle echoed from every direction. Nothing was visible. With luck, he planned to keep it that way.

Running too quickly to reverse his momentum, he rounded the corner. A cluster of Sanheel reared up, hooves flailing like deadly clubs. He ducked and twisted to avoid having his face pulverized, but one hoof glanced his shoulder and he fell, turning his ankle at a bad angle. He heard something snap and felt heat shoot up his leg—broken or sprained, he couldn't tell.

"You are Ice Claw!" the leader shouted in heavily accented English. "Death to Ice Claw. Honor to Thran'Ul."

Another Sanheel shouted something Duke didn't understand while others pushed forward, shoving each other aside to aim large pistols at him. The eight-foot-tall monsters heaved him into the air and tugged him back and forth, screaming alien sounds that hurt his ears.

"I have your death weapon," Thran'Ul said, his metal foreleg scraping against the ground, spitting the words like a curse as he ripped the patrol rifle from his hands and his sniper rifle from his back.

Duke resisted just enough to keep his arms in their sockets and avoid being thrown under their hooves.

"For honor! For honor! This victory is mine!" The metal-legged Sanheel said, lifting Duke higher.

The Sanheel mob went silent as one he recognized trotted around the corner with one mechanical front leg upsetting his rhythm. An honor guard of Sanheel, armored vehicles, and Rakka shock troops accompanied him. The newcomer slowed, narrowing his gaze on Duke and sneering. His uniform and armor matched the senior-most members of the Sanheel officer corps. Only his prosthetic and the recently stitched wounds on his face set him apart.

He took the sniper rifle and ripped open the travel case. "I have it," he said. "For the honor of my family, I have it!"

Duke spat from what was left of his long-forgotten dip. "You speak decent Terran. Maybe I'll let you live long enough to be interrogated when we take back this planet."

The pair of Sanheel holding Duke dropped him. He grunted when he hit the ground, rolling onto his knees and then his feet as soon as he could force his muscles to obey.

The Thran'Ul snapped the rifle in half. Electricity arced up the twin vanes and over the Sanheel's forearms. He tossed the pieces aside like trash.

"Buffy!" Duke staggered forward.

The Sanheel boss grabbed Duke's wrists with one massive hand and lifted the Strike Marine up. The cyborg commander pulled out a wicked knife, curved and serrated, and aimed it at Duke's belly.

"It will be slow for you," the Sanheel said.

"Hold me a little higher," Duke said just as a sniper round snapped past Duke's ear and a black hole appeared in the Sanheel's forehead. The alien's mouth moved and his head lolled to one side, blood pouring down its neck.

Duke fell to the ground and stared at the bullet hole

right between the alien's eyes. An image of Booker's attempt to dip tobacco flashed in his mind and he laughed, suddenly realizing what had just happened.

"Kill enemy!" Opal roared as he charged around the corner. Hoffman followed a half step slower, shooting on the move as they rushed at the backs of the horse-bodied aliens.

"Humans!" one yelled. "Traitors and murderers!"

Hoffman switched his gauss rifle to full auto and emptied one magazine after another while Opal grabbed Duke, tossed him over one shoulder, and fired his rifle with one hand. At near point-blank range, he was accurate.

"Go, go, go!" Hoffman shouted.

Opal turned and ran. "Sir!" Worry filled his voice as he bounced Duke this way and that.

"I'm right behind you, Opie," Hoffman said as he chucked grenades to discourage pursuit.

****

"Put me down, you big dummy," Duke said when the doughboy finally stopped running.

"No. Sir said carry stupid sniper."

Hoffman, in the lead now, slowed to a walk. "Drop

him."

Opal let Duke fall unceremoniously to the pavement and Duke grunted on impact. He stood and brushed pink snow and ice from his uniform.

"Thanks, Opal. Real nice."

Booker dropped from a fire escape. "You shouldn't have used yourself as a lure. I wasn't sure I could make that shot."

"I wasn't thinking that far ahead." Duke looked at the medic in sniper training, then at Hoffman and Opal. "Just wanted the rest of you to get away."

"Thanks," Booker said.

"Sloppy shot."

"You complaining?" she asked.

"Just don't forget your breath control. We've been working on that since before the Dotari mission."

****

Hoffman reached the top of a long, gentle slope into the center of the city and made a note to dress Duke down and document his reckless hot-dogging in his file. It would fit nicely between the previous entry and the next entry. The man was a recidivist.

He studied the wide terrace that marked the end of this hill and the beginning of a residential area that hadn't been evacuated. Almost a plateau, the inhabited portion of the city had been built on a solid foundation as well ordered as the winding streets and canals below. The outer city had been beautiful to look at, not a place to live or work.

"Take five. Rest, recover, drink water if you have any," Hoffman said, then looked over the growing conflict. "We have PDF en route to our location. I'll need to brief their commanders, then get to the police station and see what's going on with King and Garrison."

Koensuu City convulsed as the Kesaht attacked in waves. Their pursuit of Duke had been a major distraction, but now the enemy forces seemed to have regained order and purpose. The Kesaht airborne assault troops still rampaged the lower ring, but the Sanheel and armor advance had stalled…for now.

Hoffman looked toward the isthmus that had protected this city from ancient invaders. Partially covered with a white forest and marshes, the narrow landmass was just big enough to move a major land force. Beyond were foothills and mountains Hoffman had already seen enough of.

Duke and other PDF irregular forces had slowed the

Kesaht advance and nearly held them until the sheer number of Rakka and Sanheel grew too large. The battle raging across the west and south portions of the city looked like a picture from Dante. Beyond that hellscape, the Kesaht formed up several divisions of infantry, armor, and combat engineers.

PDF tanks rolled down from the heights and parked on Hoffman's terrace facing the main attack. Below them, two kilometers distant, Kesaht forces reduced the outer wall to rubble and tanks rolled over the debris as Rakka infantry followed at a loping run. Hoffman and his team watched as the main force joined the shock troops.

Behind the tanks and infantry, artillery batteries set up and renewed the bombardment.

"Lieutenant Hoffman," a man said as he jumped down from a tank and strode forward. "Lieutenant Colonel Hague Mattern, PDF Tanker Corps."

"Sir." Hoffman saluted. "Lieutenant Thomas Hoffman, Strike Marines."

"Good to meet you. My men admire the hell out of your sniper. Good work. Really stuck it to those bastards."

"How many tank squadrons do you have?" Hoffman asked.

Mattern hesitated. "Just this one. Everything was in

storage the Kesaht blew up or scheduled for delivery. We're lucky to have a force this size. Koen isn't…wasn't…central to the war against the Kesaht."

Hoffman gave his after-action report to Mattern, all the time wondering how long it would be before Koensuu City fell.

Mechanized infantry arrived and deployed on the high ground. Men and women went to work fortifying the heights with concrete road barriers instead of trenches. Cranes rearranged ugly blocks of concrete and steel as fast as the engineer crews could move.

"It won't be enough," Hoffman said.

"I know." Mattern stood with both fists clamped behind his back. "Don't tell my men."

Planetary Defense Force rockets launched from the Koensuu City heights. One small artillery battery fired at regular intervals while shells from the Kesaht artillery slammed apart barriers and caved in buildings.

"Duke, Booker. Set up and start doing what you do," Hoffman said.

"We need to get to the jail," Booker said.

"I know."

Hoffman thanked the Saint for having the high ground. Without the elevated position, Koensuu City would already be overrun. He looked out across the panorama. Even when clouds weren't dumping snow, the wind blew up loose powder and smoke. Sounds arrived from a great distance, out of sync with what had caused them. He heard a man scream but never saw him. Rakka squad leaders barked orders that sounded like a chant.

"I wonder how deep that snow is in the canals. Might be worth it to push that far and fortify the line there," Mattern said.

"The canals are deep. The Rakka chasing us sank up to their necks," Hoffman said.

"Interesting. You have firsthand knowledge."

"Yes, sir."

Mattern considered the battlefield for a long time. "Thank you, Lieutenant. I need to confer with General Allan."

Lines of Sanheel trotted forward in synchronized quickstep with Rakka shock troops behind them. "Out of range," Duke said. "They'll be a challenge to hit at a full gallop."

"Strike Marine Lieutenant Hoffman for command HQ."

"HQ for Hoffman, go ahead."

"Hoffman for HQ, I have eyes on significant

Sanheel movement. Right flank. Looks like they're going to storm the defenses in that quarter."

"HQ received. We are aware. Stand by for reinforcements. Will need you to assume command of that sector," the voice said.

"Negative, HQ. Can't do that. I'm on mission."

"Not negotiable. HQ out."

Hoffman tried three times to reestablish the radio link but couldn't get through the radio chatter. "Booker, I'm heading back to HQ. I have to settle something."

"I'm just a field medic right now. Just make sure you don't forget me when we finally get the chance to get off world."

Hoffman ran to the nearest command tent, saluted the guard who was little more than a teenager stolen from the militia, and went inside. He saw few people he knew and those only from brief encounters. Captain Pine was there, whom he'd never seen but Duke had referred to him. General Allan seemed to be in command of the city at present.

Hoffman saluted and stood at attention. "General Allan, may I have a moment?"

"At ease, Lieutenant," the general said.

"Permission to speak freely, sir?" Hoffman asked.

The general looked at him with tired eyes and let out a slow breath.

"Sir, my team has two high-value targets in custody. Getting them off world and back to Earth for interrogation is vital to unraveling the Ibarran infiltration into the Terran—"

"There's no viable way off world," General Allan said. "The Kesaht have the high orbitals and everything we've sent to make a break for the Crucible has been destroyed. You're here until we break the Kesaht invasion or we all die in place. Those are our options."

Hoffman hesitated.

"Your Strike Marines have been a blessing to our defenders. Great for morale. I also happen to think you know what you're doing," General Allan said. "So relax, Lieutenant. Do what you can, while you can, for our defenses. I was sent a communiqué about your mission and I understand its importance and intricacies."

Hoffman wasn't sure how to respond, so he just stood at parade rest.

Allan stared at his tactical map for a long time. None of the other officers spoke. Lieutenant Colonel Mattern stared at Hoffman. Sounds of the closing battle passed through the tent. Artillery shells whistled through the air and explosions shook the ground. Team leaders' distant commands echoed dryly as though from a television broadcast poorly tuned in.

"Lieutenant Hoffman, despite all this, I'm not going to blow smoke up your ass. Surrender of the city may be inevitable. I may be able to scrape together a mission to get you through the Crucible with your prisoners, but if I do that, we lose what little air cover we have. That won't happen until the defense of this city is no longer viable." General Allan stared at him without emotion.

"Yes, sir." Hoffman waited to be dismissed.

"One last thing," General Allan said. "If you are on this mission, *be* on mission. Go police up the rest of your team and wait for me to send you to the fighting. It won't be someplace quiet."

"Yes, sir." He saluted and strode away from the HQ. "Hoffman for team, check in."

"Booker."

"Duke."

"Opal."

He waited several seconds. "All team members, rally on me at the HQ. Immediately."

"Yes, sir."

"On my way."

"Sir!"

They formed up and headed for the police station.

A roar echoed across the city as the Kesaht assaulted the defenders of Koensuu City. Sanheel and Rakka charged in waves, the sheer weight of their numbers shaking the ground. Artillery and rockets hammered the first-line defenders less than a hundred meters ahead of the assault.

As Hoffman used hand signals to communicate with his team, Duke grabbed his shoulder to yell something at him, but his words made little sense beneath the barrage hammering the city.

"...help them!"

"Stay. On. Mission. You've done enough. We have to go!" Hoffman pointed toward the police station.

A civilian aircraft launched from a rooftop only to be blasted from the sky by surface-to-air missile batteries. Undaunted, several civilian and military shuttles scattered into the sky as other civilians fled higher into the city, dragging children and bundles of valuables.

Booker argued with Duke. Opal opened and closed his fists, angry veins twitching in his neck. "Enemy. Enemy. Enemy."

"Get us to the police station. Remember the

mission!" Hoffman yelled. "We need to find King and Garrison."

Opal noticed the strange missiles first and grabbed Hoffman by his shoulder. "Missiles!"

Hoffman and his team faced the snowstorm-obscured mountains. Hoffman carefully removed Opal's hand from his shoulder and stepped involuntarily toward the imminent destruction of the city.

"Doesn't seem right," Duke said. "I wouldn't have pegged the Kesaht to slag the city…especially not while they've got forces still fighting in it."

"They would've nuked us earlier if they had the intent," Hoffman said.

Booker spoke in a throaty murmur as she stared in horror. "They're coming fast. No time for the civilians to get to the shelters unless they're already in them."

A few of the civilians stood transfixed as others screamed and dove for cover. To Hoffman's amazement, a few came out of buildings to watch the new threat.

"I don't think those are nukes," Hoffman said. "They almost look like…" He blinked several times as the missiles veered toward the front lines, decelerating rapidly. They moved in diamond shaped formations of tour missiles. His brain told him to brace for impact and explosions that didn't come.

"What the…" Booker stared at the attack.

Retro-rockets fired off the front of the missiles and they slowed. A humanoid shape dropped from the missile and landed on a boulevard, sliding across the road. Three more of the fifteen-foot-tall mechanized soldiers dropped in and their missiles accelerated across the city. Gatling cannons snapped onto shoulders and spun to life. Sunlight glinted off massive double-barreled gauss cannons attached to the soldiers' forearms.

"Those are lance formations. It's Armor!" Hoffman said, watching as more missiles dropped their payload.

Opal jumped, thrusting one fist in the air. "Armor! Sir! Armor! Armor! Armor!"

Two lances fell on the Kesaht artillery batteries like ravening wolves. Rakka leapt onto the backs of Armor units only to be snatched off and slammed against the ground like sacks of meat. Ixio officers spilled away from the chaos as Rakka rushed in to die. Kesaht cannons and rockets panic-fired in every direction—at the Armor, at the city, and into the sky.

Hoffman called a halt, then scanned the scene with binoculars. "I don't see any Templar crosses."

"Not sure what that means," Duke said. "They look

like they're on our side."

"I expected Templars for something like this," Hoffman said.

"Could they be Ibarrans?"

"I'd rather not fight the Kesaht *and* the Ibarrans right now."

The bulk of the Armor counterassault touched a hundred meters in front of the still-charging Sanheel and Rakka shock troops. Armor fired their arm cannons as they smashed into charging Sanheel. Blood and debris fountained into the air from the collision of two unstoppable forces. Hoffman felt the impact, heard the amplified battle cry, "WE ARE ARMOR!"

"Kill enemy!" Opal cheered.

Hoffman could barely look away from the spectacle of Terran Armor charging forward to meet the Kesaht advance, but Opal's excitement stunned him. He laughed uncontrollably.

The doughboy turned toward him, arms wide as he advanced.

Hoffman held up his left hand, palm out. "Opal, no hugging."

"Sir. Armor came."

"Yes, they did."

"They're probably here to stomp on King and Garrison for going radio silent," Duke said.

"Don't be jealous, Duke. You had your moment of fame," Booker laughed.

Hoffman took one final look at the battle. He quickly counted at least fifty suits of armor attacking en masse. The lead soldiers formed a wedge and drove at the Kesaht center, smashing Rakka underfoot or throwing them aside like rag dolls. Double-barreled gauss cannons lit up the gloomy scene as snow cascaded down from the lead-colored sky. A second and third wave of Rakka and Sanheel surged forward to stop them.

One Armor lance ran swiftly at each of the flanks, holding their fire until they were on top of their enraged enemies.

Chapter 24

"Pull up the location of the police station on your gauntlet," Hoffman said. "Let's move."

Duke jogged forward to take point and Booker fell back twenty meters, taking rearguard. The center of Koensuu City was coming alive. Civilians crowded windows and doorways. Groups of young men and women climbed to rooftops to watch the spectacle while Hoffman wished they would get to shelter and stay there.

The police station, by contrast, was a ghost town.

"Something's not right," Hoffman said. "Stack up by the door. Treat this like an assault but try not to shoot friendlies if I'm wrong."

"Bang?" Booker asked.

"No bang. Tap up," Hoffman said. Booker was last in the stack as no one wanted the medic going down in the doorway. Keeping her eyes forward like the rest of the team, she would tap the Strike Marine in front of her when ready.

Time always dragged before a room entry. Hoffman readied himself for a point-blank gun battle.

Opal tapped his shoulder. Hoffman tapped Duke's shoulder and they went streaming through the front door, weapons fanning across the room.

A neat row of police officers lay on their sides, handcuffed, legs shackled, mouths gagged.

"We'll come back to them. Keep moving. Find the rest of our team and the Ibarrans," Hoffman said, feeling the mission slipping away.

They cleared room to room until they found the jail cells. Hoffman found Garrison sitting on a cell bunk, hands cuffed behind his back, looking down at his feet as if thinking deep thoughts. King sat against the bars.

Hoffman tapped his knuckles on the cell.

Garrison's head snapped up and he chewed on his gag. He leapt to his feet and stumbled toward the door in his unpowered armor, mumbling furiously.

King looked up, his shoulders slumped.

"Sir," King said, "the targets escaped a little over an hour ago. The police were Ibarran agents."

Hoffman pulled the gag out of Garrison's mouth.

"What he said, sir," the breacher said, working his sore jaw from side to side.

"Gone?" Opal asked.

"We dragged them across frozen wastes and ice-capped mountains…" Hoffman said, "…and they got away?"

"Gone?" Opal looked around frantically.

"We were ambushed." Garrison shook in his armor. "From behind! By cops! You think if anyone on the planet would be trustworthy, it'd be the boys in blue!" He leaned forward and let Hoffman see the black-and-blue welt on his forehead from the taser needles.

"Can you see this bullshit?" Garrison asked. "Does it look bad? Booker, you can fix it, right?"

Opal thrust his arms through the bars, grabbed Garrison by his sides, and lifted him off the ground. "Why gone?" the doughboy asked. "Why gone!"

"Not my fault, big guy." Garrison's feet kicked in the air. "Sir? Little help here."

"Drop him." Hoffman rubbed a hand against his face.

"We have to find and catch those two assholes…" Booker said. "…again?"

"They can't get off world," Hoffman said. "We'll find them. Again."

"Sorry, sir," King said.

"My mission. My responsibility," Hoffman said. "I assumed the local cops would be screened against Ibarra influence. And assumptions are the mother of all foul ups." He grabbed the bars and heaved, using his armor's strength assist to rip the door free of its hinges.

"She had a message," King said. "We catch up to her again, she'll kill all of us."

"She could have capped us both pretty easy, but she did say thanks for the escort back to the city," Garrison said. "So that was nice."

"We're not done with her," Hoffman said. His gauntlet screen chimed with an alert. He stepped aside as Opal and Duke went into the cell and freed the other two Marines.

"Kesaht have broken through the city's outer defenses," Hoffman said. "PDF are calling Ice Claw to the front."

Duke took a factory fresh rail rifle off his back and gave it a pat.

"She ain't Buffy, but she'll do. Doubt I'll get the Ibarrans in my sites again." Duke said.

"The city's in a full on panic with the attack," Booker said, looking out a window. "You want to try and find them in this? Almost half a million people in this city, sir."

Hoffman looked at King, who kept his face turned from the lieutenant, and Garrison, who had a sheepish grin as Opal popped a fresh battery pack into the breacher's armor. Garrison pulled his wrists away from his back and snapped the chain on the cuffs.

"She left you two alive," Hoffman said. "We're not done with her or Medvedev, but I'm changing the mission. We defend this city and the civilians inside of it. Soon as we kick the Kesaht back to whatever hole they crawled out of, then we're back on the hunt. Understood?"

"Sounds fair to me," Duke said.

"I like not being dead," Garrison said. "So those two get a head start. So what? Not like they're going to get off world while the skies are full of Kesaht. And Masha ain't going back out in that snow. She wasn't kidding about hating the cold."

"I need a weapon," King said, his gaze on his feet. Duke pulled a gauss carbine off of Opal's wide back and tossed it to the gunney.

"Let's move," Hoffman said. "This city needs us."

****

An open-topped cargo truck slid to a shaky stop at a bend in a road running through a thick forest. Hoffman jumped out of the back and his team followed. They made their way into the forest and passed a small logistics point in a clearing. Koen PDF milled about, a mood of excitement and victory as the battle for the planet neared its end.

Several PDF soldiers shouted, "Ice Claw!" as they passed.

"Duke's famous for something other than bad tipping at the titty bars," Garrison said.

Hoffman ignored the banter. He wasn't in the mood. Tired, injured, and facing failure on a grand scale, all he wanted was to catch Masha and carry out his threat—tie her up like the criminal she was and shoot Medvedev at the slightest sign of resistance. Failing at that, he wanted to help Armor smash the Kesaht.

A rocket streaked overhead as the distinct chatter of Rakka small-arms fire came from the retreating Kesaht forces. Dotari armor stalked through the trees. Shoulder mounted rotary cannons whirring as they fired on the retreating enemy. The boom of gauss cannons echoed off the mountains.

Hoffman took the lead and aimed his team for one of the Armor elements. "We'll follow them as closely as possible."

"Understood," Gunney King said.

PDF officers and newly arrived Terran military personnel ordered Hoffman and his team to stay within the lines. He didn't recognize their armor or standards, but at least one seemed to be Dotari Marines. He flashed his priority mission code.

"You think Armor's going to admit they need help?" Booker asked. "I'm not familiar with their unit markings. I wish Max were here. He has all their crests memorized. Something's different about these lances."

"No," Hoffman said. "They'll tell us what they need, and we'll do it."

"Here comes the welcoming party," Duke said, pointing at a lance of four Armor units breaking off from the attack to stop Hoffman's team.

Hoffman went forward to contact their team leader. He cued up the code, ready to send it the moment it was requested. The sound of the Armor soldier's voice was strange, which he hadn't expected because they all used voice synthesizers to speak externally.

"I am Armor. My lance makes this assault. What are you doing here?"

Hoffman thought it was the rhythm or syntax rather than the tone that was off. "First Lieutenant Thomas Hoffman, Terran Strike Marines. General Allan—head of the PDF—sent us to augment your unit."

"You are Lieutenant Hoffman?"

"Yes, sir."

"Of the Strike Marines?"

Hoffman stared up at the Armor soldier. "Is there a problem?"

"There is no problem! You are the *Breitenfeld* Strike Marines who saved our home!"

"You're...*Dotari*?"

"Yes! I am Fal'tir." He banged a huge fist against his breastplate and the other armor in his lance followed suit. "We must first destroy these Kesaht, but anything else we can do to assist you will be done."

"Where were they two days ago?" Booker muttered.

Hoffman winced, hoping the armor didn't pick up on the comment.

"We came soon as Admiral Valdar arrived on Dotari Prime. He asked for our fleet's assistance to fight the Kesaht here," Fal'tir said. "After bringing the Golden Fleet back from deep space, the Council of Firsts was inclined to help him. But let us focus on our enemy. The Kesaht are launching a last-ditch offensive. Their remaining Sanheel want to die with glory. We will give them death. There is no glory in wasting lives. Come, see if you can kill as many as we can."

Fal'tir walked off.

"Dotari armor's not that different from ours," King said.

"Not to besmirch our honor as Strike Marines," Garrison said, "but if we can keep them between us and the Kesaht…better tactical decision. Yes?"

"Follow me." Hoffman said. "The Marines and Ice Claw have a reputation to uphold."

****

PDF and Terran forces pushed out from Koensuu City in greater and greater numbers. Reinforcements landed at the spaceport while others deployed straight to staging areas. A continuous column of Kesaht forces marched from the foothills and across the isthmus. Rakka foot soldiers led by Sanheel officers, tanks commanded by Ixio crew and officers, and the elite Sanheel cavalry units covered fields and foothills as far as Hoffman could see.

"Do we call the Sanheel units cavalry?" Garrison asked. "Nothing freaks me out more than alien centaurs."

"They function as mounted shock troops," Hoffman said. "Call them whatever you want as long as we're winning."

"What is a centaur?"

"A mythological creature, half horse, half human," Hoffman said.

"There must be quite a romance story behind that myth," the Armor said.

"Booker and I saw one of the Kesaht landing zones. There are at least a dozen other valleys where they could have put down troops," Duke said.

"That's a lot of brute force," Hoffman said.

Fal'tir led the lance toward the Armor front line.

"Can I ask a favor?" Hoffman said when they stopped.

"Yes. Anything for Valdar's Hammers."

"I need to gather intelligence reference our original mission. If you locate a high-ranking officer or anyone among the enemy who has seen two Ibarrans, I might be able to interrogate them. My assumption is that the Kesaht would have tried to capture or kill the people I am looking for."

"We will help you capture one of the Ixio officers. These are the upper caste of the Kesaht and will be valuable to interrogate for your purposes and also for the liberation of Koen."

"Thanks, Fal'tir. My sniper's setting up," Hoffman said.

"Ah, the Ice Claw. The Kesaht urinate on themselves at the sound of his name," Fal'tir said.

"Duke for Hoffman, I've got eyes on an Ixio armored transport moving close behind the line of Sanheel."

"Lieutenant Hoffman, I am patching you into the Armor channel." A high-pitched squealing noise cut into Hoffman's earpiece, followed by apologies.

"Now we can communicate directly. Can you hear me? Is the connection loud enough?" Fal'tir said.

"That's plenty loud. Maybe down just a notch?"

"Humans have unprotected ears. I forget," Fal'tir said.

A new voice joined the conversation. "This is Dotari Expedition Commander Shen'yun. The situation is as follows: Rakka infantry and Ixio armor are pushing forward in the center. Sanheel cavalry units are sweeping around the flanks. I see nothing complicated about their tactics. It is likely they wish to draw us into their weak center so they can collapse upon us."

"Where do you need us?" Hoffman asked.

"Take command of whatever PDF assets you can and hold the center. We will attack the Sanheel left flank and destroy it. Assume the Sanheel right flank will continue to charge. My lance commanders believe they will lose heart when their flank breaks."

"Received and understood," Hoffman said. "King, contact as many of the forward PDF unit commanders as possible and explain what we need. Duke, set up an overwatch position. I'll need real-time information and lots of kill shots. You have a green light on anything you can drop."

Hoffman switched to the Koen radio frequency. "Hammer One to HQ actual."

"HQ actual, go."

"I've joined forces with Armor. Their commander has given me an assignment. I need to take command of forward PDF units."

"This channel may not be secure," General Allan said. "I'll assume you are going to break the center. It looks weak. Don't give me details on this channel."

Hoffman hoped Allan understood Fal'tir's plan and was merely maintaining OPSEC as best he could on a compromised commlink.

"King for Hoffman, I directed forward PDF officers to stand by via radio. I'm told it will take the Kesaht awhile to break the crypto, which means we have a secure commlink for a limited time."

"Understood," Hoffman said. He waited until the unit commanders checked in and gave them assignments.

King took control of a leaderless infantry platoon that had just come off the line. Several squads that had been separated from their platoons and were looking for direction formed around Hoffman. He ordered them into squads oriented toward the enemy and went down the line he had created, giving encouragement to battle-weary soldiers.

"Hammer One to frontline PDF. Your orders are to hold, then advance on my command—but on my command only," Hoffman said. Officers and squad leaders checked in by the numbers.

Sanheel blared some type of horn as they exploded into action. The left and right flanks of the Kesaht advance galloped forward, covering three times the amount of ground as the infantry and tanks did in the center of the battlefield.

In an uneven but spirited charge, Rakka roared at the sky and brandished weapons. Ixio tanks followed methodically, keeping a perfect line behind the horde.

"Hoffman for King, we need one of those Ixio tanks if the opportunity arises." He looked to Fal'tir. "Can you help us capture one of their officers?"

"If it can be done, it will be done."

Hoffman aimed his gauss rifle. "Fire." He selected each target with care, conserving ammunition and steadying his breathing. His heart galloped in his chest despite all the battles he'd been in. He checked his stance and his cover. Every third or fourth shot, he lowered his rifle and looked up and down his line to be sure his team and the PDF soldiers were using cover and firing effectively.

Rakka bullets peppered his position. A rocket streaked overhead and landed somewhere behind him. Smoke rolled across the battlefield. Ixio tanks shook the ground as they rumbled forward.

Fal'tir stood up and the gauss cannons on his firearm boomed. "Yes, come closer, Rakka. Show me your fury!"

"They are just like human armor," Garrison said. "I'm so glad."

"Kill enemy!" Opal said.

A round struck the berm in front of Hoffman, throwing dirt and rocks into his field of vision. He leaned to one side and returned fire.

The Rakka were less than two hundred meters away now. The tanks were farther behind.

"Hoffman for frontline team leaders. Advance fifty meters under Armor cover fire. At fifty meters, hold position as the Armor bound ahead to drive a wedge into the Rakka infantry."

"Received and understood."

"I like this plan," Fal'tir said.

Hoffman jumped over the defensive berm and rushed forward fifty meters. He took cover in a frozen creek bed and aimed his gauss rifle. King and other unit leaders shouted orders and Hoffman's ragtag unit opened fire.

For several moments, the barrage of gauss fire deafened him. He saw the first Armor unit jump over him and land, facing hundreds of charging Rakka. Fal'tir opened fire with his double-barrel gauss weapon. A Rakka squad leader exploded in red mist, pieces of his armor splattering against other Kesaht forces. Another Dotari Armor kicked a Rakka into the air.

Hoffman expected the Dotari to shout war cries, to repeat their famous declaration of who they were. All he heard was explosions and screams.

"Lieutenant Hoffman, bound ahead of us. We cover you," Fal'tir said over the commlink.

Hoffman rushed forward with his team and the PDF infantry, looking for a good position to abandon the advance and hold in place.

King went down and Hoffman thought the gunnery sergeant struggled back to his feet. With no time to search for his top NCO or hail him on the commlink, he prayed silently and swore out loud.

Opal ran beside Hoffman, firing on the move and shouting war cries. A bullet ricocheted off the side of the doughboy's helmet and another impacted him solidly on the thigh.

Garrison screamed savagely over the commlink, but Hoffman couldn't see him. He thought Booker was moving toward King.

Before he could set his assaulters in place, Fal'tir's lance charged forward, this time punching and kicking Rakka out of their way. Hoffman saw Fal'tir grab an Ixio tank and turn it on its side.

"King!" Hoffman shouted.

"I'm good," King replied, pain and exhaustion in his voice.

"Shen'tun for Fal'tir, hold that position!" came through Hoffman's commlink. *"We crush them now!"*

Hoffman rushed up and down his line, ordering PDF and Dotari Marines into better positions. "Get down and use what cover you have! Pick your shots. Weapons free! Light them up. Keep their attention on us," Hoffman said.

He looked to the left flank and saw the bulk of the Dotari Armor standing from their concealment. The Sanheel accelerated toward them. Gauss rounds lashed between the two colliding forces faster than the eye could follow. Hoffman checked his own field of fire, then raised his field glasses with one hand to observe the left flank.

Fal'tir leapt forward and swung a hook into the head of a Sanheel. The blow sent the alien's head arcing into the air while the rest of the body kept running for a few seconds.

The fifteen-foot-tall Dotari war machines braced themselves against the ground and opened up with shoulder-mounted rotary weapons and their gauss cannons.

The front ranks of the Sanheel charge collapsed under the torrent of fire. The boom of cannons melded into a single roar as the rapports echoed through the city. Some Sanheel stumbled over the dead and met Dotari armor that were well trained in melee combat.

Hoffman's jaw went slack as Fal'tir ripped the spear out of a Sanheel's hands and rammed it into the alien's chest, the Dotari buried his farm up to the elbow in the alien. Then ripped the top half of the Sanheel away and slashed the spear tip across the throat of another Kesaht officer.

Fal'tir threw the spear with enough force to pierce through the shoulder of a Sanheel and impale another alien behind it. The Dotari armor stomped the skull of a dying Kesaht and beat his fist against his beast plate.

"Dotari'hul! Nov ani, Caas ed Ar'ri!" boomed from the speakers.

The other Dotari armor repeated the words and they advanced on the Sanheel, cutting them down methodically.

The Sanheel wavered, and the aliens began fleeing from the battle. A few escapees became a steady movement away from the Dotari, then a full en route.

"What did they say?" Hoffman asked.

"'Dotari who hear my voice,'" Booker said,

"'follow them,' and he used an honorific for the dead. Caas and Ar'ri are the names, I think."

"How do you know that?" Garrison asked.

"We got language packs to study before the mission to the Golden Fleet," she said.

"Caas and Ar'ri." Garrison tapped the butt of his rifle. "Sounds familiar. Aren't there two Dotari armor that're part of Memorial Square in Phoenix?"

A bullet zipped overhead and the Marines ducked.

"History later," Hoffman said. "There's still Kesaht in this city. Let's go kill some before the Dotari do everything for us. Strike Marines, advance!"

Hoffman vaulted out of cover and charged across the street, the roar of Koensuu soldiers and his team filling the air.

Chapter 25

Hoffman kicked a Rakka corpse. The alien's blood- and ice-encrusted body tore from the ground with the impact and flopped over. Its chest was an ugly mass of blackened flesh; its face frozen in a death scream.

More bodies lay in a rough circle, the aliens' weapons and gear scattered around.

Hoffman looked around the small clearing, silent but for the rush of wind through treetops and the crinkle of blown snow. Clusters of Rakka bodies dotted the glade.

"Sir," King said. "Team's checked all the other groups. No survivors."

"Looks like they clustered around a grenade to end it." Hoffman bent over and picked up a Rakka weapon. He unloaded the magazine and showed King that it was still loaded. "They still had the means to fight…"

"Storm blew through last night," King said. "They'd rather go quick than freeze?"

"Booker." Hoffman waved to the medic. "How long they been dead?"

Booker withdrew probes from her medi-gauntlet out of a corpse and her head bobbled from side to side.

"There's still some core heat," she said. "Maybe eight hours?"

"After the storm passed," Hoffman said.

"The Dotari Armor reported they eliminated a pocket of Sanheel early this morning," King said. "Haven't seen any other contacts with Sanheel since."

"No one's taken a single Kesaht alive," Hoffman said. "Even that Ixio pilot had no intention of being a prisoner. The Rakka must be conditioned to suicide if their leaders are gone. Maybe it's over?"

"Should be." King lowered his rifle and removed his helmet. "That being said, you'll have my resignation soon as we're back in garrison. The Ibarrans got away because of me. My failure."

"Funny," Hoffman pulled his helmet off and felt the bite of winter air against his face, "it was my decision to dump them in a jail. I'm responsible for everything this team does or fails to do. Besides, you were ambushed. I don't hold you at fault…unless you and Garrison switched jerseys on me."

"The Ibarrans can have Garrison," King huffed.

"The hammer will fall on one place." Hoffman tapped his chest. "As it should. You and the team will be just fine. I may have finally earned a job making coffee for some colonel at the Camelback Mountain HQ. All it takes is one 'ah shit' to erase every 'attaboy' in a career. Doesn't matter how successful the Dotari mission was in the end. That was a Charlie Foxtrot for the ages."

"I won't take offense if you highlight my screw-ups in the after action report," King said. "Non-comms like me don't get to make coffee. We pass out basketballs at the gym."

"And waste a perfectly good gunnery sergeant of Marines? Never." Hoffman checked his gauntlet screen and looked to the horizon. "Got a bird inbound. Friendly."

"Hammers." King raised a hand in the air and traced a circle, then pointed to the middle of the clearing.

A Mule transport came over the tree line and landed on vectored engines, blowing snow into a white gale just before Hoffman could get his helmet back on. The lieutenant found his team in the sudden blizzard.

"I swear the pilots just love dusting us," Garrison

said.

"Bet they're giggling like schoolgirls about it," Duke said. "Planning their next crew rest cycle and which nurse to hit up later tonight."

"Hey," Booker said, "at least we don't have to walk back to base."

"She thinks a Mule means no walking," Garrison said. "Isn't she adorable?"

"Feet hurt." Opal shifted from side to side.

The ramp lowered and a man in pristine Strike Marine waved them aboard.

"You guys need a lift?" Max asked.

"He lives!" Garrison hugged Max and hurried into the cargo bay.

"Now he shows up," Duke punched Max on the shoulder as he passed. "You missed all the fun."

"More fun than a bunch of blood transfusions and a couple surgeries?" Max asked. "Next time, I'll remember to duck. Where's that sonofabitch that shot me?"

"That guy," Garrison said. "He's…somewhere. Somewhere on this planet, pretty sure of that."

"What are you talking about?" Max traded nodes with Hoffman as the lieutenant came aboard last. The ramp closed and the Mule lifted into the air.

"They escaped," Hoffman said. "But they should still be on Koen. I'll tell the pilots to get us back to the space port. We can get them before they get off world."

"Space port's been open for almost a full day," Max said. "Full traffic load. And this bird's not going back to the city. We've been recalled to the *Breitenfeld*."

Hoffman felt the Mule's engines kick in and saw the planet fall away as the shuttle gained altitude.

"Then Masha and Medvedev are in the wind," Hoffman said.

"Biggest fish always get away," Duke said as he tucked a wad of chewing tobacco between his gums.

"They…" Max looked from Duke to Hoffman. "They what? You mean I got shot for nothing?"

"I'm sure there's a Purple Heart in it for you," Garrison said. "Or not. This mission was off the books."

"Why are you even on your feet?" Booker asked. "You were at death's door last time I saw you."

"Docs took good care of me." Max sat down and buckled himself in. "They said I was a friend of 'Ice Claw' and put me at the head of triage. I don't know who the hell they're talking about, but it meant getting out of the hospital faster and back in the field with you all, so I kept my damn mouth shut."

"You sure it was 'Ice Claw' and not 'Claws'?" Booker asked. "Plural?"

"Let it go," Duke said. "We get back on the *Breit* and we're all just jarheads again."

"Now he's modest." Booker crossed her arms across her chest.

Booker was the first onboard the Mule. She hugged Max, driving him back a step. "Good to see you made it."

"Jeez, Doc. Was I that bad?" Max asked.

"You still look like a can of hammered shit," she said.

"Not sure how I feel about that."

"Max," Hoffman motioned for the commo specialist to sit next to him, "come help me draft a letter to your family explaining how you got hurt. You know what'll upset them and what won't."

****

The first thing Hoffman saw when he stepped off the Mule was a formidable security force guarding a front loader and the cargo it was moving. The giant black Keystone that was part of the mobile Crucible gate carried a certain menace to it. It took up most of the cargo bay, leaving scant room for Mule transports and a few Eagle fighters towards the fore.

A *Breitenfeld* armsman led them to Valdar at the opposite side of the landing bay and Hoffman and his team saluted.

Valdar acknowledged with a quick nod. "At ease."

Hoffman's team stepped back and stood at parade rest behind him.

"It's good to see you, Hoffman," Valdar said. "Pleasant surprise to see your team listed among the defenders. Since we're in a state of war with the Kesaht, I have local authority over all Terran Union forces. Which is why I pulled you off world to the *Breitenfeld.*"

"Our last assignment to capture Ibarran spies is still—" Hoffman stopped as Valdar raised a hand.

"The Ibarrans can wait. Traitors or not, whoever you were after aren't an existential threat to innocent lives or the Union. The Kesaht are. I'm reassigning you from your clandestine status to my command," the admiral said. "There aren't any flag officers from the Strike Marines to override me and I need you and your team's expertise."

Hoffman looked back at his team.

Max wore his armor but was still gaunt in the face and limped when he walked. Booker and Duke had that ten-thousand-yard stare of warriors who'd been in battle too long. King carried an air of shame about him, and Garrison looked ready for a fight with anything that crossed his path. Opal…was Opal.

"We're Strike Marines," Hoffman said. "We fight where we're sent and we win where we fight."

"Good. Soon as I can pull the Dotari battle group away, we're jumping to Syracuse. The colony's under blockade from a Kesaht force a hell of a lot bigger than the one the *Breitenfeld* and the Dotari just wiped from space. And for the record, you are being volun-told. I need all the tools I can muster for this fight. Finding you here is a stroke of good luck. You ready to fight more Kesaht?"

A chill shot up Hoffman's spine. He could feel the presence of his team behind him even though he could not see them.

"Semper fi, Admiral."

Chapter 26

"Because you are a terrible pilot," Masha said as she steered the stolen ship through a congested space lane on the way to the Crucible. Civilian and noncombat military ships clustered around the jump gate as a wormhole opened and a squadron of Terran destroyers flew into the system.

"I'm rated on this class of cargo ships," Medvedev said.

"You almost knocked off the antennae array of a Dotari frigate," Masha said. "Damn good thing we're flagged as a medevac flight. That Dotari captain was pissed."

"I *almost* knocked off the antennae array."

Masha looked over her shoulder to the empty racks of stretchers in the cargo hold. The Koen police loyal to the

Ibarras sat strapped on benches, looking nervous.

"We are too close to success to let your crap piloting skills ruin it," she said.

"You call what happened down there a success?" the bodyguard asked.

"We got what we came for…despite a few setbacks."

"'Setbacks,' she says." Medvedev shook his head.

Masha touched a blinking screen and tapped instructions into the navigation controls.

"We're clear for the next jump to Sasebo Station," she said. "They're directing traffic away from the Earth Crucible—lots of moving pieces out there—which is fine. We can slip away to Ibarra space a lot easier from Sasebo. We're on autopilot. You think you can handle this part while I encrypt a message to control?"

"Yes," Medvedev deadpanned. "I can handle this."

She removed a small case from inside her jacket and opened it. The artifact within glowed with lime-colored light that washed over her face. She took the two discs out and held them gently between her fingertips.

"My my," she said, "what do you have for us?"

"That Lady Ibarra wants it is all that matters," Medvedev said, his brow furrowing as an alert message came through. "Our flight pattern's been locked...priority transport coming through. The *Breitenfeld*."

He looked up as the strike carrier lumbered across the sky, flying straight for the center of the Crucible, followed by Dotari navy ships.

"I never thought I'd see that ship with my own eyes," Medvedev said. "Saint Kallen served aboard her." He touched his fist to his heart.

"Lady Ibarra wants that ship." Masha nibbled on her bottom lip. "We need to find out where it's going."

"We do not have a source on the Crucible," Medvedev said. "Not a single agent."

"They'll keep jump records." Masha checked one final time to be sure the capture device was secure. "I believe it's time to develop engine trouble and stop for repairs. You up for a quick smash and grab?"

"Anything for Lady Ibarra," Medvedev said.

THE END

Hoffman's Strike Marines return in ***Valdar's Hammer***, coming Summer 2018!

FROM THE AUTHORS

Hello Dear and Gentle Reader,

Thank you for reading The Dotari Salvation. We hope you enjoyed Lieutenant Hoffman and his team's adventure, much more on the way!

Please leave a review on Amazon and let us know how we've done as storytellers, you're feedback is important to us.

Drop us a line at Richard@richardfoxauthor.com and scottmoonwritesanovel@gmail.com.

Also By Richard Fox:

The Ember War Saga:

1. The Ember War

2. The Ruins of Anthalas

3. Blood of Heroes

4. Earth Defiant

5. The Gardens of Nibiru

6. The Battle of the Void

7. The Siege of Earth

8. The Crucible

9. The Xaros Reckoning

Terran Armor Corps:

1. Iron Dragoons
2. The Ibarra Sanction
3. The True Measure
4. **A House Divided (Coming Spring 2018!)**

The Exiled Fleet Series:

1. Albion Lost
2. The Long March
3. **Their Finest Hour (Coming 2018!)**

About Scott Moon

Scott Moon has been writing fantasy and science fiction for over thirty-six years. When not reading, writing, or spending time with his awesome family, he enjoys playing the guitar, Brazilian Jiu Jitsu, and watching movies. Dog guy. Fan of the military. A career law enforcement officer, he served on the SWAT team, Gang Unit, Exploited Missing Child Unit, and helped catch a serial killer. He is also a co-host of the popular Keystroke Medium show (www.KeyStrokeMedium.com)

More Books and Stories by Scott Moon

The Chronicles of Kin Roland

Enemy of Man
Son of Orlan
Weapons of Earth

Read the entire Chronicles of Kin Roland trilogy on Kindle Unlimited!

SMC Marauders
Bayonet Dawn
Burning Sun

Son of a Dragonslayer
Dragon Badge
Dragon Attack
Dragon Land

The Fall of Promisdale
Death by Werewolf

Grendel Uprising

Proof of Death
Blood Royal
Grendel

Darklanding
Episode 1: Assignment Darklanding
Episode 2: Ike Shot the Sheriff
Episode 3: Outlaws
Episode 4: Runaway
(A new episode of Darklanding will be published every 18 days!)

Please visit http://www.ScottMoonWriter.com for more information.

Join the Scott Moon Group on Facebook to talk about books and stuff:
https://www.facebook.com/groups/ScottMoonGroup/

Printed in Great Britain
by Amazon